The Journey of Elizabeth Ann Rose
The Prequel
Seasons of Love and War

A novel by
Brenda Ashworth Barry

Published by
Melange Books, LLC
White Bear Lake, MN 55110
www.melange-books.com

The Journey of Elizabeth Ann Rose

ISBN: 978-1-68046-117-6

Cover Art by Caroline Andrus

This book is dedicated to my family and friends who inspired me to write about best friendship and love. The friendship I found in Novato, California has lasted a lifetime.

Also to my wonderful husband who always supports me.

To my children, a mother couldn't be any prouder and more grateful.

To my childhood BFF, my first true love.

Cindy Watson, thank you for all the support and love and hours of listening to sentence after sentence.

I want to also thank Barb my editor, who is amazing and helped me so much. You rock!

Thank you to my Melange family who also inspires me.

Chapter One

The desert wind fanned its way around Beth Ann, bringing the scent of her mom's chocolate chip cookies drifting through the hot dry breeze. At the age of nine, she sat holding her Shirley Temple doll and had just slammed the door to their small house. "I'm going to run away, because I'm not moving."

Maybe breaking something would have been better, especially her daddy's guitar.

Living on the Indian Reservation had just started to feel like a real home and now they were moving again. To what? Live in their old beat up car or stay in dirty, stinky hotel rooms again?

Just thinking about it made her angrier than the summer heat. After a few minutes, she felt the sweat start to dribble down her back. Great. Now she was sticky and sweaty. She rose from the front steps, thud, thud, thud, stomping into the yard, making the dust fly through the air, and hoping it made a holy mess.

Once the dust was flying around, she plopped down on the tree stump. Not only was she dealing with a sticky back, but she could also feel a swarm of angry bees stinging her heart. Maybe that was a sign of one of those heat strokes her mama always talked about. If she did have one, it might be a good thing, because she'd go into the hospital and they wouldn't be able to leave.

With that, she dropped her Shirley Temple doll and pretended to pass out.

She laid her hand across her forehead to see if anyone was watching. "Ohhh, I've fainted." She sighed.

All she heard were her brothers cracking up. The numbskulls were smirking at her.

"Fine." She got up and dusted off her clothes, then picked up her doll. That obviously didn't work, so she sat back on the tree stump.

She looked up at the white, bulgy clouds, just waiting for them to turn into a giant elephant or a herd of wild horses when a tear slipped out. *No, I'm not going to cry. I'm not a baby, and I don't care how sad I am.* She swiped the tears away and chewed on her bottom lip.

Most days, her imagination would make her smile, but nothing could cheer her up, not today. She hugged her Shirley Temple doll and heard the radio blasting as both her brothers belted out, "*Do you love me ... Now that I can dance.*" They were throwing the ball around while they sang their favorite song. Her song was better than theirs, and it had only come out a few months ago. Teen Angel, was the best song ever, even if it was sad and made her cry every time it got to the part that said. "*They said they found my high school ring clutched in your fingers tight.*" Why did she have to get hit by that train? She could have found her boyfriend's ring, another time.

Maybe she did like her brother's song better, even though the stupid girl didn't like him cause he couldn't dance. What kind of girlfriend was that? Who wrote this stuff?

Right now, she was so upset that she didn't care about anything. How could she? Her parents wouldn't listen to a word she said. Not even when she told them she didn't want to be called Elizabeth anymore. Why weren't they happier that she put on five pounds? They were always telling her to eat more and she was tired of it. So she'd eat when she was good and ready and not a minute sooner. Besides, all she wanted to do was help her family out and the only way she could do that was by eating less.

"I'll take you and Rusty with me, and we'll run away, It's nineteen sixty and times have changed and I'm old enough to be on my own." She whispered to her doll and she hugged her.

Where was Rusty? She looked around. He was probably out chasing bugs again. The thought of him doing that made her want to giggle.

Beth Ann loved her family, but hated the lifestyle. She told her parents how much she disliked it and her daddy snapped and told her to stop complaining.

All she'd done was ask him why they had to move again. Well, maybe, she said a couple other things, like she wasn't leaving if she had to leave Rusty behind. And, maybe she had also yelled at how sick she was of traveling all over Timbuktu. Then, when she said they were being awful parents, her daddy's face got all red. Afterwards, he told her to go outside and think about her words and tone.

So here she was, thinking about it, and all it was doing was making her angrier. He was the one who should've thought about their lifestyle. Why did they have to follow his band around everywhere? Maybe he should go alone.

After she laid down her doll, she picked up a dirt clod and hit the cactus right upside the head. "Take that, you stupid cactus, and you better call me Beth Ann and not Elizabeth."

Cole started laughing. "Bull's eye." He glanced over and met her gaze. "You got an arm on you little sis. Wanna come and play? That's if you can keep from passing out."

"No." She shot him her best evil eye. Neither of her brothers cared that they were leaving, so why should she talk to them? She stuck her nose high in the air.

James laughed and picked up the ball. "Little sis has a big temper."

Cole nodded, then they went back to playing ball.

Since they became teenagers all they cared about was baseball and pretty girls. What she cared about was having a home and a bed of her own.

"Cookies are ready." Her mom stood at the front door and waved for them to come inside. Just then Rusty, their family dog, must have heard, because he came up to Beth Ann and barked, then ran towards her mom.

"Good boy." Her mom patted him and opened the door so he could follow her inside. "I made one just for you with no chocolate or nuts."

Her brothers dropped everything, turned off the radio and made a mad dash up the stairs.

"Elizabeth, come here and get yourself a cookie," her mom said in her deep southern accent.

"No Mama. I don't want any cookies," she mumbled. "And my name is Beth Ann." She kicked the dirt and knew she shouldn't be mad at her mama. It wasn't her fault. She didn't want to move either.

"Okay. I'll put some away for you." Her mother went back inside, then said over her shoulder, "Rusty is enjoying his treat."

The door shut, and Beth Ann really did want a cookie, but she'd learned to go without, to save money for the family. Although, the aroma was out of this world and she was glad Rusty got his. He was the best dog in the world.

Beth Ann thought about how most summers she lived at Gram's, besides being there, the reservation was her favorite place in the world. The Indians cooked yummy food, maybe not as good as Gram's, but nobody cooked like her. The problem was Gram always tried to make her eat more and Gram didn't have a lot of money either. Everyone was always telling her how skinny she was, and it was starting to get on her nerves. Maybe if they had a real home, she'd stop being so skinny and stop worrying about being so poor.

The truth was it wasn't just the house that made it feel like home. It was all the animals and people on the reservation. There were no kids her age; most of them were really little or much older. But that didn't matter, because they had treated her nicely.

3

Her family had been able to live with the Indians even though they weren't full blood. They were only a quarter Indian. That was like twenty-five cents out of a dollar her dad had told her.

Rusty came tearing out of the front door and rushed to her side, wagging his tail.

"Hi boy." She felt tears build in her eyes. "You're my best friend in the world," she whispered.

Almost as if he knew something wasn't right, he whimpered and laid his head in her lap. She rubbed behind his ears. "I love you, boy, and no matter what, I won't leave you behind." She sniffed. "I'll run away and we can take care of each other."

Why did her dad have to play music in a dumb band anyway? Spending so much time in a nine-year-old car, doing homework, sleeping in cramped areas in the back seat, and staring out the window wasn't her idea of fun.

Oh sure, every now and again his band would get a job for a few months. "Woopy doodle." They'd get to stay in a dirty hotel room that had a TV and a small kitchen. Heck, some even had pets, like cockroaches and mice.

What Beth Ann really dreamed about was a friend with whom to share her secrets. Every day since she was little, she prayed for a best friend and a dog. At least she had the dog. Rusty took off chasing a bird and she watched him tearing across the yard.

"Hey, little redheaded angel, why do you look so sad?"

She looked up to find Charlie, the tribal chief, standing in front of her. He was the smartest man she knew. Every day he had been trying to talk her parents into staying. He'd even found her dad a job at a local pub, but her daddy wouldn't take it.

Charlie was a large man with dark hair and deep black eyes, which seemed to smile with kindness.

"Because we're leaving," she said and chewed her lip so she wouldn't cry. She was almost ten and shouldn't be a baby.

In one swoop, Charlie picked her up off the stump and hugged her, then placed her on the ground. "You're going to have a wonderful journey. Your travels will take you to a new home and you will have many friends." He touched the tip of her nose. "And you know what else?"

Beth Ann couldn't smile. "No." She looked down.

"In this new land, you will meet what white men call your Prince Charming." He kissed her head. "I've had a vision, and this man will love you with all his heart and soul. Someday, he will be your husband."

"I don't want a Prince Charming." She kicked the ground. "I just want to stay here with you. You're better than any Prince Charming. Besides, he'd just expect me to cook and have babies. I hate cooking and no babies. And if I ever get married, my husband has to know how to make food, like you." With her shoulders stiff and head held high, she stood strong.

She watched Charlie try not to laugh. "When you meet your special one, you will forget all about an old man like me."

"No, I won't." Her voice quivered. "Besides, San Diego's my home, and you said the wind knows my name, because I was born here. Now, the wind won't know my name."

He sat down on the old tree stump. "Come here, my special girl."

Beth Ann walked over and sat on his knee, trying her best to swallow all the emotions. He lifted her chin. "You have a special mission on Mother Earth. And, Great Spirit," he pointed to an eagle flying, "Needs you to do what you were sent here to do." His eyes locked on hers. "One of those things is to protect the animals. Another is to bring great joy to the world. When you sing, your voice makes people stop and listen. Even the deer have no fear of being near you because of your melody."

Beth Ann couldn't help but feel excited because she loved to sing and she wanted to look after the animals. But still, she didn't want to leave. Living out of that car was harder than most people could possibly understand, unless they had done it.

Stopping at rest stops and eating had sometimes been fun, but when it was cold, it was hard to wash up in those bathrooms. Her mom had to be their teacher, making sure they were up to date on their homework and learning. When they did stay in one place long enough to go to school, they were always given many tests. So far, they were all up to speed, so her mom had been a good teacher. The simple truth was, she hated living in that ugly, old car and wanted it to stop. Was that really too much to ask?

Maybe she really could pack her clothes and run away. There were tons of places to hide on the reservation, old barns, caves, and even some old houses. Nobody would find her and she could take Rusty with her; they would keep each other safe. Rusty was protective and had once growled at another dog for coming too close.

Charlie took her hands. "To make sure you're safe, because you're so special, I'm sending the Angel of Protection to watch over you."

As much as she tried to prevent it, a tear trailed down her cheek.

"But who will watch over you, Charlie?" She choked on her words. "You're all alone since your beautiful wife went to heaven." In a whisper she said, "I know you're lonely and sad."

His eyes filled with tears, so she placed her hands around his neck.

"Charlie, I want you to keep the Angel. You need her more than me." She tried to smile.

"Ah, you are the most precious of all the angels, but don't you worry, little one, I'll be just fine."

She hated leaving Charlie. His wife had died from her head bleeding. One minute playing with the tribal children and the next, she fell to the ground. Dead instantly, the elders had said. Everyone kept saying that the Great Spirit needed her badly, but Beth Ann felt Charlie needed her more. He was handsome and strong, with dark hair and skin that was almost chocolate. Someone needed to take care of him, even if he was an old man of thirty-two. If she stayed, she could keep him from being lonely by singing to him every day.

"Want me to sing to you, Charlie?"

He nodded and helped her stand. "How about that rainbow song?" His grin was wide.

With that, she closed her eyes and pulled up the words. "Somewhere over the rainbow, blue birds fly." When she finished singing, she saw Charlie wipe away a tear.

He hugged her. "If I ever have a little girl, I would want her to be just like you." He touched her nose. "Now, I have to talk to your mom and dad and steal one of those cookies I know she's baking." He stood and strolled towards the house.

Her mind was made up. She was not going to leave San Diego, it was her birthplace and Charlie was right; the wind knew her name. That meant the land would take care of her. She would pack tonight and leave first thing tomorrow morning. Even though she'd miss her family, she had to stay and take care of her dog. She loved him and he needed her. Someone had just thrown him away and it was her job to watch over the animals. Great Spirit expected her to do that, so that's exactly what she was going to do.

Chapter Two

Kaylob woke to the sound of the TV coming from his mom's bedroom. He'd just arrived home last night after spending most of the summer at his aunt and uncle's farm. They lived in Sonora, California and even though Novato was in the same state, it felt a million miles away. He loved his time up there, between riding horses and getting to know all their foster kids, he'd always had a good time and it was the one place where people didn't judge him by where he lived.

This summer they had a new foster daughter named Mary Ann. She was sure nice and really pretty. That last week of his visit, they had gone down to the pond, and while he had been enjoying the sun, she had kissed him. Man, he was sure surprised, especially when she stuck her tongue in his mouth. He'd never had a tongue in his mouth before. Not that he was complaining. She said she had more to show him, but in truth, he was nervous about it. So afterwards, he'd made darn sure his cousin Bill was there with them, all the time.

Kaylob rose from his bed and slipped on his robe. Now that he was home, he wondered what chores his dad would make him do. His dad was actually at home instead of on one of his business trips. Usually, he kept Kaylob working around the house so much that he had little time to hang out with his friends. That was another one of the reasons Kaylob liked being at the farm. He didn't have to work every day and be his dad's slave.

Kaylob tried not to feel resentful and bitter, but some days it was hard.

The one thing he did miss while he was away was the ocean. He loved to surf, and wanted to do that before the end of the summer. In fact, he was darn good, and had beaten some sixteen year olds in competitions. He wished his parents could afford to send him to some of those surf camps, but they were too poor so he taught himself. He had a plan though, and that was when he turned fourteen he was going to get a job at the corner store and pay for things he wanted to do.

Since his dad was home, he'd more than likely have him cutting the grass, pruning the rose bushes or something worse, such as scrubbing the bathrooms. Last summer he had painted both bathrooms. Thank Moses, there were only two of them.

"Kaylob!" his mother called out. "Please come in here."

Kaylob opened his door and shuffled down the hall, wondering what they needed him to do now. Once he entered the room, he could hear his dad taking a shower. Wow, his mom was actually smiling and her brown eyes sparkled with happiness. That sure made his day. More than likely it was because his dad was home for two weeks. That always lifted her spirits.

"How would you like to go to the ocean today?"

"Really? You and Dad are going to take me?"

"We sure are, and we were thinking picnic and watching you surf."

"Hot dog." He pumped his fist in the air. "I was just thinking about the beach." He started to leave.

"Kaylob, wait." He turned and saw her questioning eyes.

"Did you have fun this summer up at the farm? How did you get along with Mary Ann?"

"It was great, Mom." He stuck his hands in his robe pockets. "We hung out a lot."

"She's a bit older than you." His mom met his gaze. "What did you two do?"

Kaylob felt his cheeks heat and hoped it didn't show. "Oh, we just went swimming, and played with the horses, and stuff. I learned how to build a fence, and paint it." He felt proud.

His dad entered the room. "Good, you can start to work on our fence. That thing is falling apart and a good coat of paint will make it look a helluva a lot better." His dad walked over and kissed his mom on the head.

"How are you feeling today, Jackie?" his dad asked.

"Fine, Harold. As a matter of fact, I'm looking forward to watching Kaylob surf." She glanced back and forth between Kaylob and her husband. "Harold, I hope you are okay, you sure have lost a lot of weight."

"I'm fine. I've just been walking more and cut back on all those sweets." He rubbed his stomach.

Kaylob often wondered how he ended up with blond hair and blue eyes when both his parents had dark hair and brown eyes. Not to mention he was already taller than both of them. They had told him he had some relatives in

Ireland that he took after. He hoped to meet them someday. The truth was he'd never even spoken to a single-family member back there.

For whatever reason, his grandma was sick on his dad's side, and his grandpa didn't seem to like him much. His mom would never talk about her parents, and he had never even met them.

Kaylob's dad pointed. "Okay, boy, go get ready and let's get started. I want to go to Bodega Bay." He walked over to the dresser and pulled it open. "I like that place."

He didn't have to ask Kaylob twice, he was more than excited. Once he entered his room, he threw on his clothes and headed out to the shed to get his surfboard ready.

He would tackle that fence later, and he could rebuild most of it. But it needed wood and that would cost money. After that thing Blake Tanner said about his house needing to be bulldozed, he wanted to make it look better. Blake had laughed and said he was only kidding, but Kaylob was fully aware of living on the wrong side of the tracks.

Right here and now, he was going to surf and that took his mind off everything, including his mom's depression. She was having a good day and that's all he would focus on. He'd learned a long time ago to enjoy his mom's blue sky days; she had so few of them. With his dad gone most of the time, he usually had to cook and clean while she stayed in bed. Although, he loved cooking. Someday he wanted to be a chef and own a restaurant.

Today he'd surf and do a good job at making his mom proud. But *nothing* ever made his dad proud.

He flipped on the radio and heard, *You belong to me.* He sang along and polished his board. He had waxed it before he left for vacation so it was pretty much ready. When he turned, he caught sight of the kites. For many years, his dad would bring those home, and every now and again, they'd go fly them. Those times were long gone, but he treasured the memory of those moments.

He felt content today and held his surfboard close and kissed it. "Ah baby, it's you and me against the surf. We're going to kick some giant wave ass today." He laughed and stepped outside, noticing the greyhound bus pull up. Two people stepped off and scurried down the street. He wasn't sure why he always had to watch who was getting off that bus, but something deep in his gut made him feel as though he was waiting for something. What it might be, he hadn't a clue.

* * * *

One week later, Beth Ann climbed into the old station wagon loaded with everything they owned.

Cole had caught her packing the night she was running away and that was the only reason she stayed. He had hugged her tightly and told her that he couldn't live without her. When he said, *I only have one sister and I love her. I'd be sad for the rest of my life if she ran away.* There was no way she could leave and let him die without her.

Her brothers were horsing around outside the car, falling down in the dirt.

"Good gravy, stop your horsing around and get yourself into that car." Her mama scolded. "Don't make me come over there," she shot them both, her parental *I dare you to ignore me* look.

That's all it took.

"Okay, Mama," they said in unison. Then high tailed it into the back seat where Beth Ann sat, minding her own business. They smelled like sweaty dirt. She pinched her nose.

Cole reached over and tried yanking her hand away. "Come on sis, you know you love the way we smell." He tickled her arm and almost made her laugh, but she was too sad.

James leaned over and winked, so she gave him a tiny smile. She had learned a new word and it fit perfectly here. That small smile was all she could muster.

Both her brothers were older and handsome. Cole had brown hair, deep brown eyes, with big muscles and golden skin. James had black hair, with olive skin, like their mom, and blue eyes like their dad. And here she was a redhead with freckles and brown eyes. Life was not fair.

Charlie and some of their friends were standing around the car, saying goodbye. Beth Ann felt bad to see her mother shedding tears as she hugged everyone. Then there was her dad, shaking hands and laughing without a care in the world. Didn't he notice how upset her mother was? Beth Ann felt like yelling at him, or calling Gram and having her do it since she was really good at telling him a thing or two.

There was one more thing Beth Ann had to do, but the thought made her eyes burn. She had to say goodbye to Rusty because her parents would not let her take him. It was clear he sensed something, because he was pacing around in circles outside the car. With reluctance, she jumped from her seat and ran to give one last nuzzle to her favorite golden mutt.

"I love you, boy," she cried and sat on the ground, holding him close.

Afterwards, she ran back to the car, and scooted into the back seat with her brothers, burying her face in her hands. She didn't want to look at Rusty when they drove away. The dogs were all barking, although Rusty was the loudest. Sadness trailed down her cheeks and she thought about running away again. Her heart felt like it was busting into pieces.

Just as she thought about making a mad dash out of the car, her parents climbed in, her dad into the driver's seat. Before they could shut the doors, Rusty jumped in, right on Beth Ann's lap. She wrapped her arms tightly around him.

"Please let me take him. Someone just dumped him off and I love him," she pleaded.

Her mom looked sorry when she sighed and shook her head. "I'm sorry, honey, we can't take a dog to live in the car. It wouldn't be fair to him." Her mom turned and had tears of her own. "Besides, everyone loves him here and he has a good home now." Her voice trembled. "Charlie's taking him to live at his house."

"Nobody loves him as much as me," she argued. "I love you, boy." She held on to his neck as he licked the salty tears from her face. "I'm going to miss you so much."

Rusty let out a loud howl and Beth Ann wasn't sure who finally picked him up, but she was fully aware of his cries as they drove away.

That was one of the hardest days in Beth Ann's nine-year-life.

"It's okay, sis." Cole wrapped his arm around her while she tried to catch her breath. "He'll be fine."

At least she had Cole. He was not only her brother, but her good friend.

James was nice to her too, and handed her a lollipop. "Here, you can have this." His eyes softened.

"Thank you," she managed to say and took the lollipop. That was his way of showing her love.

The one thing about her big brothers that was so special. They never liked to see her cry and always tried to make it better.

For miles, no one said anything, and the car was filled with an uncomfortable silence. Beth Ann couldn't help but think about how much she hated her life. Every time she got attached to someone or something, it was taken away. How much more pain could she take before she sunk down a hole and never came back? Maybe that was another reason she didn't eat very well, her stomach was always upset from stress.

In her mind's eye, she saw herself sinking into quicksand, so she tried to focus on the wheat fields as they drove down the lonely highway. In those moments, it felt like a dark cloud was hovering above them.

They were on the road again, on their way to Nashville, Tennessee, where her dad promised he'd make it big this time. His band had at least four gigs booked all over Tennessee. She turned around to grab her Shirley temple doll that was sitting on her dad's dumb guitar case. She wished she could throw that thing right out the window. How could her parents not see if it wasn't good for a dog to live in *the car*, that it might not be a good idea to have their own children living in one either. She exhaled and tried to let out her frustration. It just didn't make any sense.

Beth Ann made up her mind. She was going to plead with her parents to let them go back to the reservation. They could stay with Charlie and he would take care of them, plus she could be with her dog again.

That way her parents could stay on the road. At least the three of them could have a stable life, like other kids. It wasn't fair the way they lived, and she had to find a way to make them understand. If her daddy wanted to play in a band, good for him, but why did they have to tag along? Yep, she was going to find a way to tell them a thing or two, she'd learned that from Gram.

* * * *

Eighteen months after they left the reservation, they headed away from Nashville. They continued on the road because her dad was still trying to become famous. She had spent a good part of those eighteen months begging and pleading to go back to the reservation. However, it did no good. All she'd done was make her daddy mad, and her mom sad.

Speaking of her mom, she looked really pretty today with her new hairstyle and yellow dress with polka dots. As a matter of fact, she hadn't seen her mom look so nice in a long time. Her jet-black hair now styled around her shoulders, and that dress did show off things. Beth Ann might be young, but she knew that her mom had a great figure.

This week, they'd be staying in a hotel room with two bedrooms and a small kitchen. That meant having a TV, which was something Beth Ann really enjoyed. One reason was that on Sundays her mom had always let her watch Shirley Temple.

Her dad was playing music at a downtown bar for a week, maybe longer. It all depended on how well he did. Usually her daddy didn't come home while he played in bands at bars, mainly because he stayed with the guys practicing or playing music. Beth Ann missed him a lot when he was gone, but since he was never around, why did they need to be there with him? It still made no sense. Weren't they supposed to be adults and figure out what was good for their kids?

Beth Ann was fed up, and had a feeling her mom was, too. Pretty soon, her mom was going to put her foot down and make her daddy find them a house. Beth Ann could feel a change coming.

* * * *

Her mom had been quiet lately, leaving them alone at night and going out. She'd always call to make sure they were okay, and a few times, she brought home pizza. Beth Ann managed to eat one piece, although, her brothers tried to get her to eat more. They'd even tried to bribe her by saying they would play jump rope. She almost did it, because she thought it was funny to see her brothers doing that, but she wanted to save some of the food for her parents.

The weird thing was her mama had never spent extra money like that before, and she seemed happier somehow. Beth Ann wished she felt that way.

As much as Beth Ann tried not to complain, the words just fell out of her mouth. Her daddy had told her to think before she spoke, and that's what she had done. The problem was her mouth had a brain of it's own, and when she tried to tell them that, they all laughed really hard. That was confusing. What was so funny about that?

Weeks later, early in the morning, they were on the road again and it was still dark outside. This time they were heading off to the small town in Hanford, California. Her brothers were sleeping, while Beth Ann stared out the window at the boring freeway. Her parents were silent for most of the trip.

"Is something bothering you, Jean?" her dad asked.

"No. Why would it be?" She paused and took a deep breath. "Just tell me this, how long will you be gone this time? Never mind, it doesn't really matter anymore."

"Guess someone woke up on the wrong side of the bed, this morning," he chuckled.

"What bed? You call that thing we were sleeping on, *a bed*?" her mom shot back.

What Beth Ann saw next told her something bad was wrong. He reached over to stroke her mom's hair, but she pulled away. Uh oh, her daddy was in the doghouse. But they'd make up soon, they always did. And maybe this was the first step in her mama putting her foot down so they could get a house.

As they continued down the road, Beth Ann observed a long silence fall between her parents. That made her sad. She just wanted them to all be happy, even if she wasn't.

Once they pulled up at the hotel, Beth Ann didn't want to get out of the car. The place looked scary and the only good thing was a guy on a walk with his dog. The hotel sign was missing some letters and weeds were everywhere. The Dumpster was overflowing with garbage, flies swarmed all around. Beth Ann noticed a lady wink at her daddy; she had on shorts with fishnet stockings.

Her daddy's cheeks grew pink, and her mom shook her head.

"Come on, kids," Her mom's nose wrinkled. "James, Cole. Get up right now and let's get our stuff inside this god forsaken place."

Beth Ann heard James whisper. "Cole wake up, we're at the Ritz and there's some classy lady waiting for us, maybe she's the hostess." He shook him awake.

Cole opened his eyes and scrunched his eyebrows. "Great. First class all the way."

Chapter Three

They walked inside and darkness seemed to bleed from the walls. At least it had a TV and two bedrooms with a small kitchenette. The scent was moldy and the cigarette smell made Beth Ann gag. The stuffing was falling out of the couch and the dark green carpet was almost brown.

Beth Ann was certainly happy she could use her imagination, because in this room she would need it. She weaved her way through the room, trying to convince herself that it wasn't all that bad. Beth Ann's gaze followed a bug crawling up the wall. Gross, was not a good enough description of what she really felt. A few seconds after standing there, a voice boomed its way through the walls and made her jump.

James shook his head. "Great, that must be the welcoming committee." He picked up his bag and moved it into a small closet. Cole just stood, staring at the walls and the floors.

Before they could even unpack, her dad made his excuses. "I have to run to the club and check everything out. We play tonight." He picked up his bag, tried to kiss her mom, but she pulled away again. He turned towards the three of them. "Be good, and mind your mama," he said, as he rushed out the door, faster than the wind.

They all stood and stared at the closed door. Nobody said a word, and then her mom picked up her suitcase and headed towards one of the bedrooms, she paused and spoke without turning around.

"James, Cole, get the broom and the cleaning stuff from the car. We have to clean this filthy room." She picked up her bag and left the living room.

Beth Ann almost felt excited, because she knew the days of living in a hotel were coming to an end. Her mama was as mad as a wet hen. That's what Gram said when someone was really angry.

That evening their mom put on a pretty black dress and said she was meeting a friend. Beth Ann knew one thing for sure; her mom had changed everything about herself. The way she dressed, her hair and even the way she

Brenda Ashworth Barry

walked. Beth Ann had a sneaky feeling that her mom and dad were going to
have a date night and make up, and just maybe, they'd be getting a house soon.
She'd even heard James whisper to Cole that their mama was sick of living this
way.

As days went by her mom stayed away a lot. Sometimes it was early
morning when she came home. James was seventeen, so he was old enough to
be the man of the house when her parents were both gone.

That evening Chinese food showed up at the door, and Beth Ann ate a
little more than usual, but she wouldn't touch the sweet and sour pork. There
was just no way she'd eat that. Not since she found out it came from cute little
pigs. Everything was getting better; her mom had even bought a pretty plant to
put in the room, and a new tablecloth to throw over the ugly table.

When Beth Ann got up that next morning, it was clear her mama had not
come home all night. Beth Ann was sure that she and her daddy just needed
some time alone. That was a good sign. She couldn't help but be in a good
mood as she poured herself a bowl of cereal and maybe she'd eat a normal size
bowl. She just had to be sure there was enough for everyone.

"What are you doing up so early, and why are you humming?" Cole
walked in half asleep, looking for another bowl.

"I'm just happy today." She grinned. "I think we'll be getting some good
news soon."

"That's a nice change of attitude, but what good news?" He scratched his
head and poured the milk on his cereal.

"Just something." She glanced up to see James walk in.

"Hope you saved me some. I'm starving," James mumbled.

That morning eating breakfast together without their mama seemed
strange, but it was worth it, because something was coming and Beth Ann
could feel it in her guts of guts.

Later that evening while they watched TV, there was a knock at the door.
James went and answered it.

A man wearing a uniform handed him a large box of something.

"Jean asked me to deliver this." The short, skinny man looked around the
room and his face crinkled, like he smelled a rotten egg.

"Thank you," said James as he shut the door, then walked over and placed
the box on the coffee table.

Cole got up off the floor and slung the box open. "Whoa. Look at all this
food."

There was fried chicken, potatoes, cornbread, and veggies. But the best
part was the huge chocolate cake; maybe Beth Ann could have one piece. It all
smelled really good and she did feel hungry. One piece of chicken and cake

16

wouldn't hurt anything. Would it?

"Beth Ann." James shot a look at her. "You need to eat something besides one chicken leg."

"I'm saving room for a piece of cake," she said flatly. "Stop trying to boss me around." She made a face at him.

"You need to have at least two pieces, or you can't have any cake." He gave her a stern look.

"Fine." She grabbed a second leg. "I'll eat two, but I need to save some for mom and dad."

Next thing she knew he dumped some vegetables on her plate. "At least take a few bites of this too."

Cole nodded. "Come on sis, we're just worried."

The look on their faces made her eat everything. She knew they both loved her. Besides, it felt good to eat tonight, Sometimes it got hard to go to bed hungry. Their life was about to change anyway and maybe there would be more food.

"You know Daddy must be getting paid more money for this gig," she said to her brothers. "Maybe that means we'll be getting a house soon."

Both her brothers stopped and stared at her. Cole appeared confused and James looked away and started fidgeting with the box. She wondered what that was all about. Maybe he was afraid of settling down. He'd lived like this longer than any of them, so maybe he liked it.

As the days traveled by, being surprised by deliveries became a pattern, and soon they were going to the movies and getting to do things they'd never done before. It was making the icky hotel room more bearable. Her dad hadn't been home in three weeks, but that was no surprise. After all, her mama had been going to stay with him almost every night.

Usually, there was some type of room over the bar where her dad stayed. This gig was lasting two months, which made Beth Ann wonder if he'd be gone for the entire time. She sure hoped her mama didn't stay away the whole time, too. One time, they had all stayed in one of those rooms over the bar, but the thumping and loud noise kept them awake all night. For that reason, her mama never wanted to stay again.

Speaking of her mama, she wished she would come home soon, because James didn't know how to do a French braid. He'd tried, but had made a mess and really, since he had short hair, he didn't know how to deal with hers being so long.

* * * *

That evening as they watched Bonanza, Beth Ann's mom walked through

17

the door, looking unhappy. That caused Beth Ann's stomach to turn. The faded carpets and old run down curtains only added to the feeling that something wasn't right. Ten seconds later the air got thick and Beth Ann found herself wanting to open the door to let the breeze in.

Her mom cleared her throat. "Kids, I need to talk to you, right now." She walked over and turned off the TV.

"But Mom, that was in a good place," Cole whined.

"This is more important." She glanced at James and gave him a look Beth Ann didn't recognize. Maybe he knew what was up already. After all, he was the oldest.

James stood and nodded for them to sit on the smelly couch. He bent down and pulled Beth Ann up. "Come on squirt, you need to listen to Mom." He glared at Cole and nodded towards the couch.

Beth Ann noticed her mom pull over a wobbly metal chair and sat down. When Beth Ann saw her pick imaginary lint off her new dress, she knew her mom was nervous.

Beth Ann's heart fell, when her mama looked up with glassy eyes and swallowed.

Oh no, this was not a good sign at all.

"Kids, I know this is going to make you sad," she said and paused. "And, I'm so so sorry, but … I'm leaving your father." She smoothed out her beautiful green dress and finally looked up. "I love him, but I just can't live this way anymore." She waved her hand around. "I want more for all of us."

Cole spoke first. "Mama, how will we live?"

Beth Ann tried to swallow the knot in her throat. They were leaving her daddy? She wondered how they would live, too. What would happen to him? She looked over at Cole and saw the tears in his eyes, which made her lip tremble.

"I rented an apartment in a little town called Petaluma in California. It's nothing fancy, but it's home, and it's clean and cute. That's one reason we stayed in this dump, so I could afford to get us a better place to live." She ran her hand through her hair. "Since it's the summer, Beth Ann can go stay with Gram while we look for a bigger place. I will be staying in Reno, Nevada, for a short time." She continued. "However, we will not be living out of a car anymore or staying in bug infested hotels." She looked at them and wiped away a tear. "I'm exhausted, and it's just too hard. You kids are getting too old to live like this. Cole, you're almost in high school and James, you're seventeen. You've missed out completely and for that I'm truly sorry." She looked down at her hands and her lip trembled just before tears trailed down her cheeks.

Beth Ann sat there, not knowing what to do or say. They couldn't leave her daddy, they were a family and they needed each other.

Cole jumped up. "Mama, please don't cry," he pleaded and hugged her. "We can make it work. Maybe Dad will want to settle down when you tell him," he said with sad eyes. "He won't want to lose his family." He glanced around at everyone.

Beth Ann felt a flicker of hope when her brother said that. He wouldn't want to lose all of them. Cole was right, this could be fixed.

Then her mama shook her head. "I'm afraid it's too late, son."

"But Mom." Cole raised his voice. "We can't just leave Dad alone!"

Beth Ann stood. "I don't want to leave Daddy. I don't mind living out of the car." Had she caused this from being too whiny? She'd take it all back and never complain again. She could eat even less, she'd already cut way back.

"It's okay, Mama, I love traveling. I get to see so many different things. I'm sorry for complaining," she cried. "Please, don't leave, Daddy. I'll be good, and I promise to never say anything bad about any of this again and I'll cut back on eating even more, so we have more money."

A movement caught her eye along the bottom of the baseboards. When she looked closer, she saw that it was a big cockroach. She hoped her mama didn't see it, so she took a step in front of the wall, trying to hide the bug. "Please, let's stay."

James pulled Beth Ann back down. "Knock it off you two. Dad's never even here with us. Look at this place, crawling with bugs and it's filthy. Mama wants a different life for us and for herself." James looked at his mom with way too much understanding.

"Like I said, I love your daddy, and this has nothing to do with any of you complaining or not eating food. I just can't be with him anymore. It's over." She stood and swept out of the room, but not before she took off her shoe and killed the cockroach.

Chapter Four

After she left the living room, they could hear her crying. At that moment Beth Ann knew her life was about to change. What would her life look like without her daddy? Would they end up homeless? Her mama had never worked and didn't know how to bring in money. She'd heard her daddy say that more than once. How long could she live with her Gram and what about her brothers? Beth Ann felt her heart pounding. All she wanted to do was run out the door and go find her daddy. He needed to know they were leaving. Tears flooded down her cheeks, as she thought about him all alone.

James got up and walked over to Beth Ann. "Don't cry, sis. Things are going to be better for all of us." He tried to hug her, but she pushed him away.

"What about Daddy? How much better is it going to be for him? You knew and didn't tell us! You can't tell me that you didn't, because I'm old enough to know better." She ran into the other bedroom, threw herself on the bed and cried until she drifted off to sleep.

That next morning her mama arrived with a brand new spanking car. It was red and had a pull down top. As they loaded their stuff into the trunk, Beth Ann wanted to know where she got it, and how could she afford it.

She heard her brothers whispering, but couldn't make out their words. Although, she had a feeling by the look on their faces, they were wondering the same thing. Beth Ann decided she should just come out and ask.

"Mama, where did you get this car?" She ran her hand across the red convertible. "I don't think Daddy would approve of you spending all his money without telling him. Does he know you bought this?"

Cole glanced up and subtly shook his head. She knew he was trying to tell her to shut up. But she wasn't going to because she wanted to know.

"It doesn't matter where I got it. Only that we have a car. Now, get your stuff and get in the car and no more questions." Her mom's eyes narrowed and she pointed. "It's a long drive from Hanford to Petaluma. So let's get going."

Beth Ann noticed her brothers, like usual, had taken off to toss the baseball back and forth. How could they act so casual when they were on their way to a new place and away from her dad and they weren't even saying goodbye.

Beth Ann knew her mama was mad at her daddy for staying away so much, but he had to practice and couldn't do it in a hotel room. Deep inside she had a feeling that really wasn't a good excuse, but right now, she gave him one anyway.

"Come on, boys, let's get on the road," her mom yelled. "We need to get going, now."

Cole and James had to toss the ball one more time.

"Did you hear what I said? I really don't want to have to say it again." She put her hands on her hips and arched a brow.

They stopped dead in their tracks, hopped in the car, and slid across the vinyl seats.

Beth Ann started to get inside when she remembered her new book, The Yearling. She hadn't even had a chance to read it after her mama bought it.

"Mama, I left my book. I have to go find it."

"Go on, but hurry we need to get started. Don't you boys dare leave this car!" She walked around and opened the trunk.

Beth Ann ran back in the bedroom and found her book under the nightstand. While she was down on her knees getting it, she spotted her mom in the next room, putting what looked like a folded letter on the pillow. She'd heard about those dear Jack letters and wondered if that's what it was.

"Beth Ann," her mama called out.

Beth Ann stayed on her knees, pretending to still be searching. "I'm still looking for my book."

"We'll be in the car, so hurry."

"Okay, Mama, I'll be right there."

Beth Ann waited until she heard the door close to the living room. Then she tiptoed into the other bedroom across the hall and lifted the folded letter.

My dearest James,

You were my first love and I'll always carry you in my heart. But I can't be your wife anymore. I don't want to be your wife. I'm going to get a divorce and that way you can stay out as long as you want and never worry about coming home. I know you love the children and they love you just as much.

But as far as us. It's over. I'm going to Nevada and get a divorce. It should be final soon. I'll let you know when I find out.

Please take good care of yourself and thank you for giving me the three most precious gifts of my life. Our children.

Love always, Jean

P.S. I'll call you when we get settled. The children will want to speak to you.

Beth Ann placed the letter inside her book. She wouldn't let her mom leave that note, but ... her daddy might worry. So with that thought she put it back on the pillow with tears stinging her eyes. That's it; she wasn't going to leave with them. She'd stay put and wait for her daddy. With conviction, she walked into the living room and plunked herself down on the couch.

First, the horn beeped and then she heard the sound of a car door slamming. Someone was coming.

The front door opened and her mom stepped into the living room.

"Beth Ann, what in tarnation are you doing?" Her mama demanded to know.

"I'm not going Mama. I saw the note you left for daddy. Someone has to be home when he gets here."

Her mom's face softened. "Honey, this is not home. She came over and sat down next to Beth Ann. "Your daddy won't be here for a few more days and the only reason he'll be coming, is to pick up that letter. I'm going to call him and tell him it's here." She took Beth Ann's hand. "Now, I know this is hard, but we need to leave this place. You can talk to your daddy later." She reached her hand out and pulled her up. "Let's have some fun. We could put the top down on the car and have lunch at a nice place. What do you say? I promise you will see your daddy soon. Besides, we need to put some meat on those bones. I had no idea you were cutting back on food to save money." She stared at Beth Ann. "James said you've barely been eating."

"I've been eating, Mama. I just don't pig out like they do and I figured that eating less would save more money."

"Today we can all pig out and you never have to go without food again." Her mom's smile faded and her eyes got misty. "I had no idea that's what you were doing."

Beth Ann had no choice but to leave her daddy behind. Just maybe having the top down would be fun and having lunch on the road in a real restaurant would be nice. She could have a cup of soup and a nice salad. They'd never done that before.

The only good news, if you had to find something, she was going to see her Gram. That part would be a great thing. Gram would know what to do. How to make her parents behave and stop this divorce thing. Beth Ann couldn't stand the thought that her parents were getting a divorce. Did that mean that her daddy wouldn't be her daddy anymore? She wasn't sure how that worked and didn't want to talk about it with her mama. She'd wait and talk to Gram. She would fix this whole situation and there would be no divorce.

* * * *

Three months later, Beth Ann awoke at Gram's with the sun shining through the lacy blue curtains that hung in her bedroom. Actually, it wasn't the sun that woke her as much as the smell of Gram's yummy cooking. She'd always said *that's my alarm clock for you, sweetness.* Beth Ann was the luckiest girl in the world to have such a wonderful grandma. When she was at Gram's house, she could almost pretend her life was normal, no dirty walls, bugs, or sleeping in the car. For the first time ever, her mom had sworn that her life was about to become stable.

Her parents had gotten that divorce and her mom had just married a guy named Stanley. The truth was that the getting married part had been a bigger shock than the divorce. Beth Ann hadn't seen that coming.

Now, her mom and stepdad had bought a brand new home in a brand new neighborhood and would be living in a little town called Novato, California. The place was only thirty minutes from San Francisco and that's where Stanley owned his own Automotive Center. Beth Ann tried to be happy about being so close to the city. She thought San Francisco was neat, with all the cable cars, the big red bridge, and the cute sailor guys all over the place, but nothing could make her stop being sad about that divorce. She just wanted her family back together again. Her mom had said there was no way she'd ever patch things up with her dad. Beth Ann knew she had to pretend to be okay with it. Yet deep down inside she hated it.

The thing that also scared her was a new school and making friends. She'd never been in one school for any length of time and never had one friend for very long. What if nobody liked her? She didn't even know how to meet people. Living out of a car was no way to get to know anyone, going from city to city and state to state. The thought of it made her want to cry. Now, she wished she had never complained, because she had a pretty good idea that it was her big mouth that caused this whole thing.

The memory surfaced of what Charlie had said over two years ago, about a new home and a prince charming. Being almost twelve, didn't mean she wanted a prince charming. Not unless it was Little Joe from Bonanza. He would make a good one because he was so nice and liked to cook, plus, he was really cute.

The fragrance of Gram's cooking forced her to want to get out of bed. It smelled so good. She threw the covers back, rolled out of bed, and stretched out. Then she shuffled in front of the mirror and really wished she could do something about her out of control hair.

Like I'd find prince charming anyway. She wrinkled her nose.

"What's that face?"

Beth Ann turned towards the voice and found her Gram in the doorway. Love filled her heart when she saw her Grandmother's tender blue eyes.

"Oh, Gram, how does one put in a complaint to God?"

Gram's smile reached her eyes. "You pray and talk to him."

"I've tried, just like the pastor said. I prayed and asked God to take away my red hair and these freckles. She pointed to her hair. "It's still a problem, nothing's changed." She moved over and plopped down on the bed. "Maybe I need to put in a formal complaint to the Attorney Captain."

Beth Ann witnessed Gram press her lips together and almost laugh. "I think you mean the Attorney General. You're a beauty and you'll love your red hair someday."

Beth Ann mumbled, "They should have a return policy, like stores."

Gram stood and shook her head. "You need to get dressed. Today is a big day. But I do wish you would have taken a plane. That darn old station wagon your daddy drives had to break down. I don't like you taking that bus alone."

"Gram, I'm almost twelve, I'll be fine." She meant it. "I spent enough time in that old heap anyway."

"Okay, I guess you did. Besides, we have no choice." Her gram brushed some crumbs off her apron. "Right now you need to get dressed. We can't have you missing that bus." She glanced down at the floor.

"Okay, but I don't want to leave here," Beth Ann said matter-of-factly. "I like being with you and Daddy." Her dad had been staying with Gram since the divorce. He was playing music, but not traveling around from place to place, at least not right now.

"You're going to love your new home. Finally, you'll have a house and a school. You'll make a lot of new friends," her Gram explained.

"I've never had a long term friend before," Beth Ann murmured. She stared at her hands. "What if nobody likes me? Kids from the past have made fun of my freckles and my red hair." She went over to the dresser, pulled out her blow up slip.

Gram walked closer and placed her gentle fingers under Beth Ann's chin, then raised it. "You've never lived in one place long enough to have friends. And, your hair is so pretty now. It's calmed down and all those curls are beautiful." She touched Beth Ann's hair. "Look at the kids around here that wait for you to show up every summer. Especially Billy." Gram winked. "He's sure a cute boy now."

"He stares at me all the time and maybe he's cute, but he's not my friend anymore."

"Why?" Gram stared at her.

"Because, he called me a stuck up virgin the other day." She finished her slip, then walked over and laid it on the bed.

Gram's eyebrows shot up. "What did you say to him?"

"I told him I was no such thing and I was going to tell you … but, you were at the store. I will never be his friend again. Calling me a dirty name like that."

Gram walked over to the bed and patted the seat next to her. "Come here, sweetness." She waited for Beth Ann to sit down. "You are a virgin, Beth Ann."

Beth Ann felt tears swim in her eyes. "I don't want to be one." She felt upset and wondered when she had turned into that.

Gram embraced her. "It's nothing bad. It just means you've never had relations with a man and that's a good thing."

Beth Ann cocked her head. "Relations, what's that mean?"

Gram inhaled deeply. "What it means is you've never made love with a man." She smiled. "You've never let a man kiss you or touch you in a special way."

"No way," Beth Ann said. "I know how people have babies." She felt herself blush. "A girl that was pregnant on the reservation told me. But she didn't explain the virgin part."

Gram stood. "Now you know. And now, I need to go finish breakfast." She exited the room.

The stuck up part was the only thing Billy had said that was mean. She wondered why he had called her that, and decided that next summer she'd tell him a thing or two, or maybe three.

After a few minutes, she walked over to the closet and pulled out her new dress. To calm down, she turned on the radio and one of her favorite songs was playing, so she sang along with Runaround Sue.

When Beth Ann finished getting her clothes on and her hair done, she entered the kitchen. Her dad was sitting at the table reading the paper, while Gram dished up food on her Blue Ridge china plates. Beth Ann wondered how old those dishes were—way older than her that's for sure. Gram's kitchen never changed, the same light green walls and her matching curtains were there since Beth Ann was old enough to remember.

The sound and smell coming from the percolator made her sad. It had always been hard to leave, but now it was even harder. Gram's beautiful old Victorian house had been her home every summer since she was a kid. The comfort of the smells and Gram's hugs were something that Beth Ann needed and loved.

Now her dad was going to stay behind, never to live with the family again.

Beth Ann swallowed the lump that formed in her throat.

Even though her dad was gone a lot, he'd always been fun to be around. His joyful and goofy behavior had always made her laugh. Not to mention, he'd always listened to her stories with keen interest. Now, she'd be around some strange man that was her stepdad. What if he was mean and hateful? Her daddy might have been immature, but he was never ever a mean person, and she knew he loved her.

Her dad had tried everything to get the family back together, but it was too late and Gram had refused to interfere. Beth Ann had pleaded with Gram to make her mama stop with the whole divorce thing, but gram had said she had no right to tell Jean anything, and that life wasn't always fair.

While her dad was away, leaving them alone, Beth Ann's mom had met someone, and even though nobody told Beth Ann, she knew now what she hadn't known then. Like why her mom started dressing different and got her hair done. Plus, that brand new car had been a gift from Stanley. Beth Ann might be young, but knew that when someone buys you a brand new car, they must be serious.

"Hi, Daddy," she said when she finally sat down.

He winked and grinned. "Well, don't you look pretty and all grown up in that dress."

"Thank you. Pink is my favorite color." She ran her hand down her new dress and could feel the blow up slip underneath. She wanted to make an impression when she got off the bus in Novato, that way nobody would know that she had lived out of a car. She could pretend to be normal.

"I do know that's your favorite color, Elizabeth." He grinned.

"Daddy! I'm not Elizabeth anymore. I keep telling you. I'm Beth Ann. I'm way too grown up for Elizabeth." She scolded. "And Beth Ann is going to be my famous name someday."

"Yes, ma'am." He arched a brow.

Gram placed the plates on the table and sat down. "It looks like your daddy's not the only one wanting to be famous." Gram reached over and took the paper from his grasp. "James, now go wash your hands since you've touched that nasty paper."

"Mother, really. I'm a grown man."

Beth Ann couldn't help but notice how thick their southern accents got when they argued with each other.

"Really? I hadn't noticed. Now go wash those hands." She lifted her napkin and placed it in her lap. In one instant, she frowned at James, then turned and smiled at Beth Ann.

A few minutes later after they prayed, they dug into the scrumptious

26

smelling breakfast. Gram had gone all out—eggs, homemade potatoes, gravy, biscuits, and sausage. Beth Ann would not eat the sausage, because it came from a pig.

One summer in Nashville, she'd made friends with a cute little guy named Dewy at her Aunt's farm. That little pig had been so smart and followed her everywhere. Then one morning she went out to visit him and he was gone. That was the summer she found out that sausage and pork came from pigs. Since that day, she hadn't taken one bite of pork and never would again.

After breakfast, she and Gram cleaned up while her daddy loaded the suitcases into a car. He had borrowed a vehicle from some lady friend, he knew. When he walked in the door, she knew what was coming. He ran over, picked her up and spun her around. Beth Ann couldn't help but squeal, like she always did.

"James, put her down for heaven's sake. We are going to be late and she's too old for you to be doing that to her anymore." Gram stood, drying her hands on a towel.

"Yes, Mother," He winked at Beth Ann and watched Gram leave, then gave her one last twirl.

This is what Beth Ann would miss, she felt tears swimming. Her dad had always been so playful and that was one of the things she loved most about him.

"Now, what's that look?" her dad asked.

"I don't want to leave, Daddy. I want to stay here with you and Gram." She swallowed back the tears.

"Ah honey, you know Cole would never let that happen. Since the day you were born, he claimed you as his own." He gave her a tender look.

Beth Ann knew that was true, but still she wanted to stay.

"Come on you two." Gram grabbed her purse. "We need to head on out."

On the way to the bus station, her daddy glanced in the rear view mirror. "Elizabeth …" He paused. "I mean Beth Ann. I don't know why you couldn't take a plane. You would have been there in thirty minutes or so." He shook his head.

"Daddy, I don't want to fly," she said flatly. "I don't like it, and I won't do it. Besides, do you know how much reading I can get done on the bus?"

"How would you know that you don't like flying?" He glanced at her in the mirror again. "You've never flown."

Gram turned and looked over her shoulder. "I would have felt safer if you'd flown, but I do know how much you like to read."

"Okay, I'm making a list of the things that are never going to happen. I won't eat pork, I won't fly and I'll never learn to cook. My mind is made up on those issues. Oh, and I don't ever want a husband unless it's Little Joe from Bonanza, because he's so handsome and he cooks. But even if he was my husband and tried to serve me pork chops, I'd get a divorce."

Both her dad and Gram cracked up, and then her dad mumbled under his breath. "Divorce is no fun."

Beth Ann knew she shouldn't have said that. "I'm sorry, Daddy. I do need to think before I talk. " She felt horrible. More than once this summer, she'd seen her daddy's eyes droop and his mouth curved down instead of up. So she knew he was sad.

He waved his hand as if it was no big deal.

Gram changed the subject. "I bet you're going to make a lot of new friends."

"I hope so, Gram." Beth Ann tried to feel happy. "I want a best friend so bad. Oh no, Gram we need to go back. I left my comic books under the bed."

Gram turned around and glanced at Beth Ann. "I'll mail them to you. If we turn around now, you'll miss that bus."

"So I can take the one tomorrow or the next day." She chewed on her bottom lip and felt her stomach jitter.

"We are not going to turn around, so you can put that thought out of your head." She gave Beth Ann a sidelong glance. "I know you're nervous, but everything is going to be good, better than good, wonderful."

Beth Ann didn't think so. How could it be? Her daddy was in Oregon, while they'd be living in California with her *new* stepdad.

When they pulled up to the bus stop, Beth Ann felt like crying, but she didn't want to upset Gram, nor did she want to hurt her daddy.

Her dad walked around the car and pulled out her luggage. When she stepped outside Gram handed her a lunch box.

"You have a sandwich, cookies, apple and lemonade in the thermos," she said. "Make sure you eat all of that."

"Okay, I promise." Beth Ann swallowed hard again.

Gram was sad, but was trying to cover it up, which made Beth Ann's heart sink like a boat with a hole in it. It was the same way every summer when Beth Ann left, and the truth was simple, Beth Ann hated to leave her Gram every time. She loved her family, but wanted to live with her grandmother. That was where she felt safe and stable.

At least she had her new book, *Charlotte's Web* to take her mind off things. She tucked it under her arm and tried to act brave.

Before Beth Ann stepped onto the bus, her Gram wrapped her in a big hug. "Call me as soon as you get home. Is that clear?"

"Yes, Gram," Beth Ann whispered and inhaled Gram's scent of cinnamon and ginger. There was no better aroma in the world, but once again, her throat burned from emotions.

When Gram released her, she swallowed her salty tears. A few seconds later, her dad stepped up and gathered her in his arms. "My sweet little girl, I love you and I'll see you soon."

"Okay, Daddy." She kissed his cheek and gazed into his blue eyes. Beth Ann was fully aware of how good-looking her daddy was, and that ladies always stared at him.

When he finally let her go, she stepped back. Beth Ann felt her heart ache because she knew the family she always loved, could never be whole again. All the days of singing and going on picnics would now be a tender memory. Beth Ann felt like she was going to fall apart at any moment. The thought of saying goodbye to a life that was forever gone, made her feel like bawling.

She was always losing people and things she loved. Would that ever change?

"I love you, Daddy," she whispered again.

"I love you, too." His voice cracked.

With that, Beth Ann inhaled deeply, turned, and walked up the steps.

Once she was on the bus, she found the quietest seat in the back near the bathroom. She sat by the window and watched her dad handing off the luggage to the bus driver. Gram was giving instructions to the man and pointing inside at Beth Ann. Gram was really good at directing.

She watched as people climbed up the steps, carrying their bags and chattering, while looking for the perfect seat. Gram and Dad were still talking to the bus driver, while he loaded the luggage for others.

Beth Ann looked up to see an old man that had boarded, standing right in front of her. He nodded and gave her a soft smile as he sat down. He seemed like a nice old man, although she knew to watch out for strangers. Gram had drilled that into her head, almost as much as Cole. Her mom had said they didn't even tell Cole she was taking the bus, because he would have had a fit.

When she blew a kiss goodbye, a feeling of loneliness washed through her. The worst part was seeing Gram's shoulders shake as they turned to walk away. At least her dad placed his arm around her and guided her inside the car.

Why did her daddy have to leave them so much when they were in the hotels? Now, she was going to have to live with some man named Stanley who could be uptight and stuck up. *I bet he doesn't even want me around.*

Her mama had explained why she had to leave and wanted a divorce. But knowing the reason didn't take away from the fact that she'd miss her daddy every day. She felt her heart sag. There was no way she was going to start crying on a bus with a bunch of strangers.

Even though she didn't want a new stepdad, her Gram had told her she needed to support her mama. Gram had also told her that sometimes life just doesn't work out how we wish it would, and God always has a plan. She also explained that her mama had a right to be happy.

"Hi ladies and gentlemen, we will be driving all night and we should be arriving in about twenty hours. We will be making stops for your convenience and ..."

His voice faded when she pulled out the crocheted blanket from Gram. The aroma had the sweet scent of the old Victorian house, and so did the hat that Gram had stuck inside the carry bag. That did it, tears slid down her cheeks, so to hide her emotions she buried her face in the small pillow that her grandmother had packed.

A while later, she was able to pull herself away from the sadness and noticed that she had both seats to herself, so she stretched out and pulled up her book. It didn't take her long to go deeper into the story, which was about a pig and a funny spider that was really smart. Someday, she'd have a pet pig and there was one thing for sure, nobody would ever eat him or her.

Chapter Five

She was already half way done with the book when she noticed fields of wild berries and patches of weeds. She had no clue where they were. Once they stopped, she felt the urge to move her legs, but decided to wait until everyone had exited the bus. The stewardess that had been sitting up front, stood and smiled at her.

"Hi, you must be Beth Ann," the lady greeted. "I thought I'd walk with you. My name is Suzie and I will be hanging out with you when you get off the bus if that's okay? This is a small town, but it's safer to be in pairs."

"Sure, that would be great." Beth Ann meant it. She liked the idea of having company, because it would keep her mind off things.

Once she went inside the building, everything changed. Among the shadows, were people buying tickets. Some were saying hello to loved ones while chatter filled the air. One girl passed by with flip-flops on and tears streaking her face. She must have said goodbye to someone she loved, which made Beth Ann feel sad.

The smell of hot dogs pulled her away from the chaos and made her tummy growl.

Suzie looked at her, grinned and touched her own stomach. "Me too."

Beth Ann bought a bag of chips and a peanut butter cup, her all-time favorite.

When the bus took off again, Beth Ann picked up her book to read, but decided to look out the window at her surroundings instead. Suzie had said they were in a city called Roseburg, Oregon. It was a tiny place with surrounding mountains and a river that seemed to run almost through the heart of the town. It was so pretty, with the sun shining its rays across the water and leaving trails of sparkling lights dancing under the bright blue sky.

Beth Ann thought about summer days and snow cones, and wondered what life would be like in the new town. Soon they were out on the freeway heading to Novato.

Beth Ann pulled out her toasted-egg sandwich and listened to everyone chattering while she continued to read. All except the old man in front of her, who was snoring loudly.

Beth Ann tried not to giggle as she continued to eat her delicious sandwich that was toasted, which was the only way she liked it. The egg squished between her teeth, so she took a big gulp of her cool lemonade to wash it down, hoping it would also wash back the giggles.

She picked up her book again and read for a couple of hours. All of a sudden, she was interrupted by the old man's pillow landing on the floor. Suzie strolled over to pick it up, so Beth Ann went back to her story. Not more than thirty minutes later he dropped it again, but this time Suzie was talking to the bus driver and didn't see it. The poor old guy just sat there, staring at the pillow. So this time Beth Ann picked it up.

"Here you go, sir." She handed it to him.

"God bless you." He took the pillow and stuck it behind his head.

Beth Ann sat back down to read and was engrossed again when she looked up to find he was staring over the edge of his seat, again at his pillow. This time someone walked down to use the restroom, picked it up, and handed it to him.

Holy pillow dropper. He kept dropping it and leaning over the edge to stare at it. Beth Ann had to cover her face with the blanket to keep from laughing out loud. For hours, it happened, over and over again. He'd drop his pillow, stare at it, and wait for someone to pick it up. She lost count of how many times she helped him, but the whole scenario was entertaining.

Finally, as the sun set and she finished her book, she wondered what the town was like. In this new town, would there be chirping robins? She could imagine the smell of budding roses and fresh cut grass along with wind chimes singing their songs.

Having this extra time not only gave way to her imagination but also gave her time to reflect on unanswered questions. Like why her mom and dad got divorced, and how they stopped loving each other? Or did they? For the first time reality hit her, she was mad at them both for letting this happen. Sure, her daddy stayed away all the time, but how much had her mama let him know that she was fed up? Had she given him a warning? She made a mental note to ask her mama about that soon.

After a while, she was finally able to drift to sleep, dreaming about the way life used to be and wondering what her world would look like now.

* * * *

"Okay folks, we'll be entering Novato in about ten minutes. Please gather your belongings and stay seated until we come to a full stop," the driver announced over the intercom.

Beth Ann rubbed her eyes, hardly able to believe she had slept so long. After a moment of clearing her thoughts, she packed her stuff into her carry bag that had her name embroidered in pink. The bag held everything, including her Shirley Temple lunch box that she'd had since she was five. She loved it, but really, it was time to get a more mature one. Next, she found a lifesaver and popped it into her mouth, deciding to wait and brush her teeth when she got to the new place.

They pulled into town and Beth Ann gazed out the window. At first glance, it seemed like a small and simple place, but tingles of anticipation ran through her. There was something about Novato that was enchanting. Maybe it was the way the shops lined up perfectly along the well-kept streets. The main street held a florist shop that had an array of colorful flowers in bins sitting out front, which reminded her of a rainbow. She watched a woman pick up a bouquet and bury her nose among the petals. People strolled down the sidewalks arm in arm, while children rode their bikes with giant smiles.

A movie house called *Novato Theater* caught her attention just before she spotted a laundry mat next door. She was sure they'd be doing their wash there. Another block down, she spotted a pool hall, along with Ben and Franklins, her favorite five-and-dime store. They also passed by a place called, DeBorba's.

The last business on the street was a modest neighborhood grocery store named, Rayburns, where a man swept off the sidewalks. Everything appeared to be spotless and storybook perfect.

When the bus pulled up to the drop off area, it wasn't a bus stop at all. It was no more than a couple of benches, next to a small travel agency. What an odd place to be dropped off, right behind what appeared to be an old abandoned train station. Beth Ann loved trains and always had, but when she studied the place, she thought it looked haunted and abandoned.

Once the bus came to a full stop, she scooped up her bag and waited to see who else might be getting off. Only one other lady left and seemed to be in a hurry. Beth Ann stood and exited the bus. She guessed everyone else must be getting off at the final stop, a place called San Rafael.

The bus stewardess waved goodbye and Beth Ann nodded since her hands were full.

The minute she stepped outdoors, the scent of eucalyptus filled her senses. As a cool breeze tickled her skin, the sounds of birds serenaded her with their special songs. Something inside of Beth Ann felt drawn to all the surroundings. There was an odd feeling, like something was about to happen, then when she looked at her arm, there were goose bumps.

The bus driver lifted the luggage door and pulled out her two suitcases.

"I'll set these here and someone will be here to pick you up, right?" He looked around. "We are about ten minutes early."

"Yes. My mom's coming and she's always on time." She looked around and was surprised that her mama wasn't there yet.

"Okay." He nodded, then sat down the bags and climbed back onto his bus.

Beth Ann took a seat on the bench, placed the hat on her head and waited for her mom.

Chapter Six

Kaylob continued to paint the fence while he watched the tiny girl step off the bus. He had seen the bus driver take out two suitcases and set them down. Either she was visiting or moving to town. He watched as she leaned back, slipped on a hat and turned her face toward the sky. When the wind lifted her hair, Kaylob became mesmerized by its color and his heart fluttered. He'd never seen red hair like that before. He wasn't even sure he could call her long, curly hair red but a deep coppery gold was a better description. What he wanted to know was why couldn't he take his eyes off her. It's not like he hadn't been around other girls and right now he was hanging out with a high school girl, who was almost eighteen.

Oh crap, he thought and ducked. She looked right at his house. He couldn't let her see him ogling her. *She looks kinda young, what if she's too young? Too young for what, idiot?*

He watched as she stood and waved to someone. Kaylob followed the direction of her attention.

A groovy red convertible pulled up, driven by a lady with dark hair. He'd seen her a few times lately and was pretty darn sure she was new in town. Could this be her daughter?

When she parked, she hopped out of the car and ran to the pretty, copper-headed girl. It had to be her daughter because they both squealed and embraced each other. Well, that wasn't the only reason that they must be related. The older woman was good looking too, dark hair and curly like her daughter's, with a great body. *Oh, shut up! What kind of pervert are you?* First, he was checking out the girl and now he noticed the other lady's figure. Even though it was hard to miss, he shouldn't be noticing.

When they stopped hugging, the wind blew her hat from her head and it was moving towards the tracks. He wanted to help her, but she caught it and held it up to show her mom.

God, she was tiny, but such a beauty, and the way she walked. He looked down to see if his shoes were still on his feet, man oh man she was knocking him for a loop.

Was this what I've been waiting for all these years? For some reason he thought the answer was yes.

Her mom picked up the suitcases and stuck them in the back of the car. Just as the girl reached the convertible, she stopped and glanced around. He had to duck again as she was looking down his street. Why did she keep looking in his direction? She hadn't seen him, had she?

He was saved by her mom when she opened the door and waved for the cute girl to get inside.

They were going to leave, and he didn't know where she lived, or what her name was. A thought hit him. He decided to pretend to wash the windows at the old train station. That way he could watch her reflection in the glass. He wasn't sure why he needed to do this, but he didn't have time to figure it out. All he wanted to do was get a long look. There was nothing wrong with that, right?

He sure as heck hoped she was in town for good.

He picked up an old bucket and a rag and tore across the street. Now, he'd go into acting mode, and watch with keen interest. Man he was twisted. *Why was he acting like this*? Well, she did have the cutest freckles scattered about her perfect complexion, and okay, she was a little skinny. Nevertheless, he'd just enjoy the view and stop asking himself stupid questions. He was a guy and she was a girl, plain and simple.

A few seconds later, he heard the train bells chiming. They were going to get stuck behind the trip arm. Man, this was his lucky day.

You dog, he scolded himself.

As they sat there, the lady waved her hand around, clearly chattering away. He saw the moment the redhead turned and looked at him. He was still pretending to wash the windows as she stared at his back. Wow! She was scoping him out. So with a slow and slick move, he turned and looked right into her amazing brown eyes and held her gaze.

Her eyes widened and her mouth fell open.

With that, he gave her the most flirtatious smile that he could conjure up, and watched her face grow from ivory to a beautiful pink. At that point, he knew there was only one thing he could do, he winked.

Suddenly, her cheeks flamed to a fire engine red and he had to chuckle. She whipped her head around to face her mom and that's when he saw the funniest thing he'd ever seen. Her mother pressed her hand on her forehead like she was checking for a fever. A few moments later, she pulled her hand away and the blushing girl slowly turned her head and glared at him.

Okay, he had no excuse for what he did next, but he did it anyway. He winked again, and observed her cheeks glow like the nose on Rudolf the red-nosed reindeer. Oh, now he was even more intrigued. He'd never seen someone blush that much. He threw his head back in laughter, holding his stomach and he couldn't seem to stop.

After a few seconds, the train ended and she shot him one long, nasty glare before they drove away.

Yep, there was no doubt that Novato had just become a lot more interesting.

* * * *

As they drove along, Beth Ann pretended to be enjoying everything her mother was saying about the town and the school, even though she was furious. *What gall that guy had, flirting like that.* He'd actually made her mom think she had a fever. She wished she could dump that bucket of water on his head.

So what if he was the most handsome boy she'd ever seen, even better than Little Joe. Big deal that he had the most divine blue eyes on the planet, all they did was make her blush. And who cared, if he had blond hair with a cute little dimple in his chin and muscles that were hunky-dory, that was just not a big deal.

"Beth Ann, did you hear what I said?" Her mama drawled big time.

"Yes, Mama. You said Cole is going to Novato High School, and he's already made a couple of friends."

"Honey, you sure you're feeling okay? I've never seen your face so red."

"It's just hot that's all." She fanned her face, then touched the end of her nose to see if it grew.

"It's only in the seventies." Her mother chuckled. "You must have gotten used to the cooler weather in Oregon."

"Yep, that's it. I got used to the weather there."

After a few minutes of silence, Beth Ann's mom pointed ahead. "We're almost there,"

Beth Ann's nerves were fried. First, the boy flirting and now she was going to her new home and would meet Stanley. Her stomach flipped and her throat got dry.

When they turned into the new neighborhood the first thing Beth Ann noticed was all the brand new houses. Newly planted trees dotted the dark green lawns along the street. White fences lined the borders of many houses, embellished with multi-colored flowers. The neighborhood bustled with activity; people cutting their grass, kids on bikes, and the sounds of laughter echoing through the neighborhood. One little boy pranced down the sidewalk, playing his flute like he was in a marching band.

Her mama glanced around. "You're going to have so much fun here. I've already seen girls your age walking around. This is a new neighborhood, and so many kids are searching for friends. And look ..." She pointed again. "We have a musician in the neighborhood." Beth Ann's mom grinned as she watched the little boy doing his routine.

Before Beth Ann could respond, they pulled into the driveway and her mom turned off the car. They sat there while Beth Ann noticed a light breeze playing with the trees as if whispering of hope for the future. The yard was perfect, with flowers that bordered the fence. The grass was as green as any green she could imagine. The color of the house was white as snow, which enhanced the dark green shudders.

She loved the beautiful oversized front porch. It wasn't as big as Gram's, but it was nice. She never imagined so many trees, flowers, or the white picket fence. Nor could she believe that the aroma of eucalyptus would fill her heart with such delight. The house was everything she'd never dreamed of, because her dreams had not been big enough.

After a few melted moments, Beth Ann's mom reached over and caressed her hand. "Welcome home, my precious daughter." She wiped away a tear and asked, "Are you ready to go inside and see your bedroom?"

Beth Ann felt another lump in her throat and nodded in response.

Before they could open the car door, Cole rushed out to greet her. She jumped out of the car and ran into his arms.

"Sis, I'm so glad your home." He swung her around then set her down.

"Me too." Her hat fell to the ground and her mama reached down and picked it up.

"Where's James?" She looked around, wondering where he was.

Her mom touched her arm and said, "He's away right now. I'll explain later."

Beth Ann was sure she saw sadness in her mom's eyes and wondered what was going on. Stanley must have sent him away and just maybe she and Cole were next. Once again, her stomach took a dive just thinking about James and what had happened.

"Mama." Beth Ann tilted her head.

Cole seemed to duck her question, went over to the car and pulled out the luggage. Something was way off and Beth Ann intended to find out later.

"Come on, honey, let's go inside." Her mama was clearly trying to take her mind off James.

Right now, she'd do what her mama asked because she didn't want to take away from her excitement.

The minute she stepped inside, she was mesmerized. The living room was overwhelming with floor to ceiling windows. The gorgeous hardwood floors were strewn with green and white throw rugs. All the furniture was new and matching. Beth Ann couldn't believe how beautiful it all was.

"Well, what do you think?" Her mom walked over and switched on some lights. "I love this room." She nodded towards the hallway. "Now, you need to see your bedroom and afterwards you can look around at the family room, kitchen, and the backyard. We also have a laundry room, complete with washer and dryer." Her mom's voice went up a notch.

"Wow! No more laundry mats?" Beth Ann was surprised. "This is wonderful, Mama." Although she wondered how long she'd be there to enjoy it.

Her mom nodded and opened up a window to let the cool breeze flow inside.

"Where's Stanley?" Beth Ann questioned.

"He's at work, but he is going to try to make it home early." She took Beth Ann's hand and led her around the corner and down the hall.

They stopped in front of a door and her mom slowly opened it. Cole stepped up with the luggage, giving Beth Ann a cute wink.

Beth Ann's hand went across her heart as her eyes fixed on a canopy bed with pink lace and everything matching. Even the curtains were pink and white. They must not be sending her away or why would they buy all this stuff?

"Mama, how could we afford this?" Beth Ann felt worried. She looked at the animal pictures flanking her wall. Then her eyes came to rest on a photo of her and her daddy. It was a special one of them together on Christmas two years ago at Gram's. The memory made her heart plop down into her stomach, but she pasted on a smile, and turned to face her mom.

"Honey, Stanley works hard and we are comfortable. It's my job to worry about that stuff from now on. In the past, I shared too much of our financial issues with ya'll. Now you kids just have to stop worrying and have fun." Jean walked over to the closet and slid it open. "Look at this," her mom exclaimed.

"Oh, Mama," She felt her eyes flooding as she stepped closer to the closet, staring at all the beautiful clothes. Pink dresses, sweaters, pants, blouses—all brand new. In the past, most of Beth Ann's clothes came from second hand stores, except when Gram had put a few things on layaway. It had never bothered her because her mom always made sure things were fresh, clean, and looked new. This was a lot to take in.

"Look at this dress." Her mom pulled it from the closet and held it up. "Pink with black stripes, will look so good on you. Of course we can go shopping and you can pick out some of your own styles, but I thought these were all pretty and hip." Her mom's smile spread.

In almost a whisper, Beth Ann said, "Thank you so much, they are all really nice and I love them." She wiped away a tear.

"Come on you two." Cole spoke up. "Let's go look at the rest of the house."

Her mama laughed. "Come on honey, your brother wants to show off his new bedroom." She linked her arm through Beth Ann's as they headed down the hall.

Beth Ann couldn't believe they had four bedrooms and two full bathrooms, along with what her mom called a powder room. The family room was humongous with space for everyone. It even had a wet bar across one wall next to a fireplace. She'd seen one before in a magazine. With all this room, why did James leave? Maybe he just didn't like Stanley.

After the grand tour of the entire house, her mom and Cole led Beth Ann out back.

"A swimming pool! Oh my gosh!" Beth Ann ran over close to it. "I can't believe we have a pool."

Cole ran over next to her then picked her up and pretended like he was going to throw her in. "Isn't this the most bitchen' thing you've ever seen?" Cole laughed and sat her down.

"Cole Samuel Rose!" Beth Ann's mom scolded. "Do not curse in my presence."

"Mom, it's not cursing. It's a cool word." He shook his head.

"I won't have you using anything that starts off with that b word in this home. Do you understand me?"

Cole nodded and said in a smarty-pants tone. "So what do you want me to call bread and butter, and what are we going to rename Beth Ann?" He stifled back a laugh.

Her mama's look was one they knew well, which told Cole she didn't find him funny at all.

Beth Ann giggled and Cole did a half shrug.

"Yes, Mom." He shuffled his feet. A few seconds later Cole grabbed Beth Ann's arm. "C'mon, let's go swimming."

He ran with her through the house and they heard their mom yell. "Don't y'all run in the house, you're gonna break your neck."

They both laughed and Beth Ann sprinted to her room, where she threw open her suitcase and pulled out her swimsuit. Before she went out to the pool, she went into the bathroom brushed her teeth and changed.

The rest of the morning was spent swimming, but nobody had mentioned

James.

Okay, it was time. Her mama was sitting out under the umbrella that was attached to the new patio furniture. Beth Ann climbed out of the pool and headed her way. Cole was floating around on his inner tube.

Beth Ann knew she must have somehow given her mama a clue, because she took a deep breath and met Beth Ann's gaze.

Beth Ann sat down at the table. "Where's James, Mama?"

She stared at her.

Just then, she heard Cole getting out of the water and he shuffled over and sat down next to Beth Ann.

Her mom's eyes filled with tears and Beth Ann felt her heart sink. "Mama is he hurt?" She felt dizzy.

"No," she cried. "He joined the Navy. And … I'm just worried with this war going on and everything." She took a deep sigh. "I tried to talk him out of it. So did Stanley and your daddy."

Cole reached out and held his mom's hand. He's going to be fine, Mom."

"I didn't even get to say goodbye." Beth Ann felt tears building as a tear slid down her cheek. "When will I see him again?"

"He'll be home for a few days after boot camp."

Beth Ann had no idea what that was. "What is boot camp, Mama? Is that where they learn to wear those big boots?"

Cole chuckled through the tension. "It's where they learn how to do everything. It's like survival training." He stared at his Mom. "James is smart and strong and he's going to make it through with flying colors."

The gate to the side opened and a man stepped into the backyard. It had to be Stanley. He was handsome with dark hair and green eyes and appeared nervous.

Her mom stood. "You're home, darling." She rushed over to him and gave him a hug. "Come meet Beth Ann." She took him by the hand.

Beth Ann felt her pulse shoot up. Not only because she was seconds away from meeting her new stepdad, but she hoped her brother would not have to fight in that bad war. She knew guys got killed over there, and she just didn't like the whole idea.

Beth Ann stood and watched as they walked toward her as she kept hearing the word *darling*. Her mom had never said that to her daddy.

Stanley walked up to her. "It's so good to finally meet you." His smile spread into his green eyes.

"Hi." Beth Ann stuck out her hand, but instead he pulled her into a hug. After a few seconds, he released her.

He grinned again. "I feel like I know you already." He reached over and put his arm around her mom. "Jean has told me so much about you."

Beth Ann couldn't say the same thing. She hadn't been told much of anything. But her Gram told her she had to be polite.

"It's nice to meet you, too," was all she could conjure up.

Cole walked over and broke the ice that Beth Ann knew was freezing everyone. "Hey, I played ball and the coach was out there and said he was impressed," he said to Stanley.

"Wow! No kidding. From what I've seen you will have no problems." They walked away, but not before Stanley turned back and gave Beth Ann a nod.

Her mom took her arm. "Isn't he wonderful?" She met Beth Ann's gaze.

"Yes, Mama. He seems wonderful," she lied. She didn't like her mama calling him darling at all, and she didn't like him taking the place where her daddy should be.

"I'm going to make some sun tea for everyone," her mom said, looking so happy that Beth Ann thought she might outshine that sun. There was no way that Beth Ann wanted to spoil that. So she sat down on the lounge chair and tried to let the heat of the sun wash away her irritation.

A few minutes later, Beth Ann glanced up at all the clouds that were floating high in the blue sky. Cole was tossing his baseball up and down in his glove and Stanley was swinging his arms like he was batting.

Beth Ann was surprised at how much Cole and Stanley were laughing and getting along. Didn't Cole miss their daddy? What was wrong with him?

As she sat there trying to relax, her eyes started getting heavy, then she heard the back door open. Her mom came out carrying a tray with sun tea and glasses filled with ice.

"Anybody want some tea?" Her mom glanced around when she sat down everything.

Beth Ann couldn't help but notice the way her mom and Stanley gazed at each other. It was nothing like she'd ever noticed between her parents. Sure, she'd seen the love, but not like this, at least not for a long time. Beth Ann felt her stomach turn and thought she was going to throw up. She needed to escape and do it soon.

"Mama, I'm going inside for a while." She stood. "I'm feeling a little tired."

"Okay, sweetheart," her mom said, and gave her a tender look.

Stanley glanced at her and smiled. "Have a nice rest." He sounded sincere.

Why did he have to be so dang nice? She tried to smile, but scooted off to her bedroom.

Once she got into her room, she leaned against the wall and stared at everything. It was her dream. Hadn't she asked for her own room with her own bed and dresser? There was even a bay window, with a seat to look outside at the hillsides that cast shadows from their presence. She sank down onto her bed, thinking of her grandma's words. *God has a plan and sometimes we don't always understand what it is.*

Along with Gram, she thought of Charlie's words. *'This time your travels will take you to a new home and you will have many friends,'* his voice echoed through her mind.

Could all his visions be true?

After thinking about her time on the reservation and where life had taken her since then, she drifted off to sleep.

Chapter Seven

Sometime later, noises from another part of the house woke her, so she rolled off the bed and opened her bedroom door. She was still trying to pull the cobwebs out of her stupor. Was that her mother laughing? Beth Ann couldn't remember the last time she heard her laugh like that.

As soon as she approached the family room, her mom's voice became clearer. What a lovely sound, almost like a song that she hadn't heard in forever. When she entered, she found her mom and Stanley cuddling on the couch, eating popcorn together, watching the television and something must have been extremely funny.

Her mother looked up, still catching her breath and waved for her to join them. "Come in, sweetheart. We are watching, *I love Lucy.* It's so funny. I looked in on you, but you were still sleeping, so we left you alone. Want some popcorn?" She patted the seat next to her.

"Help yourself." Stanley held up the bowl. "As a matter of fact, you can have the rest if you want."

"No, I was wondering if I could go downtown. I really want to look around and see what's there. I saw a Ben and Franklin and I was hoping to find a book. I finished mine on the bus. I thought about reading it a second time because it was so good, but a new one would be great. Maybe Cole might want to go with me?"

"Your brother took off to go play some baseball with a couple new friends." She grinned and then started to stand, but Stanley touched her arm.

He rose and pulled out his wallet. "Here, go buy yourself some treats. Just try to stay on Grant Avenue so you don't get lost. Also, there is a wonderful deli called Perry's if you want to grab a sandwich and check the place out." His eyes were kind, but he could be pretending, or at least that's what she told herself. "Take the phone number just in case." He held out a twenty-dollar bill.

Beth Ann looked at her mom, not sure if she should take that much money. There was a time when that would have put food on the table. Beth Ann remembered her mom having to shop with a twenty-dollar bill. Sometimes she'd have to put a couple things back, because there wasn't enough to pay for everything. It was always so embarrassing when people would stare at them. One time a lady got angry with her mom, because she was returning things and the lady had to wait. That's one reason why Beth Ann learned at a young age to try to eat less and ignore the hunger pains.

Stanley pulled her back from her memories when he took her hand and placed the bill inside. "Take this honey, go treat yourself." He wrote down the phone number and handed it to her.

"I feel so spoiled today already," Beth Ann said. "Thank you both for all the wonderful clothes and my new furniture. I don't even know what to say." She held up the twenty-dollar bill. "Are you sure about this?"

He nodded and touched her cheek. "Yes, I'm more than sure." He sat back down. "Now, go have fun."

Her mama nodded. "Maybe you'll meet some other kids along the way, but be sure to grab some food. Beth Ann you don't have to worry about anything anymore."

"I will, Mama." Beth Ann went over and gave her a hug, then dashed out the door.

Just maybe she would meet some friends and maybe she could get a special treat today.

On the way out of the neighborhood, she saw a lot of little kids, but it wasn't until she got to the stone entrance that she saw a girl her own age. She had long brown hair and was sitting on the passenger side of a car. Their eyes locked, and the girl smiled a welcoming smile then waved. Beth Ann couldn't help but grin and wave back. The lady driver nodded as they turned the corner down Ferndale Drive. How cool would it be if they lived on the same street?

Beth Ann continued on her way and once she was out of the neighborhood, she passed by many older homes. One yard was filled with roses of every color. She just had to stick her nose in a red one hanging over the fence. The aroma was out of this world, like strawberries, pears and apples all mixed together. There was a saying that a rose by any other name wouldn't be as sweet, but she could think of a lot different names for roses that would still smell wonderful. She chuckled to herself as she thought of some. Okay, what if the name was, bunny, shiver, or twinkle. Those all smelled good, so maybe she'd have to make up a story or something.

While she strolled along, she found herself following the train tracks until she came to the old haunted train station. It had only taken her about five minutes to get there. The bucket and rag were still sitting out front. Just why had that boy been washing those old windows? The place was run down and appeared to be abandoned. She was glad he wasn't there, wasn't she?

Well, forget about him, she knew right where her first stop would be. She skedaddled along, passing by some of the little shops along the way. When she arrived at Ben and Franklins, she waltzed in and heard the bell jingle above the door, announcing her arrival. The smell of chocolate and popcorn was intoxicating. Then when her eyes came upon a giant size case filled with hundreds of different types of candy, she was sure her tongue fell out. There were only two things Beth Ann was searching for; chocolate peanut butter cups, and chocolate orange jelly sticks.

"Good afternoon. Can I help you with something?" asked the lady with salt and pepper hair. Her nametag read, *Betty*.

Beth Ann nodded. "Yes, I want a dozen peanut butter cups and the same amount for chocolate orange sticks." She felt her mouth watering. "And I want to find a good book to read."

Betty grinned and pushed her funny glasses up on her nose. "I just got some really good books in." She set the bag down on the counter and led Beth Ann to the back. "I finished one about a dog, and it was wonderful."

"Really? I read a lot, so what's the name of the book?"

"*Beautiful Joe*." The lady picked it up from the stand. "The dog in the book is the narrator and the author is a lady from Canada. It's really good." Betty handed it to her.

"I love stories about animals and just finished reading *Charlotte's Web*." Beth Ann examined the cover as the woman waited. "I'll take it. Thank you for helping me out."

The lady headed back to the front of the store. She put the chocolate in a bag and rang it up.

Beth Ann read the back cover, then handed her the twenty and got back her change.

"Come back when you can, and let me know how you liked the book." Betty smiled,

"I will." Beth Ann nodded.

Beth Ann held up her book as she headed to the front of the store. She paused again, smelling the heavenly aroma, then opened the door and stepped outside.

The first thing Beth Ann did was place two peanut butter cups in her mouth to melt, the feel was soft and creamy, but the taste was deliciously nutty, she opened her book and started to read. She knew she should have lunch, but she just wanted candy, she'd tuck the rest of the money away just in case her mom needed it later. After standing there for a few seconds, she started walking and reading, being careful not to run into street poles.

The first page already hooked Beth Ann, and when she looked up, she was back at the old train station. She wanted a closer look, so she placed her book back in her bag and tiptoed her way to the bottom of the steps.

She crept up the stairs leading to the old building. When she peered into the bucket, she couldn't believe her eyes. There was nothing. No water, no cleaning stuff. Holy numbskull, didn't he know you were supposed to wash windows with water? She found herself chuckling, while she pressed her face against the glass and saw just how old everything was. The floors were torn up and a counter looked as though a bull had rammed it. Nobody had used this place in many years.

"What are you doing?" A deep voice startled her.

She turned to see Mr. Blue Eyes standing there with a grin and, oh, that dimple in his chin. Oh god, her teeth were covered with chocolate and she couldn't say a word, so she swiftly started to exit the area.

"Let me try this again." He stepped in front of her. "Can you tell me your name? My name is Kaylob." He was grinning like he had eaten not only the bird, but the early worm too. Or was that saying he'd eaten the worm and saw an early bird. Oh well, no matter.

She held his gaze and felt her knees wobble. So she scurried down the stairs without so much as a word.

"What's wrong, cat got your tongue? Or are you afraid of me?" He cracked up as he continued following her.

With that, she swallowed hard and swung around. "No and no. I just don't like boys who are so fresh." She whipped back around to leave.

"Fresh?" He laughed even harder. "Did you time travel from the olden days?" He ran again to catch up with her.

"No!" She glared at him and saw his grin get bigger.

He reached out and touched her cheek. "You're cute."

Oh, for crying out loud. She felt the heat crawling up her cheeks. He was flirting again, so she pushed his hand away and scrunched up her nose.

He ignored her dirty look. "Whatcha got in the bag?" He leaned over and peeked inside. "So what's your name?"

"My name is Beth Ann, but I'm really Elizabeth Ann Rose. I took Beth Ann because it's a better stage name." She jerked her bag away and closed it up.

"Stage name? Are you an actress?" He acted like he really wanted to know.

"No, well … yes, but mostly I sing." She felt rude by not offering him a candy so she opened the bag and held it up. "Here, you can have some."

He reached in, took a peanut butter cup and plopped it in his mouth.

47

"Thank you. So I'm talking to a future star." He took her hand and bowed. "Nice to meet you Miss Rose and tell me, how old are you?"

"I'm almost twelve … are you making fun of me?"

"No. I never make fun of anyone. I'm seriously happy to meet you, and I'm glad to hear that you're almost twelve." His face softened and his eyes held hers.

At that moment, she wondered if those peanut butter cups were filled with butterflies because something was fluttering in her stomach. Not to mention that her head felt funny. Holy midnight, she must be coming down with something.

"Beth Ann, you okay? You look a little pale." He reached out to steady her and she stumbled into his arms. She couldn't help but notice how tall he was, that his shoulders were so wide and strong, and he seemed so mature that it made her wonder how old he was.

In the next instance, he stumbled backwards and gently held her away. Now, his face was all red and he looked nervous.

She steadied herself. "Are you okay, Kaylob?" She stared at him and tried not to bust up.

"Yes. I'm fine," he said, his face still red. Then he shook his head, like he was trying to clear cobwebs out of his brain.

"Sorry if I made you nervous." She giggled. "Your face is all red." She stared at him, then turned to leave.

But she only took a few steps before he was right in front of her again. He took her hand and gazed into her eyes. "I'm not nervous, Beth Ann. It's just that it's not every day you meet the girl you're gonna marry." With that, he brought her hand up to his lips and kissed her palm.

She froze for a minute and felt her heart melt. What was wrong with her? She didn't even like boys. Well, except little Joe, but she had to admit Kaylob was much better looking and there was something about his eyes.

A memory of Charlie's voice washed over her. *'In this new land you will meet what white men call your prince charming, and someday he will be your husband.'*

Holy midnight she had to swallow and breathe, but he was making it hard. With pure determination, she found the strength to run away like the roadrunner, trying to escape the coyote. Only this one had incredible blue eyes, with the most amazing smile she'd ever seen.

He was dangerous!

* * * *

Kaylob watched Beth Ann run away. Man, oh man, his heart ignited.

48

Maybe she was a little young, but he couldn't help how he felt. One thing he knew for sure, at age fourteen he'd never had a girl make him feel that way before. Not even Dusty who was tall, blonde, and filled out in all the right places.

He continued to stare until she turned the corner, hoping she would look back, but no such luck. After a few minutes of gathering his bearings, he placed his hand across his heart. *It's beating a million miles an hour*. Whoa, just maybe she'd cast a spell on him.

After his heart calmed down, he took a deep breath and counted to a hundred. It was time to head home and fix lunch for his mom. She would be wondering where he was. Most days he worried about her because of her mood swings with depression. He just wished his dad were around more to help her snap out of it.

The minute he got back to the train station, he collected his fake window washing junk, and headed back home.

"Kaylob!" He heard his mom calling when he walked into the shed.

"I'll be right there," he yelled back. "I'm just putting stuff away." He rinsed out the paint brushes and put everything back on the shelves. He would finish painting that fence tomorrow. The place was starting to look better, but he wished they didn't live so close to the old train station and in such a small run down house. Next month he'd paint the house and that would make it look better. At least the flowers in front of the white fence looked good.

Fifteen minutes later, he was in his house and saw his mom sitting in front of the television with her TV tray. It would've been nice if she had at least heated up everything, since he had done all the cooking. But, she was out of bed and moving around. That was a good day for her. Some days she never even changed out of her robe. With resolve, he took out the food and turned on the oven.

He'd made fried chicken, which he soaked in his own recipe—buttermilk, cream, olive oil, salt, pepper, basil, along with minced garlic. After he had placed it in a large bowl and covered it, he marinated it all night. Afterwards, he'd dipped it in the eggs first, and then in flour, paprika, basil, garlic powder, red pepper, and a few pinches of other spices. It was beyond tasty and the aroma was out of this world. He couldn't wait until he became a chef. That was the reason why he'd started putting money away from his job at the corner store, because he also planned to own his own restaurant someday.

He grinned to himself, because it reminded him of what Beth Ann had said. *Someday she'd be a star*. He sure hoped he would get a chance to hear her sing, and even more, he hoped he'd run into her again.

Maybe next time she wouldn't run away.

He carried both plates into the living room and prepared to watch *Father Knows Best*. His mom loved that program and he thought that maybe it was because the dad actually stayed home and took care of his family.

During the commercial, his mom glanced over at him. "Kaylob, who was the little redhead you were talking to at the station? Is she new in town?"

He almost choked on his soda pop. "She just moved here. Her name is Beth Ann."

"How old is she?" She studied his face. "You seemed a little smitten with her."

"Almost twelve and she's an actress and singer." He took another sip of his drink. "Really nice girl and yeah, I like her."

"Sounds like you have a new friend." She patted his arm as she met his gaze. "Does she live close by?"

Kaylob nodded. "I think so." He hoped she lived close by and he hoped she didn't get disgusted when she found out where he lived.

Once dinner was over, his mom did the dishes and cleaned up, which was a nice change. Usually he had to do the dishes, too. Today was the best day he'd seen his mom have in weeks. He'd learned from a very young age to treasure those good days.

He spent some time just hanging out with his mom, then later, took a walk down to the pool hall. Some of his friends were there and Dusty spied him the minute he walked in. She was sure a fox, with her blonde hair hanging down below her waist. Man, he loved the view—she never wore a bra. Every guy in the place was checking her out, which made Kaylob wonder why she wanted to hang out with him, when he was so much younger.

He was sure he saw a few of the seniors' tongues fall out, as she sashayed towards him.

"Hey, I was hoping you'd show up." Dusty's voice was sultry. Then, she took his arm, pressing her very large breast into him. "My parents are gone away again, how about coming to my house for a swim?" she offered. "We can have some fun."

How could he pass up an offer like that? Besides, his body answered before he did. Then his mind flashed to Beth Ann. Hadn't he just kissed her palm and told her she was going to be his wife? Although, she had run away from him. What was a guy to think? He liked Beth Ann a lot and hoped to get to know her more. But for now, he was with Dusty and he had to do the right thing. Besides, seeing her in that tiny bikini was something to watch. Just maybe, he'd get a chance to touch her under that swimsuit.

He stood debating with himself as Dusty chatted with her friend. Then, out of the corner of his eye, he saw Blake Tanner walk in. As usual, he had three girls hanging from both arms. The guy was definitely popular with the female crowd and dated all ages. He had broken a lot of hearts and Kaylob didn't like to see girls cry.

Dusty took his arm. "C'mon, let's go." They headed out the door.

Kaylob stopped by his house, grabbed his swimsuit, and told his mom he was going swimming. She was on the phone laughing with someone and waved. That made him feel happy. He knew, though, that she'd be asleep by the time he got home, because she always went to bed early.

When he climbed into Dusty's car, she leaned over and brushed her soft lips across his. Then she started her car and headed off to her house.

She had sweet kisses, no doubt about that. Once again, his mind drifted back to the new girl in town. Beth Ann, she was so intriguing and there was just something about her.

Kaylob resolved himself to the moment. It wasn't nice to be thinking about another girl. Even though he and Dusty weren't serious or going steady, they still had been spending a lot time together. He'd slightly touched her and boy that sure made him want to at least get to second and third base.

He took a long, lingering look at Dusty and felt things going on that he hoped didn't show. She was almost eighteen and knew how to touch him in a way he'd never experienced. Before he could pull his eyes away from her very large breasts, she stopped the car and gazed at him.

"Ready to go for a swim?" She rubbed her hand slowly up his leg and sent shivers through him.

He nodded and opened the passenger door, but before he stepped out, he glanced down to make sure nothing was showing. Once they were inside her house, she turned and kissed him, pressing her body against his. In the next instance, she took his hand and placed it on her breast, and man did she ever feel good. While he fondled her, his mind conjured up all kinds of things they might do.

Chapter Eight

Kaylob tiptoed into the house the next morning, trying to be quiet after spending the night with Dusty. He heard the TV on in his mother's bedroom. He stepped inside his room and took a deep breath. God, last night had been so bitchen, and boy, oh boy, he was ready for more.

Dusty kept reminding him throughout the night, that he couldn't get *serious* because of their age difference. He kept telling her not to worry, because the truth was, he didn't feel that way about her. Being with Dusty was like being on a roller coaster ride and waiting for the best thrill. The truth of the matter was, he was having fun and knew it couldn't last and would be fine when she ended it.

"Kaylob Shawn O'Brien! Get in here." He jumped. Damn it, she knew he was home.

"Okay, Mom, coming." He ran into the bathroom, brushed his teeth, and tried to wash off any evidence of what he'd been doing the night before. His face looked tired and Dusty had put a giant hickey on his neck. There was no washing that off. He pulled up his collar, knowing he needed to stop daydreaming about last night.

Right now, he had to face his mom, which made his stomach surf a giant wave. Kaylob looked in the mirror again and sighed. If she knew what he'd been up to, she'd panic or get even more depressed. Any type of stress caused his mom to sink deeper into depression.

"Kaylob!" His mother yelled again.

He rushed down the hall. "I'm right here."

He stood in the archway looking at her, still in bed. He wondered if she would be getting up today. It was just hard to know from one day to the next. She looked too old for her age. Her once black hair was mostly silver now, and her skin was as pale as the white bed sheets. It made him feel bad to see her looking so aged. He thought about Beth Ann's mom and bet they were close to the same age. Man, there was no comparison.

"Where have you been young man?" she asked.

"I stayed the night with Dusty. Her parents were out of town and she was nervous to be alone." He wiped his hands down his pants and shifted his stance.

"Your friend could have stayed here."

"We had fun swimming and she has a pool table at her house." He glanced down to the ground. "I would have called, but I knew you'd be sleeping and I didn't want to wake you."

"I understand that, but from now on if you're going to stay the night with a friend, you need to let me know. I realize you think you're all grown up, but you're only fourteen." She frowned. "I trust you, Kaylob, because you're a good boy, but I like to know where you are."

If she knew what he had been doing, she wouldn't think he was such a good boy. Furthermore, if she knew what he'd like to do, she'd send him away to a religious school for boys, or make him live up at his aunt and uncle's house. Little did she know that Mary Ann spent most days trying to seduce him up there.

"Okay, Mom. I will from now on, but remember I'll be fifteen in a few months. I don't feel like a boy anymore. Look at everything I take care of." He waved his hand around.

She cocked her head. "You're right son, but your birthday is more than just a few months away and you're still too young to stay gone all night and not call."

"Okay, I want to go over again this afternoon. Her parents called and said they'd be gone another night." He shook his head. "They leave her alone way too much. I feel bad for her."

"Oh, the poor darling. But why can't she come and stay here with us?"

Kaylob had to think of a good reason so he thought of her cat. "She has animals and her parents want her to take care of the house while they're gone."

His mom looked down and paused. "Well." She sighed as she straightened up her bed sheet. "You can spend the night, but is there any food left over?"

"Yes. I'll be sure to put it on a plate for you."

With a tenderness that only his mother had, she reached her arms towards him and gathered him in a warm hug. "Kaylob, I love you and I miss you when you're gone too long."

He kissed her cheek and moved out of her embrace. "I won't leave until the afternoon. I need to finish painting the fence. When's Dad coming home anyway?"

"Next week." She looked sad. "He's only going to be home five days this time."

Kaylob nodded, but inside he was boiling. His dad stayed gone more than he was home. All that traveling and leaving everything on his shoulders made him resentful. Sometimes he wondered if his dad made excuses to be gone longer so he didn't have to deal with his mom's depression. At one time, his dad had sold Encyclopedias in Novato and the surrounding areas. Now he went to bigger cities because he said he had run out of options in the Bay Area. Even though he still did San Francisco and Oakland from time to time, he didn't come home.

He left the room, ate breakfast, and went out back into the shed to gather the things he needed for painting. The day was warm and a slight breeze blew through the yard. He turned on the radio and *Blue Velvet* came floating through the speakers. The strong smell of paint surrounded him as he brushed it onto the wood, He couldn't help but think about what Dusty had done to him last night, which was not good because it made things happen south of the border.

He also loved what she had taught him to do to her. Man, they had come so close to going *all the way*. Just as he paused, a red convertible drove by and sure enough, the little redhead was inside. She glanced at the old train station as though she was looking for him. Holy hell, Dusty fell from his brain and seeing Beth Ann made his heart jump out of his chest and run down the road in her direction. He'd better go retrieve it fast.

He jogged into the house and yelled to his mom. "I'm going to the store, I'll be right back."

"All right, will you pick me up some lady things?"

"Aww, Mom. Some of my friends are down there. Can I do it later?" He waited.

"Okay, but I'll need them by tomorrow afternoon."

That he could do, even though he hated shopping for lady's things.

"Sure thing." He slammed the door and ran.

The minute he walked into Rayburn's, he spotted Beth Ann's mom. No missing her. She wore tight yellow Capris, a snug polka dotted top, and a scarf around her hair. She was squeezing a big round melon, when she turned and saw him. The lady gave him a gracious smile and his cheeks heated instantly, but he grinned back anyway. Little did she know he was stalking her daughter and noticing things about her he shouldn't.

Kaylob picked up a hand basket and moved past the produce. He walked through the store, acting like he was searching for something. Good thing Mildred wasn't paying attention, since he worked there. She would have been on to him faster than an eagle on a field mouse.

Right on, he said to himself. He honed in on the little fox giggling with her nose in a magazine. She looked amazing with her copper hair flowing down her back. She wore a pair of pink shorts and a top to match. He couldn't seem to find his breath when he gazed at her from top to bottom. He'd never known he even liked red hair, but he knew now.

Once he steadied himself, he decided to approach. He tiptoed behind her and saw she was reading Archie.

"What's so funny?"

She jumped and her hand went across her heart. "You scared me to death," she scolded. "Do you always sneak up behind people? This is the second time you've done that." She held his gaze and he saw her swallow.

At that moment, staring into her eyes, he shriveled on the spot. There was something about this girl—the way she tilted her head with those cute little pouty lips—not to mention how good she smelled, like fresh strawberries. He wanted to kiss her right then and there. He'd never had a girl make him feel like this. Not only was he looking into her eyes, he felt like he was connecting to her soul.

He took a giant step back and stuck his hands in his pants pockets. The last thing he wanted to do is to scare her. "Sorry, I saw you and just wanted to say hello. How do you like Novato so far?"

"So far things seem great." She put down the magazine.

"You should try the pool hall right down the street. A lot of kids go there, and the afternoons get busy." He wished he could take her, but he already had plans.

He heard someone behind him with a cart, and he was just about to move when a thick southern drawl pulled at his attention.

"Beth Ann, honey, I'm done shopping." She looked at Kaylob and nodded. "Ah, you met a friend, how nice. And what is your name?" She held out her hand to Kaylob.

"I'm Kaylob Shawn O'Brien and I just met your daughter yesterday when she came into town. I was just telling her about the pool hall down the road." Kaylob shifted from one foot to the other. "That's where a lot of the kids hang out." His mouth went dry and a lump formed in his throat.

"Well, isn't that sweet of you." Her eyes lit up.

Beth Ann cleared her throat. "I'm ready, Mama." She moved over next to her mom's shopping cart.

"Well, thank this nice young man for taking the time to tell you where the kids hang out." She gave him a tender look.

"Thank you, Kaylob. I'll check it out." Beth Ann grinned.

"You're welcome. I'm sure I'll see you around." He watched as they both strolled away. Just when they were almost out of sight, Beth Ann stopped and flashed him the most stunning smile he'd ever seen in his life. Now, he understood that song by Elvis, All Shook Up. His head was spinning and his knees were weak.

He grinned back and watched her cheeks flush. *Damn, she's cute*. What in the heck was he going to do? He could feel himself falling off a hundred foot cliff and where he was going to land, he didn't have a clue. But he knew if she was involved, it would be paradise.

* * * *

Beth Ann stood by the car after putting the groceries away and watched her mom push the basket back to the store.

She couldn't help wondering why she even noticed a guy in the first place since she wasn't interested in boys. Maybe Novato had something that made a girl change her mind …

Yeah, like a boy named Kaylob.

"Beth Ann, you didn't tell me you met someone downtown yesterday." Her mom raised a brow. "He sure is a handsome young man."

Beth Ann felt heat swimming up her face. "I guess, Mama. I don't notice things like that." She lied. "I ran into him at the old train station and we talked for a while."

"You didn't notice?" Her mom grinned. "Well, my sweet daughter, maybe we should get your eyes checked. Or maybe you're pulling my leg."

Beth Ann looked in the grocery bag and quickly changed the subject. "Yummy, you're making fried chicken, that's my favorite."

Her mom played along. "How would you like to help me cook tonight? You really should learn."

Beth Ann wrinkled her nose. "Mama, I don't want to cook, but I can help set the table and do the dishes."

"Someday, you'll need to learn, but okay, you can set the table. You and Cole can wash and dry the dishes," she said.

"So long as I never have to cook, I'm as happy as a lobster." She sighed.

Her mama chuckled. "You are a funny girl." She hugged her daughter before they climbed into the car.

Once they pulled in to their driveway, Beth Ann saw the same girl strolling down the street that she had seen yesterday.

Her mom turned off the car. "Honey, why don't you talk to that young lady? I saw her next door today." Her mom nodded in the direction of the girl. "I only have two bags, I can carry them inside."

"Okay, Mama." She slid out of the car and closed the door. Afterwards, she strolled to the end of the driveway.

"Hello," said the girl with long brown hair and a friendly face.

"Hi. I'm Beth Ann and we just moved here." She pointed to her house.

"I know. I saw the day you guys moved in. But I didn't see you until yesterday."

"I was at my Gram's up in Salem, Oregon. I usually spend summers up there with her," Beth Ann explained.

"Oh groovy, I've heard it's pretty up there. I'm Denny, by the way," the girl reached out her hand. "We moved into this neighborhood three months ago."

Beth Ann accepted the gentleness of Denny's touch and noticed her beautiful long nails and olive skin.

"What grade are you in?" Denny asked.

"I'm in sixth this year."

"Groovy, we are in the same grade." Her dark brown eyes sparkled, with what Beth Ann hoped was excitement. "Would you like to come next door and meet my grandparents?" Denny asked. "I'm here a lot and my grandma and grandpa are the best."

"Sure, I'd love to meet them. Where do you live?" Beth Ann inquired.

"Right behind you." Denny pointed. "We can yell out our back door to each other."

"That's really neat." Beth Ann was thrilled. Today she was going to push all the worries out of her mind and make it just about friendship and meeting new people. Nothing else had to be thought about.

Chapter Nine

Once Beth Ann returned home from Denny's she couldn't have been happier. She plopped onto her bed, daydreaming about the town, going to school, and now having a friend.

Denny's grandparents were cute like Gram. Generally speaking, though, Beth Ann didn't remember much about her grandpa. She had been told stories of how happy they were. That must be why Gram would look so sad from time to time, because she missed her husband.

Beth Ann understood feeling sad. She missed her dad every day and now her brother was going to that darn old boot school. She'd sure be glad when he got back home.

After a few minutes of staring at the ceiling, the phones loud shrill tore her from her trance.

"Beth Ann!" her mom called out. "You have a call."

She hopped off the bed and darted towards the phone. "Who is it?" Thinking it was Gram.

"I think it's your new friend from next door." Her mom gave her a big grin.

"Hello," Beth Ann said, happy she had given Denny her number before she left.

"Heya, Beth Ann. It's me. Would you like to go to the pool hall tomorrow? They have all kinds of fun things to do there."

"Is the pool hall for kids and adults?" Beth Ann asked.

"Yes, but there is no alcohol served, if that's what you're wondering about. It's mostly for kids with soda pop and stuff like that, and really great hot dogs."

"That sounds fun. I would love to go. Hold on though." Covering the phone, she called out. "Mama, can I go to the pool hall with Denny tomorrow. It's mostly for kids, no grownup stuff." Beth Ann was almost jumping up and down.

"Of course you can."

With that, Beth Ann and Denny made a date. She was over the moon that

Denny asked, because she must have a lot of friends. Sure, she was new in the neighborhood, but she'd lived in Novato all her life. Still, she had invited her and she was going.

The rest of the afternoon Beth Ann hung around the house. Cole left with his new friends and her mom had gone on a lunch date with some ladies from her quilting group. Beth Ann had the entire place to herself and loved it. She was extra glad her stepdad wasn't home because all he did was make her miss her daddy. Stanley was a good actor, though, he pretended to want her around, but deep inside she knew he didn't.

While she spent time swimming and soaking in the sun, she listened to their new transistor radio. The station was KFRC, which played the groovy kind of music she loved, like Sonny and Cher, and Leslie Gore.

As she floated around the pool, she had to sing along with one of her all-time favorite songs.

"Crazy," Beth Ann belted out by Patsy Cline.

When she reached the end, she was startled by clapping and saw Denny and the same woman that was in the car. They were both looking over the fence into the backyard.

"Wow!" Denny said. "Your voice is amazing!"

The lady who had to be her mother, nodded. "Yes, it is!"

Beth Ann slid off the inner tube and climbed out of the pool, grabbing a towel. "Thank you." She felt herself flush. "I didn't know anyone was listening." She dried off.

Denny climbed over the fence. "How could we not listen? You're so good."

Her mom's face softened. "Have you taken lessons?" Her eyes were like Denny's, soft and brown.

"Not yet, but now that we are settled, my mom wants me to receive special training." She looked down still feeling shy. "I've always wanted to be a singer."

Denny's voice climbed a notch. "Wanted to be? You are a singer, and the best one I've ever heard."

"I would have to second that." The lady agreed. Her mom was pretty. She had jet-black hair and a smile just like her daughter.

"Right now I have to get back to dinner, girls. By the way, my name is Gina Ribera and it's nice to meet you, Beth Ann." She looked over at Denny. "Did you still want to cook?"

Denny shrugged. "I don't know."

"It's nice to meet you, Mrs. Ribera," Beth Ann said. "I was wondering if you wanted to come and swim, Denny?"

59

Denny's mom grinned. "You can call me, Gina, Mrs. Ribera sounds so old."

"I don't usually call adults by their first names." Beth Ann felt uncomfortable.

"Well, I insist," she said with a laugh. "You'll get used to it."

"I'd love to," Denny interrupted. "Is it okay, Mom? Can I go swimming?"

"Yes, but just don't wear out your welcome."

"She won't," Beth Ann said a little too loud. "As a matter of fact, I was wondering if you wanted to spend the night tomorrow night." She glanced at Denny and back to Mrs. Ribera. She would say that in her mind, but she'd force herself to use Gina from her mouth.

Denny's mom tilted her head. "Are you sure it's okay with your mom?"

"My mama is happy for me to have a friend stay over." Beth Ann grinned.

Denny gave her mom a begging look with her hands clutched together in anticipation.

"It's okay with me, once I make sure it's good with your mom. I'll come over and talk to her later." She nodded and left.

Denny and Beth Ann jumped up and down, holding hands, then Denny let go. "I'll be right back." She darted over the fence.

A few minutes later, she was back with a dog and her swimsuit on. "Is it okay if Bridgett hangs out with us? She's a really good girl."

Beth Ann was thrilled. "Yes. I would love it." Beth Ann approached the dog and rubbed behind her ears. She was so sweet and playful.

A few minutes later, they both jumped into the pool, laughing and singing along with the radio while Bridgett basked in the sun. Beth Ann had no words to describe the feeling. She also noticed, as the day went on, just how much Denny was like Gidget on TV. Cute, silly, and with a great figure.

When the back door opened, Stanley walked out, making Beth Ann aware that she had lost track of time.

His face showed kindness. "Hey ladies, are you enjoying yourselves?" He reached down and scratched the dog. "Hey pup," he said in a funny voice.

Achoo. "Sorry girls." Aachoo, achoo. He pulled out a handkerchief and went back into the house.

Denny looked worried. "I better take Bridgett home. I think your dad's allergic," she said in a soft voice as she got out of the pool and grabbed her cover jacket. "Tell your dad, I'm so sorry. I'll see you tomorrow."

"It's okay, Denny, he's not really my dad and it's not your fault," she exclaimed as Denny ran off.

Darn. Her stepdad was allergic to dogs. That was the moment she knew she wouldn't be allowed to have one, or likely any other animal. She'd always wanted a pup like Rusty. Well, he couldn't help being allergic, but still. She stepped out of the pool and dried off. Now, he'd have a good excuse to send her away. She'd read a book once where the stepdad sent his stepdaughter off to a far away boarding school. Maybe, that's what he had planned, but she'd go live with Gram first.

Once she stopped dripping, she went inside to see how Stanley was. He was still sneezing, so she decided it would be best to wait in the family room after she got dressed.

About thirty minutes later, he finally appeared and shook his head. "Sorry about that, honey. I guess I still have a bad reaction to dogs and cats, sometimes birds, too. I was hoping it would clear up, because I know how bad you want a dog." He blew his nose in his handkerchief and wiped his dripping eyes.

"It's okay, you can't help it. Are you okay now?" She did feel bad.

"Getting there. Hey, you want to grab an ice cream at Berkley Farms? It's the best ice cream place in the world, and they have wonderful milkshakes." He finally tucked his handkerchief in his pocket. "Your mom won't be home for another hour or so."

"Sure." Beth Ann loved chocolate ice cream, but in truth, she loved chocolate everything. She couldn't deny he was acting nice. Could it be real, she wondered?

When they pulled up to Berkley Farms, the first thing Beth Ann noticed was the oddly shaped building painted white and gray with a hat like roof.

What was more surprising was that Stanley held her hand as they walked inside. Could he really like her? His eyes flickered something, but she had no clue what it was. As they sat eating their ice cream, he was attentive and listened to everything she had to say, even about pork.

She was even more amazed at Stanley when he said, "Don't worry, honey, I'll never bring home pork."

Once they finished their ice cream, they went for a walk together in a park not far away. It seemed he had something on his mind. She couldn't help but wonder what it was.

The place was alive with kids on skateboards and people walking their dogs. The sky was a soft shade of blue and a light breeze fanned the scent of fresh cut grass through the air.

"Beth Ann, can we sit for a minute? I want to share something with you." He pointed to a park bench as two boys drove by with playing cards in the bike spokes. Both she and Stanley listened to the flapping sound even after they were out of sight.

"Okay." She tried to smile, but felt nervous. Was he going to tell her he wanted her to go away right now?

They sat down on the bench and tears pooled in her eyes.

She didn't want to be a big old crybaby, so she tried to swallow back the emotions, but failed when one tear slid down her cheek.

"Beth Ann, are you upset?" Stanley tilted his head and gazed at her.

"Please don't send me away." Beth Ann looked down at her hands. "I'm sorry about the dog and I won't ever have one over again. I want to stay with my Mama and Cole."

"Send you away? Oh lord, Beth Ann, I would never do that ..." He seemed shocked. "I want to be the best stepdad, I can be. That's what I wanted to talk to you about. I know I can never be your daddy ..." He paused. "But, see, it's like this. I never had a child and I always wanted a daughter. I'm looking forward to spending these years with you, being your stepdad." He gently held her hand. "I love you already and don't worry about the dog. I really like animals, it's just my sinuses won't let me get too close."

Beth Ann's voice trembled. "I just thought I was in the way."

"No, honey, not at all. I want you here. I know you're sad about being away from your dad and I promise never to interfere with what you have with him." He swallowed. "I was just hoping that maybe you had a little extra love in your heart to share with me."

Beth Ann couldn't help but like this man. He wasn't pretending to like her, he really did. Plus, he hadn't said a bad word about her daddy.

That afternoon at Pioneer Park, the heat flowed around them. Beth Ann noticed the beads of sweat form on Stanley's forehead, while they sat in silence. They were both watching the natural activities on that summer day. After a few minutes, Stanley pulled out his handkerchief and dabbed off the sweat that trickled down his face

"I think we better get back home before I melt." He took her hand. At that moment, Beth Ann knew that he was going to be a great stepdad.

Chapter Ten

Beth Ann awoke the next morning with the sun peeking through her beautiful pink and white curtains. As she glanced around her room, everything still felt like a dream. That made her understand the saying, *there's no place like home,* because now she had one. She had called her daddy and Gram, but there was a strain and her dad rushed off the phone. Gram tried to cover for him, but Beth Ann knew something was wrong. Just thinking about his voice made her heart fall.

She let out a long breath. At least today, she'd be spending the afternoon with Denny. Putting those thoughts in her mind made her feel better. Holy night, she had a friend already and she was having a sleep over. Both their moms had hit it off while they spent time drinking sun tea. Wouldn't that be neat if they could all be friends and do barbecues together? Still a lingering piece of guilt about her dad tried to spoil her idea.

Her Gram had said everything happens for a reason. So just maybe there was a good reason. There were seasons in the weather and maybe that's how life was, a season of sadness, loss, fun, and joy. Today, she'd make her season a happy one. Didn't she deserve that?

The morning flew by and Beth Ann tried on three different outfits before she finally picked a pair of sky blue shorts and a white blouse that tied around her waist. She slipped on her flip-flops, then had her mama put her hair in a French braid. Now she was ready for the day.

Right at noon, the doorbell rang and Beth Ann knew it must be Denny. Once she swung open the door, Denny stood with her overnight bag and a fabulous smile.

They both giggled and ran to Beth Ann's room where they put away her bag. It didn't take them long to exit out of the bedroom.

"Mama we're leaving," Beth Ann yelled, sounding winded.

"Okay." She walked into the living room, drying her hands on a dishtowel. "Now y'all have a good time and be careful."

"We will." Beth Ann blew her mom a kiss just before they darted out the door.

As they stepped outside, the warmness of the day fanned its way around them and heated Beth Ann's skin. They held hands as they proceeded down the road to the pool hall. The aroma of eucalyptus filled Beth Ann with a sense of home and belonging. In the short time she'd been in Novato, she had fallen in love with all the delicate scents and the way the sun lingered over the mountains.

The whole area made her feel that she was in a land of make-believe, where the magic truly did exist.

While they continued down the street, there was a comfortable silence between them. It was as though they were taking in the beauty of the day and their newfound friendship. Once they arrived at the tracks, Beth Ann couldn't help but think about Kaylob.

"Denny, do you know a guy named Kaylob?"

"Yes, I've known him for years. Why?" she asked.

"I met him the other day and ran into him again at the grocery store. And … well, he flirted with me." She felt heat burning her cheeks.

Denny stopped walking, released Beth Ann's hand, and faced her. "Are you serious? Kaylob flirted with you?"

"Yes, he told me that it's not every day you meet the girl you're going to marry. And he kissed my hand."

"Wow!" Denny said with a bulging smile and placed both hands on her heart. "Do you know how many girls are going to be jealous over that? He mostly hangs out with older chicks, and he's been hanging out with Dusty. She's some high school girl." Denny shook her head. "Do you like him?" She stared at Beth Ann and waved at an older lady driving by.

"I don't know. I hardly know him," she said with a shrug.

"Well, you're a lucky girl." Denny laughed. "Some girls have been trying to get his attention for years."

Beth Ann reached out and touched Denny's arm. "Do you like him? Because, if you do, I'll never look at him again."

"No. He's just a friend. But Frankie Russo, that's a whole other story. The sad thing about Frankie is he always keeps his distance." She kicked a rock and sent it flying. "The guy kissed me once, and I really liked it, and he hasn't ever done it again."

"On the lips?" Beth Ann asked.

"Yes, right on my smacker." She puckered and kissed into the air. "It was so sweet. We were playing spin the bottle and when he took his turn, it landed on me." Denny looked up and closed her eyes. "I'll never forget his lips." She inhaled and let it out slowly.

"He's an idiot if he doesn't go for you." Beth Ann arched her brow.

"I guess." Denny giggled. "There is this other guy I like too, named Andre. He likes me also."

"I've never really liked a boy before," Beth Ann said softly.

"Well, my dear, that's going to change soon." Denny placed her arm around Beth Ann's shoulders. "You can just mark my words."

As soon as Denny opened the door to the pool hall, it seemed as though many of the kids stopped and stared. Beth Ann noticed one girl in particular who was breathtaking. She had jet-black curly hair that flowed across her shoulders. She waved to Denny and Beth Ann.

Denny pulled Beth Ann over to the table, where the girl was playing a game of pool, with a tall brown haired guy who looked older.

They both stopped and glanced at Beth Ann. Once again, Beth Ann blushed.

Denny pulled Beth Ann forward. "Lisa, this is Beth Ann, she's new in town and moved into my new neighborhood. She's our age."

"Hi, Beth Ann." Lisa's smile was stunning. "You guys want to play a team game?"

The guy grinned. "Nice to meet you Beth Ann, I'm Terry." He moved closer to Lisa. "I have to get home, remember? My aunt and uncle are coming today."

Holy smoke, he leaned down and kissed Lisa right on her lips.

Lisa looked a little sad when she nodded. "Okay."

"I'll call you later," he shot over his shoulder as he left the pool hall. He seemed in a hurry.

"Is he your boyfriend?" Beth Ann asked.

"Well, I sure hope so." She laughed. "We've been going steady for about a year, but we've liked each other since *forever*. He's a few years older, so it took my parents a while to approve us hanging out."

"Wow, I think my brother Cole would have a heart attack." Beth Ann shook her head. "He's what you might call over protective."

"Both your brothers are dreamy." Denny's eyes opened wide. "That's what I'd call them."

"Yes, they're handsome, but dreamy?" She shrugged.

They were all laughing when something caught Lisa's attention. "Hey, you! Get over here and let me kick your butt in pool." She grabbed her cue stick and finished knocking the rest of the balls in the holes.

Beth Ann turned to see Kaylob walking towards them with an older girl. Thankfully, he stopped so his date could talk to someone. Right off the bat,

Beth Ann noticed she was gorgeous, tall with a curvy figure and long blonde hair. The mini skirt was tight and, oh my god, she wasn't even wearing a bra, which was easy to see.

Beth Ann glanced down at her flip-flops and bare legs, then she stared down at her breasts. Flat was the only word she could think of. How could she compete with that?

Denny leaned over and whispered, "That's Dusty, the older girl I was telling you about. Beth Ann you are much prettier than her."

"Right." Beth Ann knew she didn't compare to that older chick. She didn't even wear lipstick yet, and she sure as heck didn't fill a dress out like that. A little lip-gloss with a hint of blush was all her mama would allow. Cole wouldn't let her walk out of her house wearing something like that.

As she watched Kaylob, she couldn't help but notice how good he looked with Dusty. He was wearing jeans and a pale blue shirt. There was no missing how handsome he was. The girl was tall, but Kaylob was taller.

Beth Ann turned her head so she'd stop staring like an idiot. Denny saved the day with her excitement. "There's Andre. Do you want to meet him?"

"Not right this minute. I think I'll go play some pinball." She tried not to look at Kaylob.

"Come over and meet him when you're done." Denny's voice shot up, then she ran over to say hello to a short blonde guy who turned and grinned at her. Beth Ann could tell he liked her.

Kaylob left his girlfriend talking to that other girl and nodded at Beth Ann as he approached the pool table.

"Right, like you could ever beat me." He shot back at Lisa, then reached over and messed up her hair.

"Beth Ann, this is my best friend Kaylob." Lisa looked between them both. "I've known him since we were toddlers, and could always beat him at everything." She smacked his arm.

Kaylob stared at Beth Ann. "We've already met, the day she got into town and again at the store." He grinned when he picked up a cue stick, then gave Lisa an ornery look. "Want to make any bets?" He threw his head back and laughed.

"Sure, I'll bet I'm going to kick your ass at pool," Lisa challenged.

"In your dreams," he mumbled.

Not even a minute later, the blonde came over and stood next to him. She looped her arm through his and pressed her large, well, objects into his chest. Kaylob's cheeks turned a glowing pink.

"Don't take too long," Dusty purred and glanced at Beth Ann.

Kaylob cleared his throat. "Beth Ann, this is Dusty, a friend of mine.

66

Dusty, this is Beth Ann." Dusty gave Beth Ann a pasted grin, along with a once over. Beth Ann felt her insides boil when she saw Kaylob looked between the two of them, then gulp for air. The jerk was nervous because he was a cheater.

Dusty reached over and kissed his cheek. "I'm going to go call my parents and make sure they're not coming home tonight." She winked at Kaylob and sashayed off, like she was trying to make a point.

It was crystal clear that she was his girlfriend. So why had he been flirting and saying how she was going to be his wife? That made flames shoot out her ears and they were headed in his direction. At that moment she was certain she didn't like him anymore and had no intentions of ever speaking to him again. There was no way she would ever have a boyfriend who cheated.

"So you're making new friends?" he asked Beth Ann as Lisa racked the pool balls.

She frowned at him then left. She wanted to go play pinball and hoped that maybe he'd leave and she'd never have to ever see his face again. How dare he act like that, when he was probably going steady. She deposited her quarter and prepared to beat the tar out the pinball machine.

* * * *

Kaylob stood staring at Beth Ann's back. *Damn it.* He knew she must think Dusty was his girlfriend. In the next instance, he felt a whack on his arm.

"Ouch! What did you do that for?" He turned towards Lisa and rubbed his sore arm.

"What the heck did you do to make her so mad?" Lisa arched a brow.

Kaylob knew he had a guilty look on his face. "I might have flirted with her twice when we bumped into each other. And well, now she must think I'm a jerk, because I'm here with Dusty."

"Are you being a jerk, Kaylob? What are you doing with Dusty?" She stepped in front of him and pointed her finger in his chest. "Are you two getting serious? You've been with her a lot lately."

"No. I mean we are friends and well ..." He looked down. "We do have some fun, but it's not serious at all. She's nice and everything, but I don't have feelings for her. Not like that."

"Not like what? Are you doing it with her? And how do you know she's not falling for you?" Lisa shook her head.

"It's none of your business, nosey." He laid down his cue stick. "I'll be right back."

As he approached Beth Ann, he watched her playing pinball, or more accurately beating the hell out of it. He was sure glad it wasn't his head or maybe to her it was.

He stepped up behind her. "Hey, are you winning?"

She jumped, causing her ball to roll away. With that, she whipped around and gave him a look that spoke volumes. Then turned back to her game again.

"What do you want, Kaylob? I asked you to stop sneaking up behind me," she retorted.

Kaylob turned her to face him. "I wanted you to know that Dusty *is not* my girlfriend. We just hang out and it's not serious. She's in high school."

"Why are you telling me? It's none of my business."

"Because, I didn't want you to think I was flirting with you if I had a girlfriend, which I don't."

"Groovy," she said in a sarcastic tone.

For a reason he didn't fully understand he reached out and tucked a piece of hair behind her ear. It felt so right, like that was his job. For a brief second he saw her eyes soften.

"We really are just friends. I mean we ... we are not serious or anything."

He liked Beth Ann a lot, even when she was angry. She had this innocence about her that made him want to protect her.

"Fine, you better be getting back to your nothing serious." She smacked his hand away and turned back to her pinball game.

He stood there, watching her play for a few minutes, then caught Lisa, Denny, and Dusty all staring at him. Lisa had her arms crossed and the look on Denny's face was like the Creature from the Black Lagoon. Oh hell, he'd better just leave, because knowing Dusty, any minute she'd be all over him, and from the looks of things, that might be worse than World War II.

Chapter Eleven

A few minutes later, they climbed into Dusty's car and took off for her house. He tried to push Beth Ann out of his head, but there was no hiding the fact that she was angry with him. If she was pissed that could only mean one thing, she was jealous, and just maybe that was a good thing. However, on the other hand, wouldn't that make him a jerk for being with Dusty and really liking Beth Ann? He knew the answer to that, and he knew he needed to do the right thing. He had never liked those kinds of games, and he sure as hell didn't want to be like Blake.

When they pulled up to Dusty's house, she turned off the car and stared at Kaylob.

"So who was the little redhead?" she inquired.

"She's a girl I met when she came to town. She lives near Denny." He played with the dial on the radio.

"Kaylob, you like her, don't you?" She tilted her head, holding his gaze.

Oh, man. Should he lie? He hated lying. He did like Beth Ann a whole lot. His mind was racing faster than a speeding car in the Indy 500.

"I do like her, a lot," he admitted, almost choking on his words. To his surprise, Dusty nodded.

"She's a little young, but cute ... although, I have something to offer you." She scooted closer to him. "I know we agreed not to get serious and I have no desire to do that, but I do have a desire for something else." She took his hand and moved it between her legs. "We can still do things, Kaylob." She moved her legs apart and whispered, "You can like your little redhead, but don't forget what I have to offer."

He cleared the giant lump that was stuck in his throat. "I really don't think that's a good idea." His words said no, but his body said yes. "And ... well, I want to get to know her better, Dusty ... I shouldn't do that with you." He forced his hand away. "I hope we can still be friends." He was feeling heated and knew he had to get out of there fast.

"Kaylob, you are my friend. I love the things we did last night. I don't want to give that up."

"I'm sorry, Dusty, but I can't. I'm trying to do the right thing." He rubbed his hands through his hair.

For a few minutes, she sat staring out the window "Do you want to come in or do you want me to give you a ride home?" She touched his hand and gave it a gentle squeeze.

He shook his head. "I think I'll walk. I need some time to figure a few things out." He squeezed her hand back. "Thanks for being so understanding. Will you be okay here?"

She nodded. "Kaylob, someday you're going to make some lucky girl a nice boyfriend. I hope it's the redhead, if she's who you want. But I'll be here if you ever change your mind." She grinned and leaned over and gave him a soft kiss. "I hope you do change your mind," she said in a throaty way that almost made him fall out of the car.

Once he collected himself, he had to get out of dodge. Holy hell, she was a fox, and he was a chicken that didn't want to lose his head.

On the way home, he decided to stop by the pool hall and see if Beth Ann was still there. He wanted to let her know he wasn't seeing Dusty anymore. That might just put cheerfulness back in her eyes.

When he entered Harry's, he saw Denny and Lisa playing pool, but Beth Ann wasn't with them. The minute he glanced around, he caught sight of her sitting in the corner talking to none other than the dog himself—Tanner. Once their eyes met, she frowned and turned her face towards Blake.

Kaylob strolled over. "Can we have a minute to talk?"

She rolled her eyes. "I guess. I was talking with Blake." Her nose went into the air.

"Can I buy you a soda pop?" Blake flirted with a wink, then glanced at Kaylob.

"Sure," Beth Ann said. "I love soda pop."

When Kaylob saw Beth Ann's cheeks get pink, he wanted to slug Blake. Not only was he way too old for her, but he had given Kaylob a smart ass grin when he turned to leave. The guy was rich and his parents were involved with the country club. They were well known in the community as one of the richest families in town.

"What do you want, Kaylob? Shouldn't you be with Dusty?" Beth Ann gave him a sidelong glance.

Kaylob sat down and stared at her. "She's not my girlfriend and I'm not seeing her anymore. I came here to tell you that." He tried to hold her gaze, but she looked away.

"You were just with her less than an hour ago and now you want to come back and hang out with me. I don't think so. Besides, I'm getting to know

Blake."

"Believe me, Beth Ann, you don't want to know Blake. Every girl in this town *knows* Blake and—"

Before he could finish, Blake was approaching with her soda. When he saw Beth Ann stand on her toes and kiss Blake's cheek. He saw fireworks and his insides heated.

"Thank you, Blake. That was so sweet." She gave him a sugary smile and Blake wrapped his arm around her waist.

With that, Kaylob turned and left without a word. He waved to Lisa and Denny and walked out the door.

She could have Blake Tanner for all he cared. Kaylob refused to play those kinds of games. If she was into that with rich boys, he was sorry he ever tried to get to know her. At least, that's what he told himself, as he marched back across town to Dusty's house.

When she answered the door, he walked in and pulled her into a kiss. He wasn't going to miss out on the fun with Dusty because of a little redheaded game player and Dusty didn't care what side of the tracks he lived on.

"So that was fast. You look upset." She touched his face.

"I'm pissed, but getting over it." He tightened his arms around her.

What Dusty did next made him forget all about Beth Ann, and Blake. She shut the door, took his hand and led him to her bedroom. Next, she lifted her dress over her head and let it drop to the floor.

That was the night Kaylob found out about manhood and he wanted to be the best man he could.

* * * *

One month later, Beth Ann woke up filled with excitement and nervousness. It was her first day at Olive School, and she hoped to be in the same class as Denny. The memory of the few schools, she had been to while on the road surfaced. It sure wasn't a fun time because many of the kids seem to know they lived in a hotel and were poor.

She had gotten a lunch for free at one of them, because the school had a few extra left over and one of the cafeteria ladies had noticed she hadn't brought a lunch. It was the one time she didn't need to worry about her family going without so she had dug right in. The students there had picked on her, calling her a pig and making fun of the way she ate. Beth Ann had promised herself she would never be accused of that again.

Now she wondered if the kids would see through her at this school, too. Would they make fun of her even though her mama ironed her clothes and made them look nice? So far, that wasn't the case, but today would be a big test. The truth was they lived in a nice house in a new neighborhood and now they weren't homeless or poor. At least for a while.

Stanley had taken them on a family vacation to Lake Berryessa for the remainder of the summer. She hadn't really wanted to go, but her mama was so excited. It ended up being a great family trip, although two people were missing, her dad and her brother James.

Since she returned from vacation, she'd seen Kaylob once, getting out of Dusty's car. She'd hidden behind a telephone pole and watched them kiss. It seemed pretty clear things had changed between them and more than likely, they were going steady now.

All she'd done was kiss Blake on the cheek. Why would that make him so dang mad? At least she wasn't crawling all over him. She had no idea he'd hate her afterwards, but maybe it had hurt his feelings even though it was just a kiss. She kissed her brothers like that all the time.

Maybe, just maybe, she had let her jealousy get the best of her.

Blake had been trying to get her to hang out with him, but he did have a lot of girls. Kaylob was right and she didn't like how Blake mentioned that Kaylob lived on the bad side of town. When Blake saw her face, he had changed the subject. He knew his comment had made her mad. Kaylob's house was cute and she loved the little white fence and all the pretty flowers.

However, Blake did have the cutest dimples she'd ever seen, but the plain and simple truth was Kaylob had already engraved his initials on her heart and there was nothing she could do about it. He was all she could think about.

"Beth Ann, time to get up." Her mom opened the door and peeked inside. "Are you awake?"

"Yes," she said and opened her eyes. "I'm so nervous." She glanced at her mom, rolled out of bed then shivered.

"You'll be fine." The phone's shrill took her mom away. "Get ready while I answer that."

Beth Ann crossed the room to the closet and knew exactly what she was going to wear.

"Beth Ann, Denny's on the phone!" her mom called out.

Beth Ann darted out to the living room and took the phone from her mom.

"Hi. I was just getting up." She caught her breath.

Denny giggled. "Want me to stop by and we can walk to the bus stop together."

"Sure, that would be great. So I'll see you in about an hour."

Denny agreed and Beth Ann placed the phone back on the receiver. She had a friend to walk to school with. This was all new and exciting.

When she got back to her room, she went over to her closet and pulled out her new pink dress with the polka dots. Everything in her life had changed—the clothes, starting at a new school, having a new friend. It was everything she'd ever dreamt of and more.

After she got dressed, she put her hair in a French braid and weaved pink ribbons through it. "Now, everything matches," She gazed into the mirror and actually admired how she looked. Even her new pink bra matched. This was her first year of wearing one, and now she actually had a reason to, maybe not a big reason, but nevertheless, a reason.

Her mom had a hot breakfast waiting in the dining room. Beth Ann could hear her singing Dinah Washington's, *What a Difference a Day Makes,* while she did the morning dishes. Cole had already left early and Stanley was out the door by five A.M. for his drive to San Francisco.

Never had Beth Ann experienced her mother so incredibly elated at doing dishes. Thinking about that, made Beth Ann remember how hard her mom worked at keeping their clothes cleaned and ironed while they lived on the road. She had used a long stick in the back that stretched from one side to the other so she could hang up their shirts. Not to mention at many of the rest stops, she would pull out the iron, go into the bathroom and iron clothes on a cardboard box upon which she had tacked a tablecloth. The dishes normally had to be done in cold water in a bucket. Her mom had done an amazing job at being organized while living out of a car.

When they did get a chance to stay in hotels, her mom would restock and replace everything. Keeping things marked, like the boxes that they used for each of their dressers. It was constant work and Beth Ann witnessed how hard it was and remembered her mom's hands being red and chapped. One time, they even started bleeding. Oh man, Beth Ann looked over at her mom again. Even though she hated being away from her daddy, she had to face the truth; her mom deserved a better life.

Just as Beth Ann was getting lost in her sad memories, she heard the doorbell chime. It was a welcome interruption.

When she opened the door, Denny stood there looking pretty and in pink. Her hair was also in a French braid. They looked at each other and cracked up.

"Twins." Denny laughed.

"Mom, I'm leaving with my twin." She ran over and grabbed her book bag and lunch.

Her mom stepped out into the living room with a wide grin.

"Well, you twins are absolutely lovely." Her eyes warmed. "Y'all have a great day."

"We will." Beth Ann ran up and kissed her cheek. "Bye, Mama."

Once they stepped outside, the sounds of car horns and children's laughter

Brenda Ashworth Barry

swept through the air. The excitement that ran through Beth Ann was more than she ever dreamed. Even the little boy, who wanted to be a musician, took a break from playing his instrument to run down the street with another kid.

Denny paused and glanced over at Beth Ann. "Are you nervous?"

"Yes and no." Beth Ann felt both nervous and calm. "I feel more joyful than nervous and in some ways peaceful." She started walking again.

As soon as they turned the corner all that peace went to hell in a picnic basket. There he was, standing against the bus stop, looking all hunky-dory.

"What's Kaylob doing here? He's in junior high." Beth Ann wanted to turn and run.

Denny studied Beth Ann's face. "This bus drops us off first and then drops off the junior high and high school kids. I think this is the closest to him now. Before, he had to walk to the grammar school to catch it."

"Great," she winced. "He hates me."

"Oh, I don't think hate is the issue. You just made him angry when you kissed Blake." She grinned.

As they approached the bus stop, she couldn't help but notice how amazing Kaylob looked in his white shirt and off white pants. She really wanted to hide before he saw her, but it was unlikely since the other kids were staring her way.

Kaylob turned around and nodded to Denny. The minute he glanced at Beth Ann, his eyes cast dark shadows towards her, and his jaw tightened. He was not happy and it was obvious by the way he turned his back. He was talking to a guy with dark curly hair, who was wearing a green polo shirt.

Beth Ann saw the guy with dark hair study her with curiosity. "Who's that he's talking to?"

"That's Frankie Russo, the one I was telling you about. He's a dream with the most divine green eyes." She let out a deep sigh. "All the girls love him, but he doesn't seem interested in anyone."

"Wow! He *is* good looking," she whispered. "Why don't you just tell him you like him?"

"No way! Don't you dare breathe a word," Denny demanded.

Just about that time, Frankie turned and nodded at Denny. Beth Ann could feel him watching her as she cruised toward them. Kaylob pretended not to be watching, but she had seen him glancing over his shoulder.

"Hey, Denny," Frankie said. "Who's your new friend?"

Beth Ann stepped up. "I'm Beth Ann." She introduced herself. "I already know your name, Frankie Russo. Denny told me."

Frankie grinned. "Cool." He stared right into her eyes.

Denny blurted out, "She's in the same grade as us." She fidgeted with her hands.

"That's good news." Frankie winked at Beth Ann. "I'll sit with you guys on the bus. I have to go remind Kaylob of something." He glanced oddly at Denny who was unusually quiet. "I'll see you in a few."

Denny leaned toward Beth Ann's ear. "He just totally sends me."

"I don't understand why you don't let him know," Beth Ann said.

She saw Kaylob shoot her another look, but once again, the minute she glanced back he turned his head.

Fine, be that way, she said silently.

"Because." Denny shrugged. "Maybe when I turn thirteen, my mom might let me have a boyfriend. If she knew I kissed someone, I'd be grounded for life."

"Well, there is more to life than boys. Like reading books, animals and spending time with good friends." Beth Ann pasted on a smile, trying to act happier than she felt.

Denny placed her arm around Beth Ann's shoulder. "I have a strong feeling we are going to be friends forever."

A few minutes later, Beth Ann saw Dusty pull up in her car that had the top down.

"Hey, Kaylob, want a ride?" She swept her hair back.

Beth Ann watched Kaylob walk over and get in her car. When they drove away, he didn't even give her a second glance.

Her stomach tightened and her heart sank. Denny must have noticed because she took Beth Ann by the arm and pulled her over to Frankie.

"Hey, Mr. Russo, did you know you happen to be looking at a girl who will be a famous singer someday?" Denny beamed.

"Well, I'm sure glad I met her now, before she becomes a hit." Frankie winked again.

Beth Ann looked into his green eyes and could tell he was smiling inside and out. She liked him instantly, and knew she'd found a kindred spirit. There was just something about him, and she had a feeling they were going to be great friends.

When Beth Ann got to school that morning she was thrilled to find out that she was in the same class with Denny, Frankie and Lisa. She knew three people and that was neat.

The teacher had given her a seat near the window, which she loved. Denny sat over in the next row and Frankie was right in front of her. Beth Ann glanced around and saw Lisa had the seat to the far left, close to the classroom door. It was sweet how the entire morning Lisa would turn, catching Beth Ann's eye and give her a tender smile. There was something special in her eyes that made

Beth Ann's heart patter.

It didn't take long for her thoughts to drift back to Kaylob. He had kissed her hand and told her she would be his wife someday. What could she do to gain his friendship back? There had to be a way. What she needed was figure out how to make him stop being mad. Man, she really blew it, but honestly, she had no way of knowing he would get that upset. Or at least that's what she tried to convince herself, she had wanted to make him jealous, but not go away forever.

By lunchtime, Denny and Lisa had dragged her up to the cafeteria, introducing her to everyone. There was Kathy, who was funny and made her laugh a lot, especially when she had a food fight with her sister.

When recess and lunch were over, Lisa walked up next to Beth Ann on the playground. "Would you like to come over to my house for lunch tomorrow?"

Beth Ann was surprised. "They let you go home for lunch?"

"Sure. It's right down the street. Only takes a few minutes to get there. But you have to be within a certain distance and your mom has to give you permission. Think your mom will write a note?"

Beth Ann was nodding before she answered. "Sure, I'd love to come and my mom will be happy for me to go. I'll get a note tonight, but what about Denny?"

"She goes home with Sharon tomorrow. That's their day for the rainbow ladies."

"Rainbow ladies?"

"Oh, it's for this group they're in. The girls get all dolled up and wear fancy dresses. It's not my thing and I'm not sure what they do." She laughed. "I am a horse girl. Cut offs and jeans are more my style."

"Well, going to your house sounds fun. Should I bring us some lunch?"

"No, my mom will be there and make us something." Lisa took Beth Ann's hand. "Let's go, we're going to be late." They ran into the classroom, laughing.

For the first thirty minutes, Beth Ann had a hard time concentrating on the teacher talking. He was such a nice guy. His name was Mr. White and he was tall and handsome with kind blue eyes.

Even though she liked the teacher and was interested in what he was saying, she kept beating herself up over losing Kaylob's friendship. All she could think about was that she would never know what it was like to kiss him or be his girl. Not that she wanted to be anybody's girlfriend, but if she was being honest with herself, she liked Kaylob a whole lot.

* * * *

That afternoon, climbing on the bus with Denny, Beth Ann saw Kaylob sitting in the back. She tried not to look, but couldn't help noticing that he glanced her way.

Denny leaned and whispered, "Why don't you go talk to him? Tell him you're sorry for making him mad. I can see you care."

Beth Ann thought about it and decided to try, before they took off. She stood next to the empty seat and stared at him. "Kaylob, can I sit down?"

"Sure." He glanced up at her as she sat down.

After a few minutes of awkward silence, Beth Ann cleared her throat. "Can you stop being mad at me now?"

He inhaled and rubbed his hands down his pants. "What makes you think I'm mad?" Kaylob gave her a sidelong glance.

"Because, since I kissed Blake on the cheek you've avoided me." A flush heated her neck and she hoped it didn't show.

Kaylob said nothing, but gave her fast glance, then mumbled, "You seem to like him an awful lot and he lives on the right side of town." His jaw clenched and he turned back towards the window.

"Kaylob, I don't want to fight anymore and what do you mean the right side of town?"

He said nothing, but continued to stare outside, not even paying any attention to her sitting there. A long, uncomfortable silence made her want to crawl under the seat.

As soon as the bus stopped, she went to stand up and everything started to spin. What the heck was going on, she wondered and clutched hard to the seat? Then, as soon as it started, it ended so she went back to sit with Denny. Tears filled her eyes and she swallowed hard.

"He's still mad at you?" She reached over and touched Beth Ann's hand. "Are you okay? You look pale."

All Beth Ann could do was nod. Why was she letting this guy she hardly knew upset her, when she'd had such a nice day? More than likely that's why she felt dizzy.

Denny whipped around and glared at Kaylob. "Screw him," she said. "Let him keep screwing Dusty. Like you said, who needs guys anyway?"

Beth Ann swallowed. "He is doing that with her? Are you sure?"

"From what I've heard, they've gone all the way."

Beth Ann tried her best to swallow the tears. After all, he was doing it with that girl. She could only hope that his thing fell off in the process, she huffed.

* * * *

Kaylob's stop was first, thank god. He was still angry with Beth Ann, and those looks Denny was giving him were irritating. Just as he stepped off the bus, he saw Dusty waiting for him. When he peered up at Beth Ann, her eyes looked so sad that his heart thumped him a good one. Jesus, she had tears, he was sure of it. What the heck was he doing? He really did like her, but damn she had made him see fire. Nobody had ever bothered him like that before. He was an ass, because she had apologized and her sweet little cheeks had flushed. All that made him want to do is kiss her, but instead he ignored her.

"Hey, Kaylob, you gonna say hi or just stand there staring at the bus?" Dusty walked up and grabbed his hand. "I thought maybe you'd want to come to my house today for a swim."

"I can't today." He squeezed her hand, then dropped it. "My mom needs me to go shopping and run some errands."

"How about I help you and you won't have to walk?" She pointed to her Dodge Dart. "I can drive you."

That was an offer he couldn't refuse, since his mom didn't drive. He could buy more than just a few things, which would save him so many trips. "Are you sure?"

She nodded and kissed his lips. "Of course I'm sure. You can get done faster and we can go swimming. My parents are gone for three days again."

Man, her parents were gone a lot. *Like my dad*, he thought. Only she had nobody at home and he felt bad for her, but at least they lived in a nice home in the good part of town. Kaylob was fully aware of what people thought about his house being behind the old train station. He'd worked hard to make it look nice, but that didn't change the location.

"Sounds fun," he lied and climbed into the passenger side.

Kaylob was pleased to have Dusty's help and she was really nice about it. He was sure as heck happy when she picked up all his mom's personal things. That was something he never liked to do.

All of a sudden, a thought smacked him upside his thick head. He was being just like Blake. He watched Dusty's eyes when they met his. He saw something there he hadn't noticed before. Could she like him a little more than he knew? Lisa had asked him that very question.

Once they got back to Kaylob's house and put everything away, they took off to go swimming. While she swam doing laps to and fro, he leaned back in the lounge chair, letting the sun heat his skin. The afternoon wind blew softly through the trees, leaving him silent with his thoughts. With his hands behind his head, he stared up at the blue sky and watched the clouds hovering above. It was really neat how they cast shadows across the pool and made odd shapes.

With time to think, Kaylob realized he wanted to be someone different, not like his dad or Blake. He wanted to grow up to be the kind of man that would be there for his friends and his girlfriend. Not someone who would abandon them, or need to prove something by how many girls hung on his arm.

"Penny for your thoughts." Dusty smacked him with a towel.

"Just enjoying the day," he lied again and summoned up a fake grin.

"Want to go inside and get your mind off whatever you're trying not to think about?" She pulled at his arm and stood.

Kaylob stared up at her and there was no doubt that she was fine, and even more so in that bikini. Every part of him wanted her and wanted her bad. His mind flooded with the cold truth, which was, if he had a smidgen of decency, he'd end this right here and right now. It wasn't right. He couldn't stop thinking about Beth Ann.

"Dusty." He glanced up at her and felt his hands trembling at the thought of hurting anyone, but even more so because she was his friend. She had told him over and over again, *don't get hung up and don't fall in love. This is just for fun.* He studied her face.

"Uh oh." She held his gaze. "You're ending it, aren't you?" Her lip trembled and her nervous voice stabbed his heart.

"I'm sorry, Dusty. You told me not to get serious and well ..." He paused and inhaled deeply. "I have feelings for someone else."

"I understand," she said, stared at the ground and paused. "Is it still the redhead?" Tears filled her eyes.

His guilt along with the sticky heat lingered in the air, which only made him feel worse. She was crying and now he felt like an ass. What the heck was he supposed to do? He'd gone and done the very thing he hated the most. He stood and pulled her into a hug, inhaling her fragrance of suntan lotion and watermelon, which he'd always remember.

"I'm sorry, Dusty. I didn't mean to make you feel bad."

"No. I know you wouldn't do that on purpose. We've had ourselves a great time. I knew from the beginning, we were too far apart in age, and I can't be with you that way either." She leaned back and looked into his eyes as she wiped away a tear. "I'm almost eighteen and you're only fourteen. Kaylob, you are the best guy and good hearted boy I've ever been with." She swallowed. "I'm going to miss you so much. You know, those older guys I hang out with don't even compare to you." She cupped his face.

There was no stopping the tears that burned his eyes. "I'll miss you too. If you ever need me, or a shoulder, I'm always your friend." He kissed her forehead. "Dusty ... you're a really special person and whoever you end up with better treat you right." He cleared his throat. "Or I'll have to hurt him."

"You're one of a kind, Kaylob Shawn O'Brien. Always remember that." She picked up her towel, kissed him softly, and walked into the house.

Kaylob put on his pants, and pulled his shirt over his head. A few minutes later, she emerged from the house with a sundress on, jiggling her keys. "Let me give you a ride, it's too hot to walk home."

When they kissed goodbye, he knew it was for the last time. Deep down, he was certain that even though he was giving up on something that had been a lot of fun, he was gaining something that would make him the kind of man he wanted to be when he grew up.

* * * *

Beth Ann sat in her room, filling out the invitations for her birthday party. The end of September had come and gone and Beth Ann had made many new friends. And that was a good feeling, but deep in her heart, she still wished that Kaylob would at least speak to her. He had only said a few words to her since the day she kissed Blake. She'd heard rumors that he wasn't seeing that older girl anymore, but he still avoided her. Whenever she saw him at the bus stop, or at the movies, he would either walk away or act busy talking to someone else. Not even looking her way. The whole thing made her feel sad, like that old song that her daddy use to sing, *make the world go away.*

However, she decided she was going to invite him to her party anyway. Lisa and Kaylob were best friends and she'd give his invitation to Lisa. All she knew was that she wanted to make up with him, and maybe let him know that she had a stomach aching crush.

"I think it's more than a crush," she said to his invitation.

She hoped he liked her a little—if he did once, maybe he could again. Was there something she could do? Maybe act more mature like those older girls he was used to, and maybe wear some pretty lipstick and stockings or something. Could she make herself look like a high school girl?

Not without being grounded by her mom and locked up for life by her brother.

Either way a pool party was going to be fun. With the weather still warm enough, and the heated pool, they could swim the day away. Beth Ann was excited because she'd never had a birthday party with friends over before. They'd always been traveling and she'd spent it with her family, which was fun, but not like this.

Beth Ann remembered being on the road for her tenth birthday. Her mom had somehow managed to get her a cake and new shoes. They had stopped at a rest stop and celebrated. Her daddy played the guitar and sung happy birthday with her brothers harmonizing. That day, her mom had fought to be happy. Beth Ann was young, but saw the pain in her mama's eyes. Therefore, she pasted on her happy face and acted way more excited than she was. The best gift of the day was when her mom started to have some real fun. They had played ball and walked down by the river, taking in the brisk fall day and watching the water flow.

One would think that she would have figured out that her mom wasn't happy, but she was wrapped up in her own unhappiness, and hadn't paid enough attention.

Someday, she'd need to tell her mama how sorry she was, or at the least ask God to forgive her for being so selfish.

A knock startled her. "Come in."

Cole stood there holding a piece of chicken. "So miss teen, are you getting your invitations done?" He winked and took a big bite.

"Yes." She held them up. "Twenty."

He swallowed and said, "That's a lot of kids for me to deal with, but my friend Carrie is coming to help out." He wiped his mouth with his sleeve.

"Is she your girlfriend?" Beth Ann was being nosey, but didn't care.

"I think so." His smile widened. "You'll like her."

"I better or you'll have to break up." She gave him a serious look.

"I'll make sure to tell her that she has to get my little sister's stamp of approval." He chuckled and took another bite.

Once he turned and left, the phone rang. Her mom and Stanley had hooked one up in her bedroom, because she got so many calls. Having her own private telephone was just another thing she'd never imagined.

"Hello."

"Hi, Beth Ann, it's me, Lisa. I called to see if you wanted some help with those invitations or did you finish them? I was coming over today, did you remember?"

"No, and yes, I'd love the help and I remembered! When can you be here? Since today is Saturday, do you want to spend the night? I already asked my mom the other day if it was okay to have you over for the night, and she said yes."

"Let me ask." Beth Ann heard her lay down the phone. A few minutes later, Lisa came back winded, as if she'd run a marathon.

"Yes, my mom said I can. Would an hour be okay? I have to do a few more chores."

"That would be great. I'll see you soon." Beth Ann hung up the phone with excitement. This would be the first time she and Lisa would spend the night together and there was no doubt they would have fun. It would also help take her mind off Kaylob. Or so she hoped.

Not even an hour later, Beth Ann heard a knock at the front door. When she swung it open she noticed just how beautiful Lisa looked, wearing her white shorts and sun top. Her skin was so dark and her eyes so blue, it was as if she stepped out of a fairy tale book.

"What are you staring at? Do I look funny?" Lisa looked down at her shorts and smoothed them out.

"Funny! No, you look like a fairy princess."

"Okay, do you need glasses?" Lisa's lips curved upwards.

Before Beth Ann could answer, her mom's voice rang out. "Beth Ann, are you going to invite your friend in or make her stand outside all day?" She wished her mom didn't talk so much like a southerner.

"Come in." Beth Ann said, and waved towards her mom who was entering the living room. "This is my mom."

"Hello Lisa, you can call me Jean since I hear your mom made Beth Ann call her by her first name. Seems to be the thing around here. It's so good to meet you." She walked up and extended her hand to Lisa, but pulled her into a hug instead. "I'm glad you're able to spend the night." She gave both girls a soft grin. "I have some things made up for y'all, since Stanley and I will be going to do some work in San Francisco. Cole will be home this evening. Our number is on the refrigerator if you need us."

"We'll be fine, Mama, and thank you for making special treats." Beth Ann took Lisa's hand and pulled her, and her overnight bag, down the hall to her bedroom.

"Wow, your mom is really nice and pretty. I love her accent, Beth Ann." She tried to drawl, but failed big time.

Beth Ann helped her out. "Well, well, bless your heart, you are a funny thing."

Lisa's eyes grew enormous. "Wow, you sounded like Scarlet in Gone with the Wind."

"Thank you, Lisa," Beth Ann bowed. "I do have a wonderful mom. I love her very much." Beth Ann was serious.

"She sounds like a southern belle. And I will just have to try some of that sun tea you were telling me about."

"Yes, you will. My mom makes the best and she always has some made."

"Trippy," Lisa said lightly. "Not many of my friends admit to liking their parents." She looked around Beth Ann's room. "Wow, this is really beautiful." She walked over and touched the lace on the canopy bed. "Did you design this?"

Beth Ann shook her head. "No, my mom and Stanley did it for me. I was so surprised." She felt her throat clog, thinking about how much her life had changed. "Now, how about we get the invitations for my party finished. Do you want to go swimming afterwards?" Beth Ann took a deep breath. "I want to invite Kaylob. Do you think he'll come?" Beth Ann sat on her bed and looked up at Lisa.

"Sure," Lisa grinned. "He likes you Beth Ann, he's just mad right now. He'll get over it. Kaylob's a nice guy with a kind heart and he's not had an easy life." Lisa sat down next to her. "So I take it you sorta like him?"

"Yes, actually, he's the only boy I've ever liked unless you count Little Joe from Bonanza." Beth Ann nodded and swallowed hard. She glanced down at her hands. "I think I blew it though and what do you mean he's not had an easy life?"

"Come on, I doubt you blew it, but let's not worry about that now. You still have Little Joe if all else fails." Lisa hopped up. "Now, let's get those invitations done and go for a swim. I don't think you know this, but I'm a fish."

"You're really beautiful for a fish." Beth Ann couldn't help but giggle. "I think you look more like a mermaid."

"Well, if I'm a mermaid, I better hurry and get my gills wet or I'll suffocate." She gave a half grin. "Now stop worrying about Kaylob, he'll stop being pissy soon."

"How do you know that?"

"He's my best friend. I know everything about him." She nudged Beth Ann.

They finished putting the time and date on the invitations and stuck them in the mailbox. Beth Ann didn't ask for an RSVP because most of her friends had already said they'd be there. Kaylob was the only one she wasn't sure about, but Lisa said he would be, so all Beth Ann could do was hope she was right.

That afternoon, as Beth Ann and Lisa spent the day swimming and sharing their thoughts on life and the world, something happened that Beth Ann had never experienced. A strong connection was formed. It was everything she imagined that falling in love was like, only with a friend.

Beth Ann strolled into the house to get some lemonade because for some reason her skin was clammy and her throat was extra dry. The minute she stepped inside, heat rushed through her and her insides felt like fire. Next, she heard a whooshing sound, then her heart started pounding so hard that the room was spinning. What the heck? Everything started going black, and then, the last thing she remembered was going down on the floor.

When she finally opened her eyes, she saw a fuzzy Lisa, with tears rolling down her cheeks.

"Beth Ann, you're awake, oh my god. I called your parents and they are on their way home. I came in and you were sleeping on the floor and I couldn't wake you up."

"I think I just got too much sun. I feel okay now." Beth Ann removed the washrag from her head and tried to sit up. "Crap, how long was I out? My mom is going to be so upset."

"I don't know, but I told them you were breathing fine and talking in your sleep." Lisa's lip trembled.

"I think I passed out and I must have gone to sleep afterwards," Beth Ann explained.

"I didn't understand why you were laying on the floor sleeping. I almost called an ambulance." Lisa's eyes were shadowed with worry.

"How long do you think I was out?" Beth Ann asked again.

"Maybe twenty minutes or so. I was afraid to leave you. Are you sleepy or do you think you might have had a sunstroke?"

Before Beth Ann could say anything, she heard the front door open and her mom was by her side, kneeling on the floor.

"I already called a doctor," her mom said, her voice trembling. "Do you remember what happened?" She gently stroked Beth Ann's hair.

"I think I just got too much sun, Mama. I'm really okay, I don't need to see a doctor and like Lisa said, I was just sleeping."

"Oh, you are going to the doctor," her mom said. "Did you eat today?"

Beth Ann went to stand, but almost went down again. "I think I forgot."

"Let's get her to the doctor, now." Stanley swooped her into his arms.

Beth Ann felt awful to worry everyone just because she got too much sun, and well, maybe, she forgot to eat.

It ended up that the doctor said she was not eating enough food. He gave her a time-consuming lecture about swimming all day with so few calories. He said it was a warning sign that she needed to eat more, but she found she didn't really want to. She had gotten so used to eating small portions, trying to eat more made her feel sick.

The words of those kids at the one of the schools, floated in her head. She didn't want to get fat. If calories would make her put a lot of weight on, she'd watch those. After the doctor made his nurse give her some crackers and juice, Stanley insisted they all go out for dinner. While they were at the restaurant, her mom sat right by her side, so Beth Ann had no choice but to finish every last bite of her food.

Great, now everyone would be breathing down her back about eating and bossing her around.

Chapter Twelve

The next few weeks went by in a flash as Beth Ann prepared for her party. At least she hadn't passed out anymore, but everyone was watching everything she ate.

Lisa and Beth Ann were inseparable, either on the phone or hanging out together. Denny was there, too. They were like the three musketeers. Denny had her best friend Gayle Williams since they were toddlers. Gayle was in one grade higher, pretty and fun to be with. Sometimes they all hung out and that was always a blast.

On Friday, the week prior to Beth Ann's party, Lisa spent the night again and they were up early and ready to go on an adventure, but not before Lisa made sure Beth Ann ate breakfast. Maybe they would kick around in town and find some adventurous things to do.

As they walked down the railroad tracks, Beth Ann saw Kaylob sitting on the steps of the old train station reading a magazine.

Lisa elbowed her. "There's the big lug, let's go talk to him." She pulled Beth Ann by the arm. "Come on, he doesn't bite."

"He might," Beth Ann said and wouldn't move.

Lisa shook her head. "Come on, chicken." She tugged her arm.

Once they arrived, he glanced at Lisa. Then slowly he turned his eyes towards Beth Ann.

He looked down at his cooking magazine and spoke. "So what are you two up too on this lovely Saturday? Causing trouble, no doubt." An impish grin spread across his face.

Why did he make her feel so nervous? Now, her cheeks heated, just because he spoke. Okay, she'd focus on Lisa and try not to look at him. However, Lisa made that impossible when she walked over and messed up his hair. "No, we are on an adventure."

He shook his head. "Wow, so much adventure to be found in Novato. Watch out for the wild animals." He threw his head back and laughed.

With that, Lisa grabbed Beth Ann by the arm. "Let's go, he's just being a brat." They turned and started walking away.

"See you next weekend." Kaylob called out.

Just those simple words were enough to let Beth Ann know he was coming to her party. Her insides jittered and her palms got sweaty. Now that he was coming, she had to make a plan, something that would make him like her again.

Lisa winked at her. "See, I told you he'd be there. He likes you a lot."

"I can't tell since he doesn't really speak to me."

"He's just stubborn and still jealous. He'll get over it. Kaylob's the most honest guy I know."

Beth Ann had to ask. "Why haven't you ever gone after him? Did you two ever like each other?"

"Oh gross, no. Kaylob's like my brother. I've known him since we were babies and I can't even think of him that way. He's my best friend. Our parents have been friends forever and don't' forget, I'm in love with Terry. I don't care about anyone else." She sighed, then continued, "Not to mention, we spent almost every holiday together, so we're family." After she paused again, she took Beth Ann's hand and met her gaze. "I have another best friend now, and I think I was waiting for her all my life." Lisa's eyes got glassy.

Beth Ann swallowed as a tear slid down her cheek.

"I've never had a best friend in my life," Beth Ann said, just above a whisper.

"Well, you do now and it's forever. And when we're really old, we will sit in our rocking chairs watching life go by." Lisa placed her arm around Beth Ann's shoulder. "But right now, while we're young, let's go find our adventure."

That afternoon, as the journey began, a cool fall breeze carried promises of a lifetime filled with bubblegum, laughter and lifelong friendship. It was the kind of day Beth Ann had never imagined, because she hadn't known what true best friendship was like.

They had found tin cans and walked on them like a pair of shoes, laughing at the clunking noise. They ate at Perry's Deli and had the most delicious sandwiches. Lisa had acted like the food police and made her eat the whole thing. After lunch, they hung out at Pioneer Park and went on the swings, trying to reach up and touch the clouds. It was a wonderful fun filled afternoon.

As they walked back home in silence, Beth Ann noticed the sunset painted beautiful colors of orange and yellow across the mountaintops. The scent in the air was of wood fireplaces and fallen leaves that smelled of pumpkin spice. That, along with the far off laughter of little kids and dogs barking, brought a sense of home and belonging that filled Beth Ann's soul.

Lisa pointed. "Look at those roses in Mrs. Oresetti's yard." She ran over to the fence and buried her nose inside a yellow one. "This smells so good," she inhaled, then swatted away a bumblebee.

Beth Ann wandered over to the flower and breathed in the aroma. "Ah, it's wonderful. I've always thought that some roses smell like all the fruit combined. Wow!" She smelled it again. "This smells so good. Do you know Mrs. Oresetti?" Beth Ann asked as she admired the white fence and the rows of colorful roses.

"Yes, and you'll meet her at Halloween. She bakes the best cookies and rice crispy balls ever." Lisa closed her eyes. "She's like everyone's grandma."

Beth Ann grinned. "That's neat." She took Lisa's hand as they skirted down the street, passing by kids playing tag and throwing balls for their dogs. That same little musician boy was marching around playing his flute, acting like he was in a band.

Lisa stopped and grinned. "That's Gary. He wants to be a musician someday. He lives in his own little world." Lisa waved and Beth Ann watched his face turned bright red. Beth Ann knew that Lisa more than likely had that effect on every young boy and the older ones, too.

When they walked in the front door of Beth Ann's house, the smell of spaghetti made her stomach do a hungry dance.

"That smells good," Beth Ann said.

Lisa nodded and stuck her nose in the air. "Good maybe you'll actually eat a lot."

"I eat better now. At least most days," Beth Ann said flatly.

"You're doing better. But tonight, let's eat a big bowl of that, okay?"

Beth Ann thought she saw concern flash in Lisa's eyes. "I plan on eating a big bowl." Beth Ann wanted to prove she ate, so that's just what she did. That should make everyone happy. She'd had breakfast, a sandwich and spaghetti, all in one day.

That night after stuffing themselves, they went swimming and played volleyball in the pool, even though it was a tad chilly. Beth Ann wanted to work off some of those calories and didn't want her family to know what she was doing.

After a while the wind picked up so they tore inside, shivering. Then they changed and ran out to the family room to find a good movie. Cole joined in and they all watched television together. At one point, Cole whispered to Beth Ann that he really liked Lisa and was happy they were friends.

Beth Ann made sure to educate him. "We are best friends for life." She gazed into Cole's eyes and saw his expression soften.

"I'm happy for you, sis." He patted her hand just before Lisa came in and sat back down.

That weekend ended and Beth Ann thought about Kaylob coming to her party, maybe, just maybe if he did, he'd like her again.

Chapter Thirteen

Monday morning was a beautiful autumn day, with blue skies that were dotted with white puffy clouds. The only thing that hinted of the approaching season change was a slight crisp breeze and the copper leaves that were starting to cover the ground. However, by noon it would be in the seventies.

As she and Denny walked in silence towards the bus stop, Beth Ann saw Kaylob laughing with Frankie. She paused and took notice of the way Kaylob tossed back his head in laughter. It was really cute.

"Shut up, Beth Ann," she whispered to herself.

"Why are you telling yourself that? I didn't hear you say anything." Denny glanced at her with a puzzled stare.

Beth Ann arched a brow as the bus pulled up. "I'll tell you later." She and Denny moved behind five other kids. Then Kaylob stepped up behind her.

Beth Ann could feel him, and his fresh scent made her head spin. It whispered of something warm with a hint of Chocolate and mint. He was making her world tilt, along with causing hundreds of butterflies to scatter in her stomach.

She glanced over her shoulder and their eyes met. Instantly, the heat crawled up her neck and she knew it was heading towards her face.

Kaylob must have seen it, because he grinned and winked. Oh god, she turned and faced the bus, willing the doors to open, so she could run and hide in her seat.

Once they got inside, Beth Ann plopped down and made darn sure not to look his way.

"Beth Ann." Denny leaned closer. "You're going to put a hole in your lip."

Frankie was sitting in the seat in front of them, and turned around and grinned. "Something got you nervous or are you just hungry. Here, you can have a bite of my sandwich." He held up his brown bag. "I hope you feel okay because your face is blood red."

Beth Ann frowned. "No, I just do that sometimes when it's warm in here." She tugged at her collar and wished people would stop talking about food.

"Well, no matter, you ladies look mighty fine this morning." He gave them both a teasing grin. There was just something about Frankie that made people feel happy.

"So are you coming to my birthday party?" Beth Ann asked.

Frankie nodded and looked over at Denny, who was uncharacteristically quiet. "Sure am, and I hope there will be dancing."

Beth Ann nodded. "Of course and swimming, too."

Before they could finish their conversation the bus pulled up to the school and the doors opened. Beth Ann stood and glanced back at Kaylob one more time. Much to her surprise, his look was tender as he held her gaze. He didn't say anything, but his eyes were whispering something that made her want to stand there and understand every unspoken word.

Denny nudged her. "Come on, girl, you can't stand here staring all day. We have to get off the bus."

Beth Ann looked at Kaylob once more. She forced herself to break the connection with his hypnotic eyes and managed to make her way off the bus without falling down.

How does he do that? She wondered. It was something she didn't fully understand.

But one thing she knew for sure was she really liked Kaylob a lot, and wondered what it might feel like to kiss him.

* * * *

As the week went by, Beth Ann and Frankie were inseparable. He was quickly becoming an addition to her circle of best friends. The thing she was happy about was he had a way of taking her mind off Kaylob. She wondered if he knew how many girls were crushing on him. He was very handsome, with his dark curly hair and that cute little dimple that emerged when he smiled. Not to mention Frankie had a great personality and could charm the honey away from bees. That Frankie Russo was a bee charmer, or better yet, a girl charmer. Maybe she could get him and Denny together. Although Denny had been hanging out with Andre more lately.

That Thursday, the ninth of October, was the first day that Frankie asked if he could walk her home instead of taking the bus. He wanted to show her the hill where everyone had fun cardboard sliding. As they climbed the dirt path towards the area, she stopped and watched a light breeze tickle the tips of the golden wheat colored hills. The perfume of eucalyptus floated all around and the old trees seemed to have a personality all of their own.

Beth Ann loved the place already.

Frankie pointed. "This is the best spot on the hill and the best cardboard sliding in Novato. You can go really fast." He whipped his hand through the air, showing her.

"I've never done that," Beth Ann confessed.

"You've never gone cardboard sliding?" Frankie questioned with his eyes wide.

Beth Ann shook her head and felt her eyes burning for some dumb reason. "No." She turned her back to him.

She could feel Frankie staring at her, just before a big tear slid down her cheek.

"Hey, there." He turned her towards him, and wiped the moisture from her face. "I'll teach you. It's no big deal." He took her hand and trotted up near one of the old oak trees.

Beth Ann stopped and looked into his soft green eyes. "I've never learned because ... we were always on the road traveling and well ..." She hesitated again, wondering if he would think less of her if he found out she had lived in a car. To heck with it, she needed to share that information with someone.

"We lived in the car a lot and I never really lived in a house, but please don't tell anyone." She sighed, feeling a big lump form in her throat. "My birth daddy is a musician and was sure someday he'd make it big, so he dragged us from state to state."

Frankie lifted her chin with his finger and held her gaze. "I'm sorry you went through that and I'll never tell anyone, but you know what?"

She shook her head no.

"You are going to be famous someday and ... You are the most special girl I've ever known." He kissed her cheek. "And you know what else?"

"What?" she asked, finding her smile.

"I know where some cardboard is stashed and I'm going to teach you right now." He took her hand again and hauled her towards two other trees.

She and Frankie stayed on the hill until the sun got dim, and what a great afternoon it was. They hit bumps and she would scream as they sailed through the air. That day flying down the mountains on their magic cardboard, whizzing over the golden wheat fields, Beth Ann found a kindred spirit and what she knew would be a lifelong friend.

After so much fun, Beth Ann and Frankie started their walk over the mountain to her house. They paused by a gate that surrounded an old farm house, and Frankie stopped and met her gaze.

"Beth Ann, you do know that Kaylob is crazy about you, right?"

She stood, letting the silence linger. "How do you know this?"

Frankie moved closer and placed his hand on her shoulder. "I know, because it's obvious. Besides, if he didn't like you, I would have wanted you to be my girl," he admitted. "But since you both like each other a lot. I'm happy to have you as one of my best friends."

Beth Ann's mind raced thinking about Kaylob and wondering if he really felt that way. Frankie's words stuck in her brain, at least the ones where he said Kaylob liked her a lot. One of the most important things he had told her was he wanted her as one of his best friends, even after knowing she lived out of her car. That overflowed her with hope, that she'd never be bullied again about the way they lived.

"Beth Ann." Frankie bent down studying her face. "Are you awake?"

Just as she started to answer, she spied a stunning white horse standing by the other end of the fence. Her mane was the most beautiful golden she'd ever seen. Beth Ann felt the horse staring right at them.

"Oh Frankie, look." Beth Ann pointed and almost lost her voice.

"Wow, what a beauty. I've never seen her before."

Beth Ann paced over to the creature and held out her hand.

"Hello there, aren't you beautiful," Beth Ann said and watched as the horse moved its large head to her hand. With ease, she stroked her mane.

Off in the distance Beth Ann saw a lady was coming towards them. She sure hoped it was okay that they were there.

"Hi there." The lady smiled, first at Beth Ann and then to Frankie. For the first time Beth Ann saw Frankie's cheeks flush a candy apple red.

"I'm Beth Ann and this is Frankie." She pointed to her open-mouthed friend. "I was just admiring your beautiful horse." Beth Ann reached up to the animal and touched it's nose.

"My name is Rhonda and I'm happy to meet you. I'm so glad you stopped by to visit my horse, she's wonderful and I'm afraid she's a bit lonely. I've been working such long hours and she's starving for company."

Beth Ann couldn't help but notice Rhonda looked like a model, her long blonde hair hung in curls around her shoulders, and her blue eyes were almost as beautiful as Kaylob's. Her legs were long and lean, and wow, what a figure that her tight shorts and revealing top showed off. Holy bareness, she wasn't wearing a bra.

Frankie finally blew out a deep breath, like he had been in a coma or something. "She's sure a beauty," he finally managed to say. "The horse," he pointed.

"Well, Frankie and Beth Ann," the lady said, "I would love to have you stop by and visit Sally Mae. She'd love that, and it would make me feel better knowing she has company."

Beth Ann glanced over at Frankie and saw his face was still glowing. But when she heard him speak, she almost laughed. His voice cracked and went up a notch.

"Sure, we'd love to," he said. "Who feeds her and stuff while you're gone?"

"My neighbor, but I've been looking for someone to do it as a job. Would you like the job, Frankie?" Her eyes lit up.

"Yes! I mean, sure." He cleared his throat.

"I could help him sometimes too. I love animals," Beth Ann said.

"Well, good, let's go over the details. Would you two like to come in and have a glass of lemonade and we can make a list of everything she'll need?" She pointed to her house. "I'm sorry, that's all I have. Working in San Francisco has left me with little to no food. I need to go shopping. But I have some graham crackers and lemonade."

They headed towards the house.

"So what kind of job do you have in San Francisco?" Beth Ann asked.

"I do some lingerie and bathing suit modeling, and lately there has been a big demand for that line of fashion," she said.

Beth Ann thought she saw Frankie's knees buckle, but couldn't be sure. Now, she had a good idea what his symptoms were. After all, hadn't she had those same things happen with Kaylob? Wait, this girl was way older, at least 20 something. Frankie had a crush on an older woman?

Frankie looked dazed and was shaking his head yes to everything. She wondered if he was going to give himself whiplash.

They entered Rhonda's home, and much to Beth Ann surprise it was decorated in a warm country theme. The place reminded her of her auntie's house in Nashville, with sunflowers everywhere. Beth Ann missed her Auntie Madeline a lot, but these days she was not in the best of health. Beth Ann hoped that someday she'd get to see her aunt again, but since she was in poor health and couldn't travel, Beth Ann knew she'd have to go to see her. For some reason she'd been ill for a long time.

Rhonda waved for them to sit on her couch.

"Do you live here alone?" Beth Ann asked as she sat down.

"Yes, this was my parents' farm and they're both gone." Her eyes grew sad.

"I'm sorry," Beth Ann said.

"Me too." Frankie nodded and plopped down beside Beth Ann.

As she sauntered away to get their lemonade, Frankie got up and stared at one of her photos, she was almost naked. A few seconds after staring at it, he rushed back to the sofa, sat down, throwing a pillow over his lap. Holy cow, he was breathing hard, maybe he was scared. What was that all about? She didn't even act that way with Kaylob. She'd have to ask him later.

After spending almost thirty minutes with Rhonda, they headed home. There was no doubt that Beth Ann had made two new friends, an amazing white horse named Salle Mae and Rhonda her owner. By the time they arrived at Beth Ann's house, Frankie seemed somewhat back to normal, but hadn't said even one word. He kissed her forehead and mumbled goodbye.

"Wait, Frankie," Beth Ann called out.

He turned and met her gaze. "Yeah."

"What happened in her house that made you run to the couch and almost hide under a pillow?"

All Frankie did is swallow hard. "Nothing, I have to go." Then turned and ran down the road.

There was one thing Beth Ann knew for sure, Frankie was one of her best friends and she had just witnessed him falling flat on his face over an older woman. Was that love or called something else?

Chapter Fourteen

Saturday morning Beth Ann awoke with happy thoughts. Today would once again be filled with new experiences. The morning air smelled of cinnamon and apples, which meant her mom was cooking something yummy. Just maybe it was her delicious savory apple cake. There was nothing like the taste. The buttery apple flavor almost melted on her tongue.

She never imagined turning twelve would ever be so much fun, just thinking about it made heart flutter. The alarm clock went off, alerting her that it was eight am, her party was at two and she had a lot to do. Beth Ann sat up on her knees and opened her bedroom window, relishing the soft breeze that tickled her skin while the sun glowed above the rolling hills, giving hope for a warmer day. While lost in the beauty of her surroundings, the shrill of the ringing phone startled her so much that she almost fell onto the floor.

Man, she needed to turn that thing down.

"Hello."

"You up?" Lisa asked.

"Yes. I'm so excited about today. It's so pretty outside for October."

"I know. I just went out front to pick up the paper for my parents. Do you want me to come over and help? I can be there soon."

"Yes. I'd love it. Just bring what you're wearing for the party and don't forget your bathing suit. The pool is heated and all set for today, and hopefully, it will be in the seventies again."

Once they hung up, Beth Ann bounced out of bed and threw on her clothes. She wondered about what kind of food they would be having, besides her birthday cake. With twenty friends coming, she needed to make sure there were enough plates and glasses for everyone. Oh god, Kaylob was coming. Her stomach crawled up into her throat, when she thought about what Frankie had told her.

Could it be possible, could Kaylob really be crazy for her?

As she entered the dining room, she glanced out back and saw her mom and Stanley putting up tables. They were laughing and giving each other kisses as they looked inside the boxes that Cole brought outside. Her mom was a changed person, always smiling and laughing. In some ways, it was sad because it couldn't be with her dad. In other ways, it was great because her mom was finally happy.

She slid open the back door and stepped outside into the most spectacular day. Everyone stopped working and looked her way.

"Beth Ann you can't be out here. You need to go away." Her mom laughed and pointed inside.

"But, Mama."

Her mom marched over and took Beth Ann by the arm, making her go back inside. "We're doing something and you can't see until your party." She waved towards the family room. "No peeking, is that clear?"

"Yes, Mama." Beth Ann plopped down on the couch as her mom left the room.

A few seconds later, her mom returned. "Here you go." She handed Beth Ann a beautiful gift-wrapped box with a big pink bow on top. "For you, my darling daughter."

Beth Ann sat, staring down at the package and knew that any moment, tears were going to speed down her cheeks. "What is it?" she asked just above a whisper.

"Open it, silly, and you will see. I hope you love it as much as I did." Beth Ann knew her mom was getting emotional, because she drawled even more.

Beth Ann took her time and opened the box, pulling back the tissue. As soon as her eyes witnessed what was inside, her lips started to tremble.

"Oh, Mama, this is …" She started to cry as she lifted it up. "Beautiful." Her voice broke.

With one swoop, her mom pulled her up and placed the dress on the chair. "Beautiful like you." She embraced her daughter. "Now, birthday girl …" She inhaled deeply. "You go try it on. I made a hair appointment for you at the downtown salon at nine. This is your special day and I've waited a long time to throw you this kind of party." She waved Beth Ann towards the room and wiped away her own tears.

As soon as Beth Ann turned to leave, the doorbell rang. She turned back to her mom. "It must be Lisa, she was coming over to help, but now I don't know what she can do."

"She can help keep you busy while we get things set up. I'll go and let her in, while you take that to your room." Her mom smiled. "Your hair appointment is in thirty minutes." She exited the family room.

Beth Ann strode into her bedroom and stood in front of the full-length mirror. When she held up the pink organza silk dress, her heart soared at just how amazing it was. So much so it made her feel like a princess. The style had a fitted bodice with a square neckline and a dropped waist seam. If she were just less skinny, she'd feel almost pretty.

As she stood mesmerized, the door opened and Lisa entered.

"Wow! Like, really wow! That's so so groovy." She walked over and touched it.

"Can you believe my mom and Stanley bought this for my birthday, and gave it to me early so I could wear it today?" She swallowed. "I've never had anything so wonderful in my life."

"Well," Lisa laughed. "You're going to knock Kaylob out with that on."

Beth Ann felt heat creeping up her neck into her cheeks. "I doubt that. After all, he's been going out with high school girls." She looked down at herself. "That's hard to compete with."

"He's not seeing Dusty anymore." Lisa waved her off. "Because he's crazy about you, and Beth Ann you are gorgeous."

A knock at the door halted the conversation. Beth Ann strolled over and opened it.

"You girls ready?" Stanley stood there, smiling. "I'm taking you to your hair appointment."

Beth Ann moved closer to Stanley and put her arms around his neck. "Thank you so much for the wonderful gift."

"You are most welcome," he replied. "You deserve it." He hugged her tightly and kissed her cheek.

Beth Ann knew, in that moment, that God had blessed her life with a wonderful stepdad. She was sure it was okay to have two dads.

"Thank you for being so good to me. I love you."

Beth Ann heard his breath catch and saw a hint of tears gather in his eyes.

After a few seconds, he replied, "I'm the lucky one." He coughed. "Now, let's get you girls downtown before your momma has my head. Both of you are getting your hair done."

Lisa looked surprised. "Me?"

"Yes." Stanley nodded. "We are treating you both to a day at the salon. We called just now and they had room for Lisa, too. You can get your nails done and have your hair styled however you want. Just nothing too wild," he said and laughed. "If it's okay with your parents." He pointed to Beth Ann's phone. "Maybe you should call and ask them first."

Lisa nodded and made the call. Her parents agreed and asked to speak to Stanley.

Stanley picked up the phone. "Hello…Yes, we are happy to do this." He paused. "It's our pleasure and you're welcome, and yes, I'll tell Jean."

He placed the phone back down and waved toward the door. Beth Ann paused, thinking about what her life used to be like and what it was now. A wonderful new step dad, a beautiful home, and her amazing best friend. She needed to take a moment, be grateful, and thank God.

In the meantime, on the way to the salon, Beth Ann spied people raking leaves and kids on skateboards. Lisa was chattering away about the different colors of nail polish. Once they crossed over the tracks, Beth Ann saw Kaylob out in his front yard. His back was turned, but she saw him hard at work, even from that distance, he gave her goose bumps. She silently prayed that he'd really show up at her party.

Stanley pulled up to the curb, nodded at them, and handed them both a banana. "Give us a call when you're all done and be sure to eat." They both agreed.

Beth Ann came to a standstill, almost afraid of going inside, but Lisa wouldn't have it. She almost yanked her through the doors of the Powder and Pout hair salon, and wow, what a place, another new experience for Beth Ann.

At least twenty rows of yellow and orange blow dryers lined one wall and sinks were scattered about. Pictures hung on the walls, showing off all the modern styles and colors with stars like Natalie Wood and Patty Duke.

While they ate their bananas, Beth Ann could hear the bells going off, and watched as some of the beauticians un-wrapped curlers and did inspections. When they were finished eating, Lisa tossed the peels away in a small garbage can by a display case.

Under the Boardwalk was playing on the radio, blasting from the speakers that hung in the corners.

Lisa spun around looking at all the pictures. "Groovy, this place is wild."

"You've never been here?" Beth Ann asked, still staring at the walls. "The place looks like it was painted with every color of sherbet ice cream ever invented."

Lisa cracked up. "No. It just opened two months ago and I think the colors are bitchen."

A tall girl was heading towards them with a hairstyle and color that Beth Ann had never seen. She was slender with bell-bottoms and a rainbow shirt. Holy hair scare, Beth Ann sure hoped she wasn't the one giving her a new style. Maybe she should grab Lisa and they should run, and run fast.

"Good afternoon, ladies. What can we do for you?" The girl smiled and waited.

Beth Ann's throat clogged so Lisa had to speak.

"We are here to get our hair and nails done. It's Beth Ann's Birthday." She touched Beth Ann's arm. "Her dad gave us a credit card to pay with. They called ahead of time."

"Ahh." The girl nodded. "I'm Heather, just follow me."

The smell was different, like ammonia and perfumes all mixed together. Beth Ann tried not to scrunch up her nose, as the girl with big frizzy rainbow hair lead them in the back.

Beth Ann glanced at ladies getting their hair done while others read magazines, waiting for their hair to dry. On the whole, everything seemed normal, at least compared to the one time she'd been in a salon, but that had been nothing like this.

Another girl who was short and round approached. "This must be the birthday girl and her friend."

Beth Ann loved her normalness. "I'm Beth Ann and this is Lisa."

The short lady stuck out her hand. "I'm Valerie, but everyone calls me Val. It's nice to meet you both. Come with me Lisa." She waved for her to go forward.

Beth Ann wanted to yell. *No, take me!* But turned and looked at the rainbow lady, who had a slight grin, almost like she was reading Beth Ann's thoughts.

A few minutes later, Heather led her over to the shampoo bowl where Lisa was sitting nearby.

Once Beth Ann sank down, Heather asked, "So what would you like me to do?" She lifted a strand. "You've got amazing hair."

"Thank you." Beth Ann wondered for how long? "I'm not sure."

"Well, now … that's what I like to hear. I'm going to surprise you, and you can see what I've done when I'm finished."

Beth Ann said a silent prayer. *Please God, when I asked to change my red hair, rainbow wasn't what I had in mind.*

She swallowed the lump. "Okay."

Miss Rainbow hair laughed. "I'm going to make you even more beautiful," she said, as she released the chair and leaned Beth Ann back.

It was too late now to run and scream.

Beth Ann closed her eyes and decided to enjoy the tender feeling of Heather's fingers massaging her scalp. It really did feel good and she might as well enjoy it since her good hair days might be coming to a dreadful end. With that, Beth Ann closed her eyes and listened to the song on the radio, which was, *Bye Bye Love,* but all Beth Ann could sing was, bye bye hair.

Despite how strange Heather seemed, she was really nice. She ended up talking about her two dogs that were like her children. One was a Chihuahua, and the other a Great Dane, apparently, they were in love. Giant was the little one and Tiny was the big one. Beth Ann found herself laughing and enjoying the stories.

Meanwhile, Lisa looked like she was having fun as Val cut and snipped at her hair. When Lisa saw Beth Ann watching, she gave her a wide grin.

Heather had stuck some kind of cap on Beth Ann's head, and she could feel strands of hair being pulled through some holes. There was some smelly solution being brushed over the cap.

Oh god, don't let it be green or purple, she prayed again.

After a while, she took Beth Ann back over to the shampoo area, washed, and conditioned her hair, with something that smelled like fresh coconut.

So far, everything seemed great, and she was having way more fun than she had expected. Kaylob hadn't popped into her head once, until now. But she was yanked away from her thoughts when Heather picked up the blow dryer and started moving to the beat of, *Dancing in the Street,* by Martha and the Vandellas.

Heathers excitement became infectious and Beth Ann started feeling a surge.

Once Heather turned off the blow dryer and did something with a curling iron, she paused.

Her brows lifted. "Now, that is a masterpiece." She had a glint in her eye. "Look how stunning you are." She spun Beth Ann around to face the mirror.

Beth Ann couldn't believe the color of her hair. Beautiful strawberry highlights sparkled like diamonds in the sun. "Wow! I love it." She gave Heather a giant smile. And boy was she glad when she saw her hair was still long, but styled in a feathery flow.

Now, she was filled with joy and tons of relief.

Beth Ann spotted Lisa and noticed she also had highlights and a new hairstyle. When Lisa turned to glance at Beth Ann, her mouth fell open and her eyes got wide.

"Beth Ann!" Lisa exclaimed. "You look gorgeous, and older."

"Thank you." She touched her hair. "I'm so happy. You look great yourself."

Lisa chuckled. "Thanks."

Heather stood Beth Ann up and guided her to a table for nails. "Now, just relax and let Mindy take care of you." She gave Beth Ann a hug. "It's been fun doing your hair."

Beth Ann nodded. "Thank you, Heather. I had a good time as well."

A few minutes later, Lisa joined her. Together they enjoyed getting a manicure and their nails polished while singing. *You Don't Own Me*, by Leslie Gore.

The trip to the hair salon had been a fun experience. Beth Ann made sure to put a big tip on the credit card, just like Stanley said. She did it for Heather and Val, before they headed outside to wait for a ride.

They stepped outside to a lot of activity. Grant Avenue was filled with cars and people trailing down the sidewalks chattering. Beth Ann watched two small kids pass by, eating ice cream cones. Right on cue her stomach growled.

Lisa looked at her and laughed. "What did you say?"

Beth Ann giggled, then got distracted when she noticed Lisa's nails. "What color is that nail polish?" Beth Ann touched her finger.

"Frosty Red. I love it." She held up her hands, wiggling her fingers.

Beth Ann showed off hers, too. "Mine is hot pink. They will match my dress."

Beth Ann looked up when she heard a horn honk and saw Cole driving their mom's red convertible.

Lisa and Beth Ann jumped up and ran to the car.

"Don't you two look foxy." Cole whistled. "I'm taking you both to Berkley Farms and getting a shake before we head back."

"But shouldn't we get home?" Beth Ann questioned. "The party starts soon."

"Nope." He shook his head. "We still have plenty of time and I want to take you two gorgeous ladies out and show you off."

Beth Ann watched Lisa's cheeks grow pink. Cole had that effect on many girls. The funny thing about her brother was, he never acted full of himself, he was always nice to everyone.

They spent the next forty-five minutes at the restaurant hearing *all about* Cole's baseball practice. Cole had ordered a big giant plate of fries, which Beth Ann didn't want to eat and really wanted a salad. But Cole and Lisa kept pushing, so she ate a few of them plus a scrumptious malty milkshake. At least it hushed them up.

Once they arrived back home, Cole gave them orders while they sat in the car. "No peeking until we call you. You can hang out in the family room or your bedroom. That's it." He arched a brow. "Mom and Stanley have worked really hard for this day, so let them do this. Got it?"

"Okay," Beth Ann agreed.

* * * *

After they were out of the car, they ran up the steps into the house and dashed into her bedroom. Once inside, Lisa ran over to her overnight bag and pulled out a beautiful red dress, two bags of chips and two apples. "Snacks for us." She handed them to Beth Ann.

Beth Ann shook her head. "I'm full from those fries and milkshake."

"From a couple of fries and a shake? Come on and eat. I don't want you falling asleep again." She shoved the apple at Beth Ann.

Beth Ann grabbed the apple and took a small bite. At least it was a piece of fruit. She took another nibble and knew in that moment she needed it, but she just hated that everybody was always pushing food on her. She'd learned to cut back on calories a long time ago. Actually, it started when her mom would run out of money and put things back in the grocery stores. Her mom was always so embarrassed and tried to cover it up.

Just as she finished her apple, she glanced over at Lisa. "That is gorgeous." Beth Ann touched the fabric of her dress. "And your nails match, too."

"It's Terry's favorite," she said with her mouth full. "I hope he shows up." She swallowed.

"What? Why wouldn't he show up?" Beth Ann asked.

"Because he's working for grumpy old Mr. Palmer and sometimes he makes the workers stay longer." Her lips turned down. "He said he'd come, even if he had to work late."

Beth Ann studied Lisa's face. "You really do love him, don't you?" She reached out and touched Lisa's arm.

Lisa nodded. "I do ..." She took a deep breath. "I'm just afraid, because I'm so much younger and can't do all the things he wishes I could do ..." Her voice trailed off.

"Like what?" Beth Ann almost felt mad.

"Oh, not that. He never pushes me to fool around. Just things like staying out later than I can, or going away camping." Lisa got a far off look in her eyes. "I mean we make out, and even touch, but he's never tried to do ... you know." She blushed.

Beth Ann meandered over to her closet and took down her dress. "We should get dressed." She hoped that would change the subject, because she'd never done anything like that with a boy before.

She held up her dress and fell in love all over again. "Lisa, look, my nail polish matches perfectly too."

Lisa nodded. "Groovy." Then got up and turned Beth Ann around. "I just have to ask this question, because well, I want to know. Have you ever kissed a guy?"

Beth Ann could see that Lisa didn't take hints very well.

"Yes! I kiss my brothers and I kissed Blake Tanner on the cheek, remember?"

"But have you ever *really* kissed a guy?" Lisa questioned.

Beth Ann took a deep breath. "No. Never on the lips." She turned around, looking for her shoes.

"Well, when you do, I better be the first to know," Lisa said.

"Okay, you will."

As she slipped on the dress, butterflies swarmed inside her. What if Kaylob didn't show up? Maybe he changed his mind or didn't really want to come. After all, he was older than everybody else. Most the kids coming were her age. And, when she saw him last, he was out in his yard working. Her heart sank at the thought.

Lisa stepped up next to her. "Wow! Girl, you are one foxy chick," Lisa exclaimed. "All the guys are going to be drooling. Especially Kaylob, who will be on the ground and might need mouth to mouth." She raised her eyebrows and a wide grin spread across her face. "This dress really shows off your boobs."

"What boobs?" Beth Ann looked down.

Lisa waved a hand across Beth Ann. "The kind every girl wants. Noticeable, but not too much. I wish mine weren't so big. They get in the way."

"Are you crazy?" Beth Ann laughed.

"Maybe a little," Lisa said. "Let's get your makeup on."

Today Beth Ann was actually going to wear makeup. Lisa helped her with eyeliner and a hint of blush with a pretty pale pink lipstick. Just as they finished up there was a knock on the door.

"Come in," Beth Ann said.

Cole peered inside. "Mom and Stanley are ready for you ladies." His eyes widened. "Holy Superman! You're gorgeous, baby sister, and you look so grown up." His grin spread.

"Thank you, Cole." Her lip quivered. He had never said that before and Beth Ann was fighting to swallow her tears.

Lisa caught Beth Ann's eyes and gave her a wink. "See, I told you."

"You're welcome, sis." He touched Beth Ann's nose.

Cole glanced at Lisa. "You look foxy, too." He arched a brow again.

Lisa blushed from her neck to the top of her forehead and Beth Ann couldn't help but giggle.

Just as they started to head out to the backyard, the phone rang and Beth Ann stopped to pick it up.

"Hello."

"Hello birthday girl. How's my wonderful granddaughter today?"

"Oh Gram, I wish you were here. I'm having my first party." She glanced at Cole and Lisa who stood watching her.

"I know you are sweetness, your mama promised me a bunch of pictures. I'm just so tickled that you are having this special day."

Beth Ann's stomach knotted. She missed her Gram and dad so much.

"I wish you and daddy were here." She inhaled.

"I know, we wish that too. I know you're going to have a wonderful time. I'm sure your daddy will be calling you later. Now, you have fun and give me all the details tomorrow. My present is there because I sent it last week. Your mama hid it from you."

"Thank you, Gram. I love you." Her voice quivered.

"I love you too and will talk to you soon. You just be happy and have a good day," she said.

When they hung up, Beth Ann took a deep breath. After a few minutes, she turned and headed outside.

When she opened the door and stepped out back, emotions rushed through her. "Oh my God," she said out loud.

Chapter Fifteen

Her incredible family had done all this for her and her heart filled with a deep enduring love.

They had worked the entire morning and part of the afternoon to make the backyard look like something out of a fairy tale. Looking around, she noticed all the little white lights were strung on the fence and on the two trees. Tables had flower arrangements that looked like something from a magical garden. Everything was pink, white, and glowing. Even the food was spread in a delicate array of exquisiteness. One long table that sat towards the back was piled high with gifts.

She was in awe of everything, from the pink and white balloons to the matching streamers. The way they had attached the butterflies that floated in the air, was like nothing she'd ever seen.

Lisa ran over and put her arm around Beth Ann. "I've never seen anything so beautiful, this is unreal." Lisa glanced at Beth Ann. "It's so cool the way the butterflies look like they are fluttering their wings."

Beth Ann nodded. "They represent coming out of their cocoon and taking flight."

"So today is your butterfly day," Lisa said and held Beth Ann's hand.

"It's all so incredible and, this is my very first birthday party." She saw Lisa tilt her head.

"Your first one. Really?" She met Beth Ann's gaze.

Beth Ann nodded. "Remember my birth father was a musician and we traveled a lot and never really had a home."

"Wow. No wonder your mom did all this." Lisa's eyelashes were laced with tears. "She must be over the moon to be able to do this." She gave Beth Ann a big hug. "I'm so happy for you and I'm happy you moved here, Beth Ann."

Before Beth Ann could get too emotional, she saw Stanley and her mom smile as they approached. "What do you think?" her mom asked when she stepped up to them. Before Stanley could join them, Cole yelled out.

"Help." Cole's voice went up.

He was trying to steady the table with the gifts on it, so Stanley made a mad dash to go help him.

"Mama, it's amazing." Beth Ann looked around, fighting tears. "I can't believe you guys did all this for me." She moved closer and gave her a giant hug. "I love you, Mama. Thank you, so much." She swallowed.

Her mom's eyes were misty when she answered. "You have no idea how long I've wanted this for you." She touched Beth Ann's cheek. "And baby, your hair looks incredible. It makes you look so grownup."

She hugged Beth Ann again, then released her and turned to Lisa. "You look gorgeous, Lisa." She gave them both a nod toward the punch table. "Now, why don't you young ladies grab a glass of punch and see what you think. It's a new recipe."

Just then, Denny waltzed in and stumbled over a chair, almost breaking her neck. As Stanley caught her and the present, they both laughed. He took her by the hand and led her to the gift table.

Beth Ann's mom held her heart. "I'm so glad she didn't fall and break her neck. Lord, have mercy." She winced and went over to make sure everything was okay.

Lisa cracked up. "Your mom and her sayings, what a trip."

Beth Ann nodded and noticed that her mom was still wearing her yellow Capris and one of Stanley's shirts, tied around her waist. Someday, Beth Ann hoped she could look so good.

They were practically tackled when Denny ran up to them. "Beth Ann, look at you and look at this place." She waved her hand around. "I love your dress and your hair." She hugged Beth Ann. "You look like a model!"

"Thank you." Beth Ann hugged Denny back and hoped they didn't fall to the ground.

"Lisa, you had your hair done, too. I'm jealous. You both look fantastic."

Lisa laughed and touched her bangs. "Thank you. Your hair looks great too. I bet you had yours done."

Denny nodded and fluffed her hair. "I'm busted, I got mine done, too."

"You look beautiful, Denny. Now, let's go taste that punch." Beth Ann laughed.

The drink was beyond yummy, the pineapple flavor melted across her tongue and burst in her mouth. Beth Ann crunched on the ice cube and realized her mom had put strawberries inside of them, which made it even tastier.

Once the music came on, Cole waved from the other side of the pool as he tested the sound and moved the amplifier away from the water. "Hey, this is for those who want to sing tonight," he announced into the microphone. "We thought that might be fun." He held it up and pointed it toward them.

"That is so neat," Denny said, while Lisa shook her head.

"You won't catch me singing on that," Lisa took a big gulp. "I sound like two cats fighting in a wet paper bag. But this punch is sure good, Lisa bit into the ice. Wow, strawberries."

Both Denny and Beth Ann were cracking up when the gate opened. Frankie and Susan walked in, carrying gifts, but stopped when they saw the back yard.

Frankie held up his thumb. "Far out," he called to the girls, while scanning Beth Ann from top to bottom "Whew! Wow! And double wow," he said, as he continued to stare at her.

Beth Ann felt the heat crawl across her face just as Cole cruised over and pulled Frankie to where the gifts were. Cole was not smiling, but Frankie had a grin as wide as the Grand Canyon.

In hardly any time, the back yard was filled with friends from school. Her parents had gone out for a while, leaving Cole and Carrie in charge. Funny she hadn't met his new girl yet and wondered why.

While music played and echoes of laughter flooded the back yard, Beth Ann felt something deep in her heart, a feeling she couldn't describe. However, there was one feeling she understood each time the gate opened, and that was her stomach doing a cannon ball as she waited for Kaylob. Maybe he wasn't going to show after all, and her spirit dropped.

She was talking to Frankie and putting on a good show when Cole came up and took her arm. "Come on, sing for us. This is my all-time favorite song that you do." He leaned close to her ear. "I've been bragging to Carrie about how good you are." His eyes pleaded.

She really didn't feel like singing. The disappointment she felt at Kaylob not being there was weighing heavy on her heart. Reluctantly, she took his hand and went to the other side of the pool to sing.

The song was *Johnny Angel*. Cole handed her the microphone. "Come on, Sis."

Her heart wasn't in it, but she loved to sing and just maybe it would cheer her up.

"Johnny Angel, how I love him, he's got something that I can't resist."

In sync, everyone stopped what they were doing and turned their attention on her. Frankie was hilarious with his mouth wide open. The one thing that singing had always done was make her feel uninhibited.

Just as she lifted her gaze toward the gate, Kaylob arrived. Within an instant, he stopped and focused on her. Without missing a beat, she met his eyes dead on and didn't look away.

His dazzling blue eyes and his slow smile enchanted her. She felt they were the only two people in the world.

As she sang the last line, "And together we can see how lovely heaven can be," a flash of her and Kaylob came out of nowhere. They were running on a beach holding hands, laughing, and then she saw him pull her close and kiss her deeply. They were maybe in their twenties and she was wearing a beautiful ring, which she couldn't see all the way.

What was that all about? She had to shake it off and, thankfully, the song ended because she almost lost her voice.

The entire place went crazy with cheers and whistles, so she took a bow. If the truth be known, she loved the attention. But today her focus was on one set of blue eyes.

Denny and Lisa ran up to her, interrupting her trance. "You were amazing," Lisa said, while Denny nodded and clapped.

"Thank you." Beth Ann felt shy all of a sudden.

"Sis, I'm so proud of you." Cole walked up, with Carrie in tow, and enveloped her.

Carrie was beautiful with warm brown eyes and gorgeous long blonde hair. "Beth Ann, you have a great voice." She had twin dimples, which reminded her of Blake.

"Thank you so much." Beth Ann grinned, trying to give them her full attention, instead of being distracted.

"I'm surprised you're not famous with a voice like that." Carrie smiled. "And by the way, it's nice to finally meet you." She nudged Cole and a guilty look splashed across his face.

"Thank you. It's nice to finally meet you, too." Beth Ann gave Cole the evil eye as he wrapped his arm around Carrie, who was much more tanned than her brother.

More school friends gathered around, filled with questions. Sharon was talking a mile a minute, telling her how great she sounded and how much she wanted to hear her sing again. Gayle asked her to sing, *Down in the Boondocks* and Kathy agreed.

When the next song came on, it was Bobby Helms' *You Are My Special Angel*. Some of her friends began dancing while others headed over to the snacks.

Lisa waved her hand in front of Beth Ann's face. "Are you in there?" She laughed and nodded to where Kaylob was standing. "Okay, go talk to him, while we throw ourselves in the pool and drink chlorinated water."

Beth Ann nodded. "Okay, have fun." Somewhere in the back of her mind, she was thinking, drink what? She turned to see her two closest friends hurry over, kick off their shoes, and dip their feet in the water. Thankfully, they weren't drinking any.

In the next instance, she saw Kaylob glance at the other couples dancing, and then he slowly turned and met her eyes, mesmerizing her. There was a shift in the air, as though the fog had rolled in, blocking out everything, except his blue eyes. The words to the song echoed through her, causing her heart to beat faster than the music.

He strolled over, not whispering a word. With a gentleness that made her heart swell. He stuck out his hand and she took hold. For a second, they stood staring into each other's eyes, which washed into her soul. He moved closer and wrapped his arms around her and they moved into the rhythm of the music. His touch melted her like an ice cube on a hot summer day. The minute she rested her head against his chest and listened to his heartbeat, there was no place in the entire world that she'd ever felt more at home.

That was the moment Beth Ann knew that she was in love with Kaylob Shawn O'Brien. She had no proof, no way to put it into words, but the truth was plain and simple. He was the guy she wanted to spend her life with, and knew that someday, she would marry him.

After a second slow song had come on, she lifted her face to study him. "So you're talking to me now?"

"Yes, I guess I am." A slow grin spread across his handsome face. "I'm hoping you're done kissing on Blake Tanner."

Beth Ann swallowed and tried to speak, but realized a frog had crawled in her throat and sat on her vocal cords.

Finally, she managed to say. "I'll … never kiss him again." She met his eyes. "You have my word."

He pulled her closer and sang the words to the song. "Unforgettable, in every way, and forever more, that's how you'll stay."

While they basked in the warmth of the sun and moved to the sound of the music, Beth Ann became aware of only one sound, and that was Kaylob's deep baritone voice with the rhythm of his heartbeat. The moment was timeless and she never wanted it to end.

"Hey, you two, the song ended," Lisa said, as she walked up to them.

Beth Ann knew she was blushing and tried to hide it, but being a redhead made that task impossible.

Kaylob released her. When she looked around, she realized that many of their friends were watching, including her brother, who wasn't smiling. Beth Ann quickly turned and pointed to the pool.

"Let's go swimming," she said, grabbing Lisa's hand and pulling her towards the back door. Some people wore their suits under their clothes, and others headed toward the house to change. Looking back towards the guy who rocked her world, she was fully aware of his eyes on her, which made a trillion butterflies take flight in her stomach with nowhere to go.

Just before she stepped inside the house, she noticed for the first time what Kaylob was wearing. She scanned him from top to bottom, and holy midnight, he looked delicious in his blue jeans and sky blue shirt.

He gave her a flirtatious grin and wink when he started unbuttoning his shirt. Beth Ann was sure one of those butterflies got caught in her windpipe, because she couldn't breathe.

Lisa yanked at her and saved the day by dislodging the butterfly. "Girl, you got it bad." She giggled. "Can we go now?"

When they started dashing through the house, Beth Ann saw her friends were lined up yakking, while waiting to get in the hall bathroom.

"Hey you guys..." Sharon and Kathy turned to look at her. "There's another bathroom outside the family room." She pointed.

"Groovy," Kathy said, then her and Sharon dashed away.

Once she stepped inside her bedroom, she moved over to the bed and covered her heart. Her legs felt like rubber bands so she inhaled deeply.

"Why does he get to me like that? Feel my heart, its racing." She took Lisa's hand and let her feel.

"Wow! It's racing fast." Lisa chuckled. "You're crazy about him. The first sign, a heart that won't behave."

Thinking about that, Beth Ann strolled over to her dresser, opened a drawer and pulled out her swimsuit. They were both changing when a knock made them jump.

"Who is it?" Beth Ann questioned.

"Me, Denny. I want to see what kind of swimsuit you guys are wearing."

Beth Ann opened the door and let Denny in.

"Wow! You guys look good. Lisa you're gonna be showing off all your private business to the world."

Lisa smacked Denny. "Shut up, I just wanted to show off for Terry."

"Well." Denny shook her head. "You're showing off alright, but remember there are a lot of guys out there."

Beth Ann looked down at her two-piece and realized she didn't come close to filling it out like Lisa and Denny. She felt skinny and like a little girl compared to the two of them. Even more so with that bikini Lisa was wearing. It was pretty tiny.

"I have no figure at all," Beth Ann said, looking at Lisa and then over to Denny.

"Yes, you do," Lisa scolded. "Look at your waist and that bubble butt."

She pointed while Denny nodded in agreement. "Kaylob's gonna want to touch that bootie."

Beth Ann looked down, rethought her bathing suit, and felt her face heat.

Denny and Lisa started laughing, then Denny walked over and hugged her. "You're so cute when you blush like that."

Beth Ann had always felt too skinny, but she wasn't going to eat a lot of food either. Maybe not because of money anymore, but it was the one area in her life that nobody could force her to do anything she didn't want.

"Let's just go swimming." Beth Ann grabbed her towel, wanting to hide under it.

A few minutes later, they were running outside. Cole and Kaylob were just walking back through the gate. Cole had his hand on Kaylob's shoulder and they didn't seem to even notice she was watching them. They exchanged a few more words, Kaylob nodded, and Cole went back over to Carrie.

What was that all about?

Lisa and Denny both jumped in the pool. However, Beth Ann stood watching Kaylob peel off his shirt and pants—she thought he'd already done that, but maybe the conversation with Cole had pulled him away.

She needed to stop thinking of his biceps so she could walk without slipping on her drool.

Well, so much for her hair, which she'd pulled it into a ponytail. All that work and now it was going to get wet, she sat on the edge of the pool and dangled her feet in the cool water.

"Hey, why aren't you swimming?" Kaylob sat down next to her.

"I was thinking about something." She studied his face. "What was going on between you and Cole?"

"Oh, he and I were just talking about baseball and surfing …" His eyes flickered with something. "He also asked me, if I liked his baby sister."

"Oh no. I'm sorry he asked you that." That was annoying. Cole needed to stop with the over protective act and thinking he owned her life.

"Why? It's no secret Beth Ann." He grinned. "The question is do you like me?" He elbowed her gently.

"No, I think you're gross." She used her foot to splash him and chuckled.

"Oh, really." He bounced up, scooped her into his arms, then jumped into the pool.

The feel of the cool water glided over her. The swimming pool was alive with movement, but in that moment wrapped in the cocoon of Kaylob's arms, the world faded and she almost forgot to breathe, but she managed to bring herself back.

He threw his head back in laughter as he held her in his arms. "Gross, huh."

"Put me down, you big brute." She kicked her legs, pretending to want down and noticed some kids laughing at them.

He had an ornery look on his face. "Take it back."

"No." She put her nose in the air and pretended to ignore him.

He held her with one hand and tickled her knee with the other. "Take it back, young lady."

"No, and you can't make me." She giggled and was impressed with his strength.

He held her and tickled her again. "Take it back and tell me how handsome I am."

She responded with laughter. "All right, fine. You're not gross and you're handsome." He released her and let her stand.

With that, she moved closer and touched his arm. His skin was wet and smooth, giving her a feeling deep in her stomach. "And yes, I do like you, too." She leaned her head on his shoulder as he wrapped his arms around her.

A few seconds later, he moved away like she had some sort of disease and dove under the water. Why the heck did he do that?

Chapter Sixteen

Lisa started splashing him as soon as he stood up. "What's with you?" She splashed him again, turned, and swam over to Beth Ann.

"C'mon. Let's go lay in the sun." Lisa pulled Beth Ann by the hand until they were out of the water. When she glanced back at Kaylob, he gave her half a grin and she could see something different in his eyes, like he was nervous.

The two best friends spread their towels on the newly cut grass while the rhythm of the music was all around. The sun warmed Beth Ann's body as the sounds of splashing and laughter filled the backyard. Frankie was yelling at Denny and telling her to catch the ball, while others joined in, trying to keep the ball from touching the water. Kaylob stayed to the side and continued doing laps.

"So …" Lisa almost whispered, "You and Kaylob are adorable together. Everyone can see he's crazy about you, and you already said you got it bad for him." She turned towards Beth Ann and propped herself on her elbow. "Next thing you know, he'll ask you to go steady."

"Ha. Not likely. One minute he's schmoozing up to me and the next he's running away." Beth Ann stared at him while he swam laps.

"Come on, you know why he moved away so fast, don't you?"

"No, and right now I just don't care." She sat up and wrung out her ponytail.

"Come on, Beth Ann. He got … a boner. That happens to a guy when they like you. They get hard, and he was afraid someone might notice. I mean he does have swim trunks on, so it would be a little tough to hide."

Beth Ann felt her cheeks turn a hundred shades of red. "He did not."

"Oh, yes, he did." Lisa laughed. "Take my word for it. I know how guys act when they get one in public."

Beth Ann opened her mouth to argue, but couldn't speak. When she spied Kaylob, he had stopped swimming and his head tilted, almost like he was trying to hear what they were talking about.

"You might want to close your mouth." Lisa chuckled. "He more than

113

likely knows what I just told you."

Beth Ann almost slammed herself backward on the grass, closing her eyes, wanting to pretend she didn't know. But the truth was she was glad she had that effect on him. She guessed maybe he did like her and at least now, she knew what that b word meant.

"Lisa …"

"Yes."

"I think I love him," she whispered.

Lisa reached over and squeezed Beth Ann's hand. "I think you guys have that thing they call love at first sight, along with amazing chemistry." Lisa sighed. "I've never seen him act toward any girl like he does with you."

"How many girls has he had?" Beth Ann asked.

"A few. But mostly older girls."

"Great," Beth Ann whispered.

"The important thing is he only has eyes for you." Lisa arched a brow.

With that said, Beth Ann nodded and tried to relax. The sun was out, but wasn't as warm as she wished. Still, she soaked it up while she listened to *Cupid*. One of the lyrics said, "Draw back your bow" and she knew right where it had landed.

Time seemed to stand still and voices faded, when all of a sudden a stupid bug tickled her nose. She swatted it away, but it came back. This time she took a swing and a strong warm hand caught her wrist.

When she saw it was him she scrunched up her nose. "You scared me."

Kaylob plopped down and started singing in his deep sexy voice. "Cupid, please hear my cry and let your arrow fly, straight to the redhead's heart for me."

"You have a nice voice, Kaylob." She looked around for Lisa, who had apparently left while she was dozing off.

Kaylob pointed. "Terry's here and they went out front to talk. He didn't look happy."

Beth Ann turned on her stomach and studied the handsome guy smiling at her. Holy marshmallows, he was so good looking. She couldn't take her eyes off his bare shoulders.

Kaylob leaned close to her ear. "You look beautiful yourself and thank you?" He wiggled his eyebrows.

She smacked his arm and rose up. "What are you talking about?" His mischievous grin told her what she already was beginning to know. Kaylob knew what she was thinking. "Want to get something to eat?" She reached out her hand, trying to change the subject.

He took it and pulled himself up. "Yes, ma'am. I sure would." He winked.

"Maybe we even have marshmallows." She laughed to herself and headed across the yard to the food area.

Everyone must have had the same idea, because many of her friends were lined up for the hamburgers and hot dogs. Cole and Carrie were cooking and handing them out. Not much time had passed when her Mom and Stanley walked back through the gate, carrying some large gifts and taking pictures again. Beth Ann almost felt embarrassed that she had so many things to open. She never had that many presents, which made her think about her dad and wonder when he was going to call.

Her mom turned, smiled, and blew her a kiss. Afterwards, she pointed towards the house, and both her parents vanished inside.

It was sweet that her mom and stepdad were giving her that space, but she had no doubt that her mom would be peeking out to see this day unfold.

As soon as their plates were filled, they headed over to join Denny and Frankie that were sitting with a bunch of friends.

"Great party!" Sharon said, her mouth full of food. Don, another boy from school, stole some chips off Sharon's plate when she turned to talk to Kathy and Gayle.

Beth Ann giggled when she and Kaylob sat down at the table, then she noticed that Lisa was nowhere to be seen.

"Where's Lisa and Terry, why aren't they back yet?" Beth Ann questioned, looking around.

Denny was chewing and pointed towards the gate. "They went out there to talk, a while ago. I'm pretty sure he was pissed about the bathing suit. I tried to warn her."

"Why?" Beth Ann wondered. "She looked great. You'd think he'd like how gorgeous his girlfriend is, and besides, she wore it for him."

Frankie almost choked on his hot dog. "Man the thing barely covers her." He swallowed. "If she was my girl, she wouldn't be wearing that *almost* bathing suit either."

Beth Ann shrugged. "I wish I had one like that."

Kaylob frowned. "No you don't." He said and took a bite of his chips, meeting her gaze.

"Yes, I do." She meant it.

He shook his head again. "No you don't." He wrinkled his forehead, so she dropped it.

Beth Ann ate a tiny bit of her hot dog and had a few nibbles of potato salad, which had a strong peppery taste, then gave the rest to Kaylob, who had no problems devouring anything left. She wasn't about to eat all those calories.

The gate opened while Kaylob was eating and Beth Ann would have choked on her food if she had any.

It was none other than Blake, holding a gift.

Kaylob spotted him and Beth Ann saw him glare. "You invited Blake?"

"No, I didn't." Beth Ann stood and made her way over to him.

"Hi there Beth Ann. I heard about the party and figured that not getting an invitation was an oversight. So I brought you your present." He handed it to her.

Beth Ann cleared her throat. "I didn't think you'd want to come with everyone being so much younger," she lied.

"I don't mind age differences." He stepped up and kissed her cheek. "Happy birthday, beautiful." She watched his eyes scanning her with something she couldn't read.

She took a step back and felt exposed even though she had a small towel wrapped around her waist.

"I need to put this with the other gifts." She turned and felt him following her as she walked over and placed it on the table.

She noticed Cole watching with a confused look, then he stood and headed towards them.

"So who is your friend?" Cole studied Blake.

Blake shot him a smart-ass remark. "And who are you, her bodyguard?"

Instantly, Beth Ann saw a scowl wash across her brother's face.

"You might call me that. I'm her older brother."

Blake's cheeks turned red. "Oh, nice to meet you." He extended his hand, which Cole ignored.

Beth Ann stepped up and fibbed to her brother. "I invited him … and he was running late."

Blake swallowed hard and once again apologized. Like a magician, Beth Ann made him disappear by pulling him over to the table, then turned towards him.

"Do you have a death wish? Sit down and join everyone. I'll grab you a hamburger or hot dog."

"Thank you. And, no I wasn't planning on death by drowning or beating today." He laughed.

"How about another way?" Kaylob said, with daggers in his eyes.

Feeling a bit irritated at the behavior of both guys, Beth Ann returned to where the food was and fixed Blake a burger. When she went back, he was sitting next to Denny and Frankie. She set down the food in front of him.

"Here you go. Hope you enjoy." She moved over next to Kaylob and noticed he seemed stiff.

Beth Ann sighed. "This is my first birthday party ever, and I'm having a really good time." She glanced at Blake and then to Kaylob. "My family worked all day on the decorations and food."

At that point, both guys seemed to understand and once again light chatter filled the area. Lisa and Terry walked through the gate and headed towards the food. Beth Ann almost laughed when she saw Terry's shirt covering her bikini.

Kaylob chuckled. "I'd be doing the same thing if my girl wore something like that." He arched a brow and met Beth Ann's eyes.

"This is the sixties, women can wear what they want." She shot her head up.

"I don't think so." He took his last bite of his hamburger and held her gaze.

"Guess as my Gram says, '*We'll cross that bridge when the ship sails.*'

"What?" Kaylob cracked up. "I've never heard that before."

"Now you have." She gave him a sidelong glance.

Once everyone finished, she noticed Blake stood. "Look, I have to get going, but I just wanted to stop by and bring you a gift and say happy birthday." He wiped his hands down his pants and almost looked nervous.

"Thank you Blake, that was nice of you." She stood and gave him a small hug.

"You're welcome and I'll see you around." He nodded at Denny and Frankie, but didn't even glance Kaylob's way.

Before he left, he stopped by the table where Cole and Carrie sat. He reached out his hand towards her brother and of course, Cole took it this time. She couldn't hear what was said since their table was further away, but could see that things seemed friendly. Just as Blake reached the gate, he turned around meeting her gaze and gave her a big smile, flashing his twin dimples.

Kaylob's eyes narrowed in that direction, and there was no doubt in her mind that Blake and Kaylob were mad at each other. It was her fault and she had nobody to blame but herself. She had to find a way to make them like each other again, because she wanted to be Blake's friend.

After everyone cleaned their plates and any stray cups, Beth Ann opened her presents and couldn't believe all the wonderful gifts she received, although there was a sting in her heart because there was nothing from her dad, not even a card.

It took a group of people to carry them all to her bedroom. They set everything on the seat under the bay window.

Every gift was special to her, but the one from Kaylob had touched her deeply. She studied the ceramic rainbow with butterflies that appeared to float around it. Then, just before she placed it on her nightstand, emotions flooded her heart. She read the precious letter Kaylob had written once more. The one musical phrase of his words made her spirit soar. "Someday I hope you will fly your way to me." With a deep sigh, she held the note against her heart, knowing she would keep it forever.

She glanced over at all the gifts—a pair of Go Go boots, stretch pants, a mohair sweater, and a beautiful opal necklace from Gram with earrings that matched. There was also a charm bracelet from her brother James. She was sad that he was away, but she was going to do her best not to think about those things today. After a few minutes, she lifted a gift box of perfume and other wonderful presents, such as a scarf, funny socks and some really neat nail polish. All these things made her feel loved and spoiled.

Now she needed to remember to send out thank you cards.

Denny stepped into her bedroom and summoned her. "Come on, girl, it's time to go back out to all the fun." Denny took her by the arm.

When she stepped through the back door, the final rays of sunshine had passed behind the mountains, leaving streaks of pink and amber. The evening breeze hinted of fall, and all the activity around, tugged at her heart. Now, she knew what magic was, because what she'd experienced was magical moments that would be sealed with every beat of her heart.

Beth Ann stood in place on the patio, just watching everyone. The little twinkling lights looked like little fireflies, which once again made her think of her daddy. Tears built up as she remembered how he'd always helped her catch them and put them in a glass jar. He would tell her they were almost fairies, and when their light burned out, it was them crossing over to get their wings. Beth Ann never knew if she believed him, but she loved the stories he always told her.

While she stood in the shadows, reminiscing of her days in Nashville with her family in one piece, she felt a tear slide down her cheek.

Before she could blink her eyes, Kaylob was standing next to her. He finished his last bite and placed his fork on the plate, then set it down.

Stepping in front of her he asked, "Are you okay?" Then took his thumb and wiped off her tear.

She nodded. "Of course. This has been the best day ever." She held his gaze.

He stepped over next to her and just their shoulders grazing made her shiver. He grinned and licked his lips. "I've never tasted apple cake like that with vanilla frosting. I might have to go for a fourth piece." He laughed. "But for now, how about you take a walk with me?" He laced his fingers through hers and threw away his empty plate.

Beth Ann felt her heart soar while they strolled through the gate. Once they stepped under the stars in the front yard, the song of the crickets filled the air while Kaylob and Beth Ann gazed up at the sky.

"There's your special star right there." Kaylob pointed. "See how it twinkles brighter than the millions up there?"

Beth Ann glanced up at the heavens and felt her heart swell. There was a star, brighter and twinkling faster than all of the others.

"Wow." She couldn't take her eyes off it. "It's amazing and so colorful." Just when she glanced over at him, he stepped in front of her again.

"You are a shining star, Beth Ann," he said under the dusky light. His words wrapped around her heart like a warm mitten on a winter's day. With a slow fluid motion, he placed a finger under her chin and lifted her gaze to meet his. "You are so special. I've never felt about anyone like I do you." He swallowed and closed his eyes.

With ease, he moved his face to hers and placed his lips so close that his breath whispered against her mouth.

"I want to kiss you, Beth Ann. Is it okay?"

All she could do was nod.

Then, in an unhurried moment, he introduced their lips for the first time, and changed her entire universe. While the fall breeze blew, at the age of twelve, her soul burst like a million falling stars. His kiss was so gentle, so sweet, it sang every love song and poem she'd ever heard. The sensation inside her heart had to be true love. The way he tasted of vanilla with a hint of apples, made her know that nothing had ever been so delicious in her entire life.

When he pulled her closer and deepened the kiss, touching her tongue lightly with his, she knew life would never be the same. The sound of the crickets, the far off barks from a dog, even the cars driving by, became a part of her soul memory that night.

This was a changing moment in Beth Ann's life and she knew it. Charlie had been right. She had met her prince charming.

Chapter Seventeen

Three days after her party she walked into the corner store. The place was slow and only a couple people walked around with carts full of food. Out of the corner of her eye, she spied Kaylob; he was stacking apples in the produce department.

Feeling a little impish and payback time, she tiptoed behind him "Are you having fun?" She giggled and watched two apples hit the floor.

"Sorry, I didn't mean to make you jump. I just wanted to surprise you." She leaned down to pick up one of the apples, while he retrieved the other.

"Hello, Beth Ann." He took the apple, avoiding eye contact and almost seemed nervous. "I have to go wash these off. I'll see you later." He turned and almost ran away, practically running into another fruit bin.

What was that all about? She picked up the sprayer he could have used and gave it a squirt. Yes, it worked. Was she making him nervous or was he avoiding her? Well, forget that, she'd just ignore him. No going back into the store again, at least that's what she thought.

However, one week later she went with her mom to pick up some groceries. The minute she saw him, he waved, and then 'Mr. kiss and run' vanished into thin air. Had he always been like that? Or, did he save this special treatment just for her?

The night he had kissed her, he told her she was a shining star. Maybe he just didn't like her, or maybe she just didn't kiss as good as the older girls he'd been with. Taking all those things into consideration, she made a choice; she was going to confront him.

"Beth Ann, honey, do you want some chocolate ice cream?" Her mom tilted her head, studying her.

"Sure. That sounds good, Mama." Beth Ann tried not to look around for Kaylob.

"Is everything okay with you?" her mom asked.

"Sure. Can I have rocky road, please?"

Her mom met her gaze. "Of course. We still need to get some meat on your bones. You know the doctor said you're still at least fifteen pounds underweight."

Oh, brother, now she was going to play the doctor card. Anything to get her to eat.

After they got home, for some reason she didn't entirely understand, she ate an entire bowl of Rocky Road ice cream and didn't even care about the calories.

On Monday morning, Denny showed up at her usual time. They were walking quietly to the bus stop and Beth Ann just wasn't in the mood to talk, and it was funny how Denny seemed to tune in on her mood. Once they got closer, she spotted Kaylob leaning against a pole. He was reading what looked like another cooking magazine. He didn't even look up, which made her angry. She stopped walking and thought about the way he'd been treating her. What the heck was wrong with him? She kicked a rock, sending it soaring through the air.

Denny glanced in the direction of the flying object, then stared at Beth Ann. "What did that rock ever do to you?"

"I don't know why he's being like this, avoiding me and acting like I don't exist. Maybe I didn't kiss good enough." Beth Ann felt her insides boiling. She glared at Kaylob, then turned back to Denny. "After all, he's used to being with high school girls."

"I don't think I like Kaylob anymore. Maybe you should start hanging out with Blake." Denny shook her head. She gave Beth Ann a knowing look. "Now, I know *he* wouldn't ignore you. As a matter of fact, he told me he'd like to get to know you better."

"I promised Kaylob I'd never kiss Blake again," she said softly.

"Forget that promise." Denny was adamant and picked up a rock. "Why should you keep your word if he's ignoring you? Maybe I should bonk him in the head with this." She drew back her hand aiming it in his direction. "It might knock some sense into his senseless brain."

"No, don't." She grabbed the rock from Denny and dropped it on the ground.

"Why should you even care about anything? Denny looked confused. She glared at Kaylob. "So what if you break your promise?"

"I like to keep my word." Beth Ann did a half shrug. "Besides, I really don't know about Blake. He's a lot older and he's got plenty of girls."

Denny laughed. "He's not that much older. When you're twenty, he'll be almost twenty-four, that's actually perfect. And look at those dimples."

"Why don't *you* go after him?" She gave her a long measuring look.

"Because he's my brother's best friend and he's my buddy." She nudged Beth Ann.

In any event, Beth Ann knew they needed to get to the bus stop, so they started walking again. Not even a minute later, Kaylob gave her a nod. What was his trip? Did he not notice she was shooting him the ring of fire look?

This guy had the nerve. She turned her nose as high into the air as she possibly could, without looking like an Irish setter.

Denny giggled under her breath. "That's the way to show him," she whispered.

While they stood waiting for the bus, Kaylob must have gathered the nerve to walk over and stand next to Beth Ann, because he leaned towards her ear. "I take it you're mad at me."

"Who, me?" She gave him a sidelong glance. "Why would I be mad at you?" That was a dose of his own medicine.

Chapter Eighteen

The bus pulled up and saved the day. She dashed her way up the steps. What she really wanted to know was where the heck was Frankie?

"Meanwhile, back at the ranch." Denny snickered as she sat in her seat. "You showed him."

Beth Ann plopped down next to her. "Well, he ain't seen nothing yet."

Kaylob slowed way down when he got closer. With a pause, he took one seat in front of them on the opposite side.

Beth Ann set her backpack down and stared out the window. "Where's Frankie?" She really wanted to know.

Denny shrugged. "I don't know."

When the bus pulled into the school Beth Ann couldn't help but worry about Frankie, he hadn't said anything about missing a day. With that thought, she decided if he didn't show up, she'd go to his house afterwards and check up on him.

The minute the bus came to a full stop, she stood and brushed by Kaylob.

"Bye, you little redheaded tantrum thrower," he said and chuckled. "Don't be beating up anymore rocks."

She turned and shot daggers at him.

"Come on slowpoke," Denny pulled at her.

That was it. She was officially pissed off, and the song that played in her head was Burning Ring of Fire, by Johnny Cash.

An hour later, she had almost pushed everything from her mind. By the time the bell rang for lunch with Halloween just around the corner, everyone kept talking about the big party at Harry's pool hall. It did sound like a lot of fun and it helped distract her.

When they arrived at the cafeteria, Lisa and Denny had already told her she was going. It would be another first for Beth Ann, dressing up like something, or someone, on Halloween. Maybe she should be a witch, so she could fly on her broom and dump a cauldron of fish guts on Kaylob's head.

"Beth Ann!" Lisa jumped, almost knocking Beth Ann off the bench. "You have to be little red riding hood." Her face lit up. "It would be perfect."

Beth Ann placed her hand across her heart, making sure it hadn't jumped out of her chest.

"You would look amazing," Lisa said in a normal voice.

Denny agreed. "That would be groovy. I'm going as Alice in Wonderland." She took a drink of chocolate milk.

"I'm going to be Dorothy from the *Wizard of Oz*," Lisa sang. "I'm off to see the wizard." Her eyes sparkled with laughter.

"Where would I find a costume like that?" Beth Ann had no clue. "I was thinking more along the lines of a witch."

"A witch!" Denny exclaimed. "No way."

Lisa agreed. "No, you can't be a witch. And don't you worry, my darling," she used her fake English accent. "I'm going to take you to the master tailor of costume making."

"Where is that?" Beth Ann inquired.

"To my house, of course. My mom and me will get you all decked out. My mom is so cool and she'd love to help you. My dad wants to meet you too, and he's so much fun." Softness swam in her eyes.

An ache of sadness welled inside Beth Ann. Her dad still hadn't called or sent anything for her birthday. It was starting to tear her heart to shreds.

Lisa touched her arm, pulling her back to the here and now. "Beth Ann, can you come over tomorrow and spend the night? We can get it done in a day, and that way you can get to know my dad."

"I'll ask my mom." Beth Ann reached over and waited for nonverbal permission before she took the last bite of Denny's sandwich. "I'm sure it will be okay, and I'll get some money to pay for the material."

"Did it taste good?" Denny grinned.

"Yes, thanks. I forgot my lunch."

Denny handed her an apple. "They do such a great job. They did it for me last year and I loved it and I love Lisa's parents. They are so neat and her mom's a great cook." She licked her lips.

Lisa placed her arm around Beth Ann's shoulder and gave her the rest of her chocolate milk. "We have so much left over material. My mom is a seamstress and owns her own business. I'm sure we'll have everything we need. What size are you anyway?"

"Almost a two," Beth Ann said, then glanced down. "I know, I'm too skinny."

Lisa shook her head. "Beth Ann, maybe if you remembered to bring your lunch, you wouldn't be. Here, eat half of my sandwich." Lisa gave her a bossy look and said, "However, you still look amazing, but I do worry about how little you eat. I do wish you'd remember to bring some food, I don't want you to faint or anything."

"I'll start remembering, but what are friends for?" Beth Ann laughed, then they all stood to leave, she sure didn't want to talk about food or her eating anymore. The sounds of chairs scraping across the floor sent a shiver down Beth Ann's back. A lot of the kids started running and getting scolded from the lunch duty teacher.

Denny took her hand on one side while Lisa clutched the other. That day, walking to class, Beth Ann realized she had never felt so loved by two friends. Who knew that having best friends was one of the most wonderful things in the whole wide world.

When the bell rang at three fifteen, declaring the end of a long week of studying and tests, she was more than ready to get out of school. She'd already informed Denny she'd be walking home because she was going to stop by Frankie's house.

She waved to Denny and a really pretty girl named Valerie, when they passed by her while on the bus.

There was a slight chill in the air, but nothing that a soft sweater wouldn't protect her from. Strolling by the houses, she noticed the golden and yellow leaves covering many lawns. One man was out raking his yard, and she couldn't help but giggle as she watched him growling at his neighbor's leaves that kept blowing into his yard.

Fall had always been a special season, her favorite in fact, she loved it. Many of the houses had been decorated with pumpkins and scarecrows, getting ready for Trick-Or-Treaters. Just the thought made her think about candied apples and pumpkin pie and her mouth watered. Ah, pumpkin pie, just thinking of the savory, nutty taste made her stomach growl. In the past, Halloween had been spent at rest stops or dirty old hotel rooms. But every now and again, her mom would bring them some treats like pumpkin pie and whip cream. Beth Ann had only been trick or treating once in her life.

All those years of traveling, the only time she'd ever had a stable life was at Gram's. It seemed over the holidays they had always been on the road. The few times they had been able to spend it with her grandmother, gave her memories she would always treasure. The summers there were forever unwavering, and she had been able to take dance lessons. Beth Ann had pretended during those times that she had a normal life.

Her grandma had paid for every one of those lessons and made sure she had at least one cute outfit to wear. Even now, with her new home and new friends, she missed her Gram something horrible.

Beth Ann turned the corner and froze, her breath lodged in her throat at the sight of the pale blue sky and trees with shades of red and vibrant orange, dancing like flames in the breeze. It was as if fall had turned into an artist and painted trees on both sides of the street.

The hair on her arms stood, as an electrifying feeling fanned through the air. Beth Ann shut her eyes and listened to the song that the waltzing trees played. She could imagine a ballet of leaves dancing as gracefully as Grace Kelly, whose manner and poise were beyond compare. Maybe someday, she'd be on stage and have a fraction of the ability to move so amazingly. Just the thought of Broadway gave her chills like she'd never had. She'd only seen musicals on TV and heard about Broadway in magazines, but one thing she knew for sure, she wanted to experience it.

That flooded her mind with memories of Charlie. He had told her that one of her missions on earth was to entertain, so today she would go home and talk to her mom.

After spending at least ten minutes admiring the fall beauty, she finally made her way towards Frankie's house. He lived near the railroad station, just across the tracks from Kaylob. It was impossible to keep from glimpsing over in that direction. Of course, Kaylob was nowhere to be found and if he did see her, he'd more than likely go in the other direction.

Just the memory of that sweet kiss swept through her with a sensation she didn't entirely understand. The taste the spicy apple and vanilla still lingered from his lips. She was unsure of anything regarding Kaylob and his feelings. With so much to figure out, which she would, because she was going to talk to him AFAP, as fast as possible. She would tie him up if she had to. He wasn't going to keep ignoring her.

Beth Ann arrived at Frankie's and wondered why she hadn't noticed this place before. It was a gigantic white house that appeared haunted and was in need of repairs. The paint was chipping and the yard was neglected, even the concrete steps leading up to the door were badly cracked. Beth Ann approached with caution.

She carefully knocked, but nobody came, so she rang the doorbell and waited. Just as she gave up and climbed down the steps, a green car pulled into the driveway. It was Frankie with a stunning woman. She was tall and lean with jet black, curly hair.

"Hey, Beth Ann." Frankie called out as he got out of the car. "Whatcha doing?"

"I came by to check on you." Beth Ann looked from Frankie to the pretty woman, who was unfolding herself from the car. As the lady climbed out of the vehicle there was no missing her amazing green eyes that looked just like Frankie's. She had to be his mom.

"I'm Rosa Russo," the lady said. "So you're Beth Ann. I've heard so much about you." She walked up and shook Beth Ann's hand. "It's nice to finally meet you. I hear you can sing like there's no tomorrow." She went around the back of the car, opened the trunk, and lifted some grocery bags. "Frankie says you're going to be famous someday."

Flames hit Beth Ann cheeks. "Thank you, Mrs. Russo. Can I help carry some groceries in?" she moved next to Frankie and wanted to change the subject.

Frankie stuffed back a laugh. "Sure, blush baby, I could use the help."

"Very funny." Beth Ann nudged him.

Mrs. Russo stopped short of the front door, and called out over her shoulder. "Frankie, be a gentleman and don't let her carry anything heavy."

"Sure thing, Ma," Frankie said, then handed her a light bag. "Want to hang out for a while?"

"Yes. That's why I'm here, and to find out why you weren't at school today. Are you sick or do you have a fever or something?"

Frankie winked as they walked inside his house.

"I played hooky with my mom today." Something in his eyes fell. "She's missing my dad, a lot. He's been gone for a few weeks now. He went back over to Vietnam and she's worried."

Beth Ann felt horrible. She'd heard about that awful war and was praying her brother didn't have to go. She stepped further into the house.

Even though she and Frankie had been hanging out, this was the first time she had been in his house.

Looking around the living room, she couldn't help but notice the old wooden floors, and once they entered the kitchen, it was yellow everywhere. Even the curtains were canary yellow.

Beth Ann saw Frankie's mom smile tenderly at him. Then she walked over and touched his arm. "Would you two like some oatmeal cookies I made yesterday with a glass of milk?"

"We would." He glanced over at Beth Ann. "Right?"

"Yes." She nodded. Great. More calories. She'd have to walk home really fast to burn them off.

With that said, Frankie pulled out the chair at the table, which sat by a big window in the kitchen.

"Sit down," he said.

His mom gathered the cookies and Frankie poured them both a glass of milk.

Frankie Russo was a good son, and Beth Ann could feel the love between them. Even though it was just a feeling, she had no doubt how close they were.

Chapter Nineteen

Kaylob stood at his window and watched Beth Ann and Frankie vanish inside the house. He hoped they were only friends, he thought as he placed his hand over his heart. Every single time he saw Beth Ann or was near her, his heart surfed on a tidal wave and he drowned in the sea of love. However, that kiss had rushed an ocean of emotions through him like never before.

He stepped outside on his front porch and heard the melody of the birds. Even the beauty of the trees and the music from the chipping sparrows, didn't stop him from wondering what they were doing. His hands clenched at his sides just imagining the two kissing. He had to push that image out of his head before he stomped over there, banged on the front door, and acted like a wild man from Borneo. Frankie was a good friend and he was pretty darn sure he knew how Kaylob felt about Beth Ann.

The truth was Beth Ann's brother had hinted big time to be careful with his baby sister. He also pointed out how young, she was—more than once. Wonder how he'd feel about that kiss on the front lawn?

Kaylob didn't want to make Cole angry, but he didn't want to lose Beth Ann either, so he was stuck between a tidal wave and a shark. Cole had said he could hang out with Beth Ann, but nothing too serious. However, he didn't say he couldn't kiss her.

He opened his gate, looked around at the cars driving by, and waved to Mrs. Jules, a school teacher at Hill Jr. High. Every time he saw her, he thought about her sad story. Losing a baby to crib death had to be hard and he felt awful about that.

Pulling his mind back to Beth Ann, he realized her brother was right; Beth Ann was way too young to do what he'd done with other girls. Now, if he could just knock some sense into his body and make it behave, he would be happy. He had to be extra careful, because he didn't trust himself around her and he didn't want a kiss to lead to anything more serious.

He had an idea, he'd think of surfing when she was around. He'd see himself on a fierce wave that was trying to knock him off balance. That would work, wouldn't it?

Speaking of stormy waters, Beth Ann was really ticked at him for avoiding her. And man, oh man, that little girl had a temper. He had to laugh at the memory of her nose sticking up in the air. She was so darn cute.

He stood staring at Frankie's house, thinking of a plan. He knew exactly what he had to do. He had to tell her he liked her for more than just a friend. Maybe she wouldn't care about the going steady part, even though most girls did. At least other guys would know she was really his girl. Other guys like Blake, who thought Kaylob wasn't good enough for her. Just because Blake had money and rich parents, didn't mean he was right for Beth Ann.

With that in mind, Kaylob walked over to the old train station and sat down on the front steps. After about thirty minutes, he laid his head back and thought about how someday his life would change and he'd show that Blake Tanner what a successful chef looked like. A few minutes passed and as he thought about his future, he drifted off.

Kaylob realized he had dozed off and had a feeling of being watched. With ease, he slightly peeked through his eyelashes. There she was, staring right at him. Hot digity dog, not just staring at him, but checking him out. After spending a few minutes watching her watch him, he slowly opened his eyes and wondered if he was dreaming.

"Hey, Beth Ann." He stood and ran his fingers through his hair. "When did you get here?"

Her cheeks turned the prettiest shade of pink he'd ever seen. "Just a second ago." She looked down and scuffed her foot.

He knew she was fibbing—she'd been watching him for a while. He stepped closer and touched her cheek. "Why are you blushing?"

"I'm not." She moved his hand and looked away.

He tossed back a laugh. "You're so cute, Beth Ann." He pointed to the steps. "Can we please talk?" He wanted to kiss her pouty lips something awful.

"About what?" She looked serious.

Kaylob stuck his hands in his pockets and stepped back. "I need to tell you something." He softened his voice. "Please sit on the steps with me."

With a shrug, she moved closer and sat down. "Okay, I'm sitting." She held his gaze.

Kaylob rubbed the nape of his neck and felt his legs tremble when he sat down next to her. He reached for her hand and surprisingly, she didn't move away. He got a hint of her strawberry scent, which threw him off track.

"I wanted to say … I'm sorry for avoiding you these last few weeks. I hope you won't stay mad at me for too long." He tried to read her thoughts, but failed.

The October breeze caught a few of her curly copper strands, making them dance around her face. For some reason he tucked the runaway hair behind her ear. Funny, he'd never had the urge to do that to other girls. Her pale cheeks slowly turned cherry, while her luscious red lips curved into a dainty smile.

God, she was the most amazing girl he'd ever met.

She looked down at their hands intertwined. "Why did you avoid me, Kaylob?" she questioned. "Did I ..." She paused. "You were my first kiss." Her lips quivered and moisture laced her eyes lashes.

That almost broke his heart and he couldn't let her think that. It was far from the truth.

"No way, I loved kissing you. I like you a lot Beth Ann ..." He raised her hand to his lips and pressed a kiss to her palm, then let go of it. "I like you so much that it scares me."

"You like me so much?" she questioned. "And it scares you?"

"Yes." He swallowed and gazed into her eyes.

"I like you too, Kaylob." She scooted closer.

The temptation to kiss her got the best of him, so he pulled her closer, feeling warmed by her presence. The sounds around him faded and all he could hear was his own heartbeat. Once he tasted her delicious lips, his resolve was gone. She had to be his girl, even if going steady was out of the question.

Once the tip of his tongue glided onto hers, he felt as though he died and was headed to paradise. Her lips were soft and moist and she tasted of nutmeg and cinnamon, blinding his thoughts. Like a giant wave rushing over him, he knew he better stop. He wanted her in a way he'd never wanted anyone or anything in his entire life.

Despite him knowing that, it was wrong, he didn't seem to have a brain left, so he deepened the kiss and pulled her closer. A dainty moan came from her throat and her breathing turned raspy. Jesus, he had to pull away and pull away now.

The surfing idea was not working.

"Ah, you've been eating cinnamon and nutmeg cookies," he whispered into her lips, trying to reverse what was happening. He had to do something to control those damn hormones because every nerve ending in his body was on alert.

"And how do you know the ingredients?" She looked curious, but dazed.

"I bake cookies all the time and I am a cookie—eating machine." He laughed and wished he could go back for more of her lips.

"You bake cookies?" She looked surprised.

"Yes. I love to cook and bake. Remember, I want to be a chef." He took her hand again, forcing himself to back away and stand, pulling her up with him. "Now, we better get you home, is it okay if I walk with you?"

"Yes, I'd like that." She gave him a bashful look.

On the way to her house, they passed by kids on bikes, people raking leaves, and ghosts with painted faces hanging from trees. When they reached Mrs. Oresetti's fence, he pulled out a pocketknife and cut her a brilliant red rose, removing the thorns.

Kaylob handed it to Beth Ann; her brown eyes grew warm, fanning his soul like a soft summer breeze.

"Thank you, Kaylob." She stood on her toes and kissed the side of his mouth. Her lips were so warm and soft and all she'd done was give him a kindhearted kiss, when everything started to spin. With that, he took her hand again and continued walking.

"Kaylob." She stopped and stared at him.

"Yes?" he answered.

"We're going in the wrong direction." She giggled. "Are you trying to take me back to your house?"

After he got his bearings, they finally made it to her front door. Once there, he gave her a gentle kiss on her forehead and looked around for her brother, hoping he didn't have to face him again.

"See you later, Beth Ann," he said and tried to steady himself because he didn't want to fall down. He was in a pickle and sure as heck didn't want to run into Cole, so he turned to leave.

"Kaylob," she whispered and met his gaze. "Thank you for telling me your feelings." She gave him the most radiant smile he'd ever seen.

"You're welcome." He left her standing on the porch and trailed away, knowing he was a goner.

That fall day, with pumpkins smiling and Halloween goblins creeping around every corner… Kaylob Shawn O'Brien admitted to himself that he was completely head over heels in love. Someday, Elizabeth Ann Rose would be his steady girl, until she became his wife.

But until that day, the big question was, *am I good enough for her?*

* * * *

Beth Ann entered the house and looked around everywhere to no avail. Finally, in the last place she looked she found her mom sitting out back with her usual glass of sweet tea.

"Hi Mama. I was wondering if you have a minute to talk?"

Her mom gave her a long look. "I always have a minute to talk to my girl." She pointed to the chair across from her.

Beth Ann sat down and fidgeted with her hands. "I want to take singing and dancing lessons and I know they're expensive. If I can't, I'll just wait until Jr. High, because they have classes." She looked out at the pool and noticed an orange leaf floating down into the water. "But, I thought I'd ask."

"Oh honey, I was just waiting for you," she said. "I found a really good school in San Rafael and they'll be ready when you are." Jean reached out and touched Beth Ann's cheek. "I didn't want to push. After all, you just made all these new friends and I wasn't sure if you wanted to give up time with them."

"I understand and I do enjoy my friends." Beth Ann paused. "I hope to still have time to be with them, and well … I'll make time. This is my dream, Mama, and Charlie said one of my missions on earth was to entertain people." Beth Ann sighed. "I miss Charlie. I wish he had a phone."

Her mom nodded. "Me too." She reached over and held Beth Ann's hand. "Would you like to start tomorrow?"

"Yes, anytime." Her voice went up a notch.

"I'll call them first thing in the morning to make sure they can get us in," her mom said.

Beth Ann stood, giving her mom a giant hug and almost knocked her backwards. "Thank you so much, Mama." She steadied her mom. "Sorry, I guess I'm excited."

Jean chuckled and hugged her back. "You're most welcome."

The emotion Beth Ann felt was out of this world, so she twirled around like a ballerina. Then attempted to do a petite jeté, but knew she failed miserably. Afterwards, she bowed and watched her mom's eyes sparkle with laughter.

Beth Ann excused herself, and ran into her bedroom. Everything was better than she ever dreamed. When she planted herself down on the bed, she couldn't help but think about the way Kaylob had treated her when he walked her home. She glanced over at the rose on her table and knew she had to put it in water. The memory filled her with joy. She stood, found a dainty vase and filled it. Afterwards, she placed the special rose on her nightstand and took a deep breath. Her fingers touched the delicate petals that were supple and velvety. She knew in that moment that Kaylob was not just in her heart, but would forever live in her soul.

A few minutes later, tears stung her eyes and emotions clogged her throat when she spied her Shirley Temple doll. Thinking about her dad made her spirits fall, and the previous excitement about Kaylob dwindled.

How could he just forget about his kids? She would have been okay with just a phone call or a card. The time had come for her to speak to her mom and get to the bottom of what was going on.

When Beth Ann stepped out the back door, she spotted her mom relaxing in the lounge chair. She looked so content and wore a soft smile. For that reason, Beth Ann couldn't find it in her heart to disturb her, so she tiptoed back inside the house, even though she really wanted to find out about her dad.

The next morning Beth Ann was awakened by the sound of knocking on her door.

"Come in." She felt sleepy and knew it was Saturday, wondering why she was being woke up.

"Rise and shine," her mom called out. She opened the door. "We have a meeting with the studio in San Rafael."

Beth Ann tossed back the blankets and almost fell off the bed. "So they can take me today?"

"They're ready for you." Jean laughed. "Here is everything we bought for you, and what we were told you needed. I spoke to them in September and got details."

Beth Ann took the box and was completely surprised. "Thank you, Mama. You must have known I was going to do this, didn't you?"

"You're welcome." She nodded. "I had a pretty good idea you'd want this sooner or later."

Beth Ann opened the box and inside was leotards and body suits. They were all different colors with dance shoes and long leggings. She loved them. Today she would choose the pink ones.

"Mama, I love these. Thank you so much." She held them up to her heart.

"You're welcome, sweetie." Her mom grinned. "Now get yourself dressed, so you can eat breakfast and we can leave. They want us there by ten."

At the appointed time, they took off and were headed to San Rafael. Beth Ann's stomach had knots the entire time so she hardly spoke and noticed nothing. Once they pulled up to the building, she was surprised because it appeared like an old church, now painted in pink, with an awning announcing the name, The Belleview Studio.

"Mama, this looks like it used to be a church," Beth Ann said. "It's really neat."

"That's because it was at one time." Her mom turned off the car and opened the door. "Let's get you inside."

Beth Ann touched her stomach. "I'm so nervous." She glanced at her mom, then opened the door and climbed out.

Her mom walked beside her and put her arm around her. "You're going to be just fine, sweetie. Just wait until they see how talented you are." Her mom's eyes got misty.

Beth Ann knew her mom was trying not to get emotional, so she leaned into her, and for the first time she noticed her mom's dress.

"Mama, we match." She gazed up at her mom.

"I hope that's okay. I don't normally wear this color. But something told me you'd wear pink."

"It's more than okay. You look groovy in pink and it's funny you knew what color I'd wear." She giggled.

"Well, thank you, sweetie." Her mom grinned. "I guess groovy means cool."

When they entered the place, it was larger than it appeared on the outside. A lady was playing a piano while a tiny girl belted out many of the wrong notes. The pianist would stop playing and start again. Both she and the little girl looked frustrated. Beth Ann wished she could help her learn to sing.

In another corner, dancers were watching a lady who wore her jet-black hair in a French braid. She was tall and moved fluidly like Grace Kelly. Beth Ann admired her style.

On a stage at the other end of the gigantic room, a play was being rehearsed, and people were acting out scenes. Beth Ann stood marveling at everything going on.

"What do you think?" her mom asked.

"I think it's amazing to have this all in one giant room." She pointed. "Look at all the stained glass with the flowers etched inside. I love that."

"Gorgeous," her mom agreed.

After a few minutes, a mature lady with salt and pepper hair approached them.

"Hi, this must be Beth Ann or should I say Elizabeth Ann Rose, which is a fabulous stage name," she said with a grin. "Follow me, my name is Linda, and I'm the owner and director."

The lady took a few steps to the right, opened a door, and waved for them to enter. As they stepped into a long hallway, Beth Ann could hear the sounds of music and tap dancing. They eased down the hallway, towards a set of double doors. Beth Ann paused to peek in each room and was even more surprised at the size. The place was marvelous and each room was about the size of a classroom.

Once they arrived at the end of the hall, Linda stopped and opened a double door. Again, she waved for them to enter. They stepped inside and right off Beth Ann noticed a piano, couch, and a large desk with chairs all around.

The lady touched her mom's arm. "Thank you for coming today, Jean. I'm excited to see what Beth Ann has to offer. Have a seat." She pointed to the chairs and sat behind the desk.

They both took a seat, then Beth Ann saw her mom pull out a check from her pocket.

"This should take care of the first three months." She handed the check to Linda.

"Before I take this." Linda laid down the check. "We have to hear Beth Ann sing because of her age. Normally, at her age we don't take people who can't sing on key." She pushed a button and asked someone named Jimmy to come in.

Beth Ann felt her throat slide down to her stomach. What if she missed some notes?

A few seconds later, a guy walked in. He appeared to be in his twenties, handsome and carried music sheets.

He nodded and sat down behind the piano. Then he propped up the first sheet.

"Beth Ann." He summoned her over with a nod and a wink.

She stood and made her way to the piano, then he handed her the lyrics. She inhaled deeply and felt almost light headed.

"So you know this song?" Jimmy asked. "We were told you love Judy Garland."

She nodded. "Yes, I love, Zing Went the Strings Of My Heart. I use to sing it to my dad." She cleared her throat and tried to hide her emotions.

He played the first key and she joined in and started singing. When she got to the part, "'Twas like a breath of spring," she moved to the beat and poured her heart into it.

When she was done, Jimmy stood and clapped. "I'm impressed." He strolled over and shook her hand.

Linda stood along with Beth Ann's mom. "My goodness, we don't get that often. Someone who can do a perfect falsetto." She had a large grin. "You are way more advanced than I expected," she said when Beth Ann approached them. "Well, Jean, I guess I'll take this check now. We most definitely want your daughter." Linda picked up the check from the desk.

Beth Ann's mom turned and hugged her. "I'm so proud of you, honey." She wiped a tear. "I'll leave and pick you up later ... at what time?" she turned to Linda.

"How about we keep her for the day, we have lunch at noon and a table of snacks we leave out."

Beth Ann felt her hands start to sweat and her heart doing the Charleston. What if she disappointed everyone? What if she couldn't keep up with the pace, and she didn't know how to professionally dance.

"Maybe I should come back another day after I get warmed up."

Linda shook her head. "That's what we're here for. To get you started." She touched Beth Ann's arm. "You'll be fine."

That day Beth Ann began her routine of rehearsing and it was harder than she imagined. There would not be a lot of free time. Regardless, she loved every minute of it. After all, this had been her lifelong dream, and she was learning to act, and dance like a professional.

Sometime later, Beth Ann sat in the small cafeteria. It had a sink, green refrigerator and oven to match. The small sitting area was furnished with couches and comfortable chairs. While she relaxed eating her crisp salad, that had the most delicious creamy cucumber type dressing on top, a little seed of worry sprouted. Would Kaylob find a new girl to hang out with if she was gone so much? Would she lose him? She looked up at the clock hanging on the wall, it read two p.m. What was he doing right now? Was he thinking about her, like she was him?

Before she could give it another thought, she saw Linda approaching. "Hey, Beth Ann." She sat down, placing her bowl of fruit and sandwich on the table. "What do you think so far?"

"I think it's fun, but hard work." Beth Ann was honest. "But, I'm looking forward to learning more."

"Once you get to know more kids your own age, you'll have more fun, too." She studied Beth Ann's salad. "Maybe you should consider eating something with more calories since you've been working so hard." She passed the sandwich to Beth Ann and she couldn't help but wonder if her mom had mentioned she needed to eat more.

Oh well, Beth Ann's stomach was pretty empty, so she took it. "Thank you," she said to Linda, who nodded.

After the day ended, Beth Ann sat on the steps outside, waiting for her mom. She was thinking about how much she had learned in one day. A wave of sadness washed over her, when she thought about her daddy. He wouldn't get to see all the things she was learning. Maybe this would be a good time to confront her mom and ask why he hadn't called. Had he really forgotten all about her?

Just as she was indulging in a feel sorry for herself party, her mom pulled up and the look on her face was pure sunshine. How could she ask her mom something about her dad? The answer was simple; she couldn't, not today. That would be selfish and immature. She swallowed down the emotions and pasted a big smile on her face.

Chapter Twenty

Weeks later, Beth Ann stood in front of the mirror in her bedroom, looking at her Little Red Riding Hood outfit. Lisa and her mom had done a great job. The red hooded cape was amazing and the cute little mini dress underneath matched perfectly. She'd never worn such a short dress and wasn't sure if she liked her legs enough to show them off.

The party was going to start in thirty minutes and her stomach was crawling up her spine, the doorbell chimed. It had to be Lisa and Denny. She picked up her basket and dashed out of her room.

When she arrived at the front door, she swung it open; there they stood in their adorable attire. Lisa was Dorothy from Wizard of Oz and Denny was Alice in Wonderland. Beth Ann looked between the two of them and laughed.

"You guys look amazing." She stepped back and waved for them to come in.

Denny touched Beth Ann's cape. "Look at you, little Miss Red Riding Hood. That's so groovy and whoa, sexy." She pointed. "By the way, I've missed you lately." She gave Beth Ann a gentle squeeze. "I feel like you're always gone."

"Me too." Lisa nodded and held up her pretend dog. "Hope this doesn't make Stanley sneeze." She laughed softly under her breath. "I'm fairly sure he's allergy free." She kissed his nose. "But honestly, Beth Ann, you are gone all the time." She pouted.

"I know." She set her basket down. "Lately it's been a lot of rehearsing." She pulled her friends into a group hug. "Hey, we have tonight and I have a break for the next five days. So let's have some fun."

They all stood together, then Denny petted Toto. "Good boy, Toto," Denny whispered.

Lisa grabbed Beth Ann's arm. "Okay, little red, let's get out of here." She opened Beth Ann's cape and whistled. "You look foxy."

Beth Ann gave her a dismissive wave. "Let's go have some fun." She stepped over to the coffee table and picked back up her basket.

In The next instant, her mom came into the living room. "Well, bless your hearts, I've stepped into storybook land. You girls look wonderful." Her mom's southern accent was thick. "Let me get my camera."

A few minutes later she had them posing and took at least fifteen different shots.

"We have to get going, Mama." Beth Ann hated getting her picture taken.

"Alright, let me get my pocketbook and I'll drive you girls to the pool hall."

Beth Ann shook her head. "We can walk, it's not far."

"No, it's a bit chilly. I'm going to drive you ladies and when it's over you call me and we'll pick you up."

"Alright." Beth Ann tried not to sound disappointed. Once in the car, she wanted to see all the sights. "Mama, go slow so we can see everything." She rolled down the window and heard laughter from kids running in all different directions. Denny and Lisa both laughed at one little boy who was walking like a monster and growling.

It was fun to watch the groups that trailed down the street with funny costumes on.

As they passed the houses, she gazed at the multitude of decorations. Many of the windows had orange colored lights, blinking like a twinkling star. Some had ghosts lighting up their trees and witches on brooms. One yard had made it's lawn look as though it was a graveyard covered with cobwebs. This was something that Beth Ann had never experienced.

When they pulled up at Harry's pool hall, the place was dark with flashing lights.

"Now, y'all have fun and make sure you eat something besides candy."

They all nodded and said in unison, "Okay, Mama." She heard her mom giggle just before they got out of the car.

All three of them ran up to the front door and stepped inside.

"Holy night." Beth Ann glanced around.

"Isn't it groovy," Lisa shouted.

"Yes," Beth Ann agreed. "Holy scarecrow, there are glowing things everywhere."

Denny cracked up and pointed. "Look at Jack. He looks like a vampire."

Lisa nodded and they giggled.

"Mr. Harry Thomson is a groovy dude and does a lot of really scary things on Halloween, music, games, and tons of treats," Lisa informed.

"Wait until you taste the candied apples." Denny licked her lips.

Beth Ann couldn't believe how the place looked. There were blinking ghosts hanging from the ceiling, and pumpkins everywhere. The smell was heavenly, like caramel and popcorn with a hint of maple. She could already taste the sweetness on her tongue. The place was scary and dark. She could see the glowing cobwebs with giant spiders that appeared to be moving down the wall.

"It's getting spookier by the minute," Beth Ann said.

"Boo!" Lisa made her jump. "I got you," she laughed. "There's my boyfriend. He dressed up like a motorcycle guy."

Denny shrugged. "He *is* a motorcycle guy."

Beth Ann couldn't help but giggle as Lisa made her way over to Terry.

The place was packed. Kids from school were playing pool, pinball, and dancing to the *Monster Mash*, while trying to scare each other.

Just as they moved over to the food table, Beth Ann felt someone tap her shoulder.

"Hey there, Little Red Riding Hood."

Beth Ann wasn't sure who it was at first, but when he smiled, there was no hiding those dimples. It was Blake, dressed in a leather jacket and pants to match, with greased-back black hair.

Beth Ann grinned. "And who are you supposed to be?"

Blake waved his hand down his body. "James Dean, of course. Rebel without a cause." He winked.

Denny touched his jacket. "Nice, Blake. Where's my brother?" She lifted a brow.

"Where do you think?" He pointed towards a tall girl who was wearing a kitty outfit. "He's got it bad for Mandy."

Denny nodded, then someone in a ghost outfit almost ran right into her. "Oh, brother." She had to find her balance then giggled. "It's a mad house tonight."

Blake stepped closer to Beth Ann. "Want some punch?"

"Of course she does, and don't forget about me, but be careful. This place is wild," Denny answered as she looked around.

Blake bowed. "I live to please and I can handle wild," he said, just before he walked away, dodging some younger kids.

Denny glanced at Blake and back to Beth Ann. "He likes you a lot."

"He's nice, but I'm wondering where Kaylob is. He said he'd be here." Beth Ann swept the room. "I hope he shows up."

Denny frowned. "Maybe he's still avoiding you."

"No, we talked about that the other day." She saw Blake coming back, juggling three bloody looking drinks, so she walked up to him and took hers.

"Thank you, so much." Beth Ann grinned and took a sip. "This is yummy." It was thick, but tasted of cranberries and ginger with some type of zingy spice. "Thank you again." She swallowed, hoping it didn't turn her tongue red.

"You're most welcome, Red." He passed Denny her punch.

Blake nodded towards the chairs and lead Beth Ann by the elbow so they could sit down. When Beth Ann took a seat she expected Denny to take the chair next to her, but instead she stood laughing and pointing at all the different costumes. Blake settled right next to her, draping his arm over the back of her chair, which left her feeling nervous.

Denny chuckled, drawing Beth Ann's attention. "Look at what Kathy is wearing! I have to go talk to her." She set her punch down on a chair and ran towards her friend who was dressed like a hippie with purple hair.

Beth Ann felt her stomach turn. Now she was alone in the darkness with Blake. The music was loud and all she wanted to know was where the heck Kaylob was. He should be here.

Blake leaned towards her ear. "So little Red Riding Hood, what are your plans for tonight?"

"I was actually waiting for Kaylob." She glanced around again.

"Well, it looks like he's a no show, so why not hang out with me?" He touched her hair.

Beth Ann shook her head. "Thank you, Blake, but Kaylob told me he'd be here." She glanced down at her wristwatch and realized he was at least thirty minutes late. "He must have got caught up at his job."

"Or with Dusty." Blake stood and held out his hand. "Well, until he gets here, let's dance."

Beth Ann hesitated. "He's not with Dusty." She scanned the room wishing Kaylob would hurry up. He better not be with her, that's for sure.

"Oh, come on. I'm not going to bite you." He laughed.

Beth Ann nodded, but felt her stomach tighten. "Okay. But I have to keep an eye out for Kaylob." They finished their drinks and stood.

Blake led her out on the dance floor, where at least eight other people had started dancing. Gayle and Sharon were doing the monster mash and cracking themselves up. Gayle was adorable in her bumblebee attire and Sharon was dressed as a the good witch from, The Wizard of Oz.

Beth Ann did love to dance and since Kaylob wasn't there, it was no big deal? Right?

As if on cue the song, *Love Potion #9* started grooving through the pool hall. Once they started moving to the music, it was like they had been dancing together forever. They both knew how to do the monkey and his moves were right on.

Blake pulled her closer. "You dance great, little Red Riding Hood." He moved to the rhythm of the music.

"Thank you." Beth Ann was starting to enjoy herself and loosen up.

As the Love Potion song ended, another one started up. It was a slow song and one she knew well. *Can't help falling in love*, by Elvis Presley.

"Thank you, Blake." Beth Ann touched his arm and turned to leave.

"Will you slow dance with me?" He turned her around and embraced her. "Come on, please?" His eyes looked just like a puppy who needed to be scratched behind his ears.

"Okay, I guess." She studied the room again, but still no Kaylob.

Blake pulled her closer and leaned into her ear. "I like you, Beth Ann."

She didn't know what to say. All she knew in that moment was she wanted to be in Kaylob's arms and wondered why he hadn't shown up like he said. So she said nothing and just moved with Blake to the music.

Chapter Twenty One

Kaylob opened the door to the pool hall and let his eyes adjust to all the flashing lights. There were people all over the place and he was over thirty minutes late, all because he had to run to the store for his mom. He started to take a step further inside, when he saw Beth Ann to the right of the dance floor. He narrowed his eyes and pulled off his stupid eye mask. It became clear who she was dancing with, which made his insides boil. Why the hell would Beth Ann let him hold her like that and why was he whispering in her ear? That was it, he spun around and started to leave the same way he came in, but not before he threw his mask in the garbage can. Screw that, he hadn't really dressed up anyway.

Once he stepped outside, he bent over, put his hands on his knees and took a deep steady breath. "Suck it up, bucko." He started walking down the street with his hands clenched at his sides. At one point, he thought about punching a wall, but decided he didn't want a broken knuckle, not because of a wall. Tanner's face on the other hand, would be worth it.

Many of the stores were closed, including Novato Theater; they did that every year on Halloween. As he stormed down the street, he couldn't take his mind off what he'd just seen.

Did she like Tanner? Maybe she wanted to be his girl? Damn it all, he couldn't ask her to go steady, and now he might lose her.

Once he got to the stop light at the end of Grant Ave, he paused and waited for it to turn green. His attention was drawn by the sound of a car honking.

Shit, he just didn't feel like talking to anyone right now.

"Hey Kaylob, need a ride?" The girl pulled to the side. "It's me, Patti. Do you remember?"

Kaylob studied her. She was pretty with dark skin and long brown hair. "Yes, I remember you." He tried to sound nicer than he felt. "I met you at Dusty's house."

"How about me?" The redhead called out.

"I do," he said. "But, I'm sorry I forgot your name."

142

"I'm Tami." She grinned.

"Aren't you going to the party at the pool hall?" Patti asked.

"I was just taking a walk first." He turned and looked down the street, still feeling pissed off.

Tami opened the door. "Come on, get in, we'll give you a ride."

Kaylob had to think about it because he wasn't sure if he'd cooled off enough to go back. His heart was still racing and his neck felt hot.

"Come on, Kaylob," Tami said again. "It's always so much fun there and you look like you could use some."

"Alright." He climbed in the back seat and tried to get a grip. But the only thing he wanted to grip was Tanner's neck.

Tami turned around and looked at him. "Something bothering you, Kaylob?" She had a questioning look. "You're usually always smiling."

"You might say that. I wanted to punch someone," he mumbled, "so I took a walk instead."

"Uh oh. Sounds like girl problems to me," said Patti.

"More like Blake Tanner problems." Kaylob informed, then looked out the window.

Tami laughed. "Better watch that hound dog. Don't let him near your girl."

Kaylob knew what he had to do. He was going to march in there, and if she was still dancing with Blake, he'd just ask her to dance with him instead. There was no way in hell he was going to run away like last time.

Once they pulled up, he climbed out of the car, then paused and inhaled deeply. "I feel better now." He opened the door to the pool hall.

It took a minute for his eyes to adjust again to all the flashing lights, but the minute he did he saw her staring right at him. Ouch, her eyes just shot him in the heart.

Tami leaned close to his ear. "So you want to dance and make your girlfriend jealous?"

"Thanks, but no. By the look on her face, I would say she's already there and I want to live." He thanked them both and headed toward Beth Ann. Her eyes narrowed and her face matched her red cape.

Once he approached, she turned her back and started talking with Kathy.

"Beth Ann." He tapped her shoulder. "Can we go talk?"

"No, go away Kaylob! Just leave me alone and go back to your girls." She started to leave, but flipped around. "At least now I know why you were late." She stormed off.

Kathy looked at him with wide eyes.

"All I did was get a ride," he said to Kathy.

He hurried to catch her. Why was she mad at him? She was the one dancing with Blake.

Once he caught up, he turned her around and held her at arm's length. "Oh, no you don't. We're having a conversation." He scooped her up in his arms. "We're going to work this out."

Blake stepped up. "Hey, put her down." He glared at Kaylob.

"Go to hell, Blake," Kaylob shot back. He could feel his heart pounding louder than the music.

Beth Ann shook her head. "It's okay, Blake. I'm fine." Her voice quivered while Kaylob held her.

Blake just stood there. "Are you sure?"

All Kaylob wanted to do was knock his block off.

"Yes. Please, I need to go talk to Kaylob," Beth Ann said.

Kaylob scowled at Blake then headed for the door, which Frankie jogged over and opened with a grin. Once Kaylob was outside, he sat her down where she immediately put her hands on her hips.

"Just what do you think you're doing?" she demanded. "You can't just pick me up and carry me around."

"I think I can. I just did. Besides, instead of me telling you what I'm doing, tell me why you were letting Blake hold you and slow dance with you," he demanded.

"I didn't know you were here. Why didn't you come and say something?"

"Come and say something? Do you want to tell me why you're mad at me, when you were the one letting Blake hold you and whisper sweet nothings into your ear?" He gave her a long hard glance. "Is this the way it's going to be? When I'm not around you're going to let other guys touch you and hold you?"

"It was just dancing." She moved closer. "I was waiting for you."

"You call that waiting? When I walked in and saw you two together, I was too angry to do anything but leave."

"I didn't want to hurt his feelings." She looked down. "Who were those girls?"

"Friends that gave me a ride after I took a long walk to cool off." He sighed as he lifted her chin. "Beth Ann if you're going to play games with me. I'll walk away right now."

Just then, a few kids came out, throwing food at each other, when they got too close Kaylob snapped, "Do you guys mind? We're trying to talk here."

The two boys moved down the street, but not before one of them shot over his shoulder, "You don't own the street."

Kaylob ignored their remarks and turned back to Beth Ann, waiting for her answer.

"No. I didn't mean to play any games. Blake was being nice to me and you were late." She touched his hand. "I thought it would be okay to dance."

He remained quiet.

"How do you like my Halloween outfit? Did I tell you that Lisa and her mom made it for me?" She fidgeted from one foot to another. "It's a little cold out tonight, but today when it was a pretty day, it was warm. I think we should get something to eat, don't you? I tasted the ..."

"Beth Ann, you're making me dizzy. Which topic do you want me to respond to?" He tried not to laugh. "Do you always do that when you're nervous?"

"Do what?" She looked perplexed.

"I think one might call that rambling." He chuckled.

"I wasn't doing that." She moved closer and laid her head on his chest. That did him in and he melted like a chocolate bar on a hot summer day.

Kaylob inhaled her sweet scent of vanilla cream and strawberries, making him dissolve into a puddle of emotions.

"Please, don't ever slow dance with him again." He kissed the top of her head. "Fast dancing I can handle, but seeing him hold you ..." His stomach clenched. "I wanted to deck him." He backed her up and held her at arm's length, but decided he should tease her for a minute. "Just maybe I should spank you."

"Oh, you wouldn't dare," Beth Ann said and folded her arms across her chest. But she must have sensed he was going to chase her or grab her, because she took off running.

Once he caught her, he took her down to the grass beside Rayburn's. There he tickled her knees.

"Tell me I'm the boss and you'll never disobey me." He laughed.

"I'm the boss and you'll always do what I say." Beth Ann squirmed.

He tickled her more. "Say it, Beth Ann. Say Kaylob Shawn O'Brien is the boss."

"No. I'm the boss." She giggled.

After a few more seconds of tickling, she yelled out, "Okay. Okay. Kaylob Shawn O'Brien is the boss." She smacked his arm.

He stopped and lay down next to her, propping his head in his hand. He reached out his finger and ran it down her neck, then close to her breast. A shiver ran through her. "Kaylob." She leaned closer to his face and gave him a soft kiss.

That innocent kiss took his breath away. He had to stop and stop now, before his hormones went insane.

"Please don't ever let him hold you like that again." He pulled her up from the grass, then he stood and took her hand. "By the way, that dress is kinda short, don't you think?"

"No, I don't think that. However, I won't ever let him hold me again, and Kaylob ..." She held his gaze. "Please don't be with other girls."

"I don't want anybody else." He leaned in and brushed another small kiss across her lips, then held her hand, leading her back to the front of the pool hall. Once they arrived, a noise from the door opening, made them both turn. It was Blake.

"Beth Ann, why don't you go inside and hang out with Denny and Lisa." He glanced over at Blake. "I'll be right there."

Blake gave him what appeared to be a sly grin and winked at Beth Ann.

She chewed on her bottom lip and looked down to the ground. "I can stay out here with you." She touched his arm.

"No. I need to talk to Blake alone. Please go inside."

"Okay," she agreed.

She looked over at Blake and gave him what appeared to be a tiny smile. Then she strolled towards the front door, but before she went inside, she looked back at the two of them. Kaylob watched her eyes droop and it made him feel bad, but not bad enough to walk away.

Chapter Twenty Two

After she vanished inside, Kaylob whipped around, meeting Blake dead on. "I want you to stay away from Beth Ann."

"Screw you." He stepped closer to Kaylob's face. "You haven't even asked her to go steady so she's not yours." Blake's ears turned red. "I like her and I'm not staying away from her."

"Fine, be friends, but don't let me ever see you holding her again." He glared into Blake's eyes.

"Why not, she loved it." He wiggled his eyebrows. "Let's face it, pal, I have a lot more to offer her than you do. Look where you live."

Kaylob was fighting hard not to deck his ass, but his temper got the best of him. He grabbed Blake's shirt. "You asshole. You get off on putting others down, don't you?"

"Hey, pool time." Frankie walked up and stepped in between Blake and Kaylob, using his hands to spread them apart. "Come on guys." Kaylob went back for Blake's shirt, but Frankie caught his hands. "It's Halloween and time for some fun and you have a girl waiting for you, Kaylob."

Kaylob gave Blake one long, daring look and all Blake did was smirk at him. Before he could do anything stupid, Frankie pulled his arm and almost dragged him back inside.

In truth, all he wanted to do was to stay outside and beat the ever-loving crap out of the asshole, but he had to pretend to keep his cool. He knew one thing for sure, Blake better watch his step, or he'd knock him out. That meant staying the hell away from his girl, even if Blake did have more to offer her in the way of material things.

* * * *

Beth Ann loved being in Kaylob's arms, but more than once she caught Blake staring at her. He had nodded a few times and she noticed Kaylob watching. The way they glared at each other made her stomach flip upside down.

147

Although, now maybe Kaylob would ask her to be his girl and give her something to prove they were going steady. That was something she was looking forward to. That way guys like Blake, would know she wasn't available and girls like Dusty would know he was her boyfriend.

There was one thing she learned that Halloween night, kissing Kaylob was better than chocolate ice cream, or her mom's apple cake, and even Gram's homemade green beans. He was kissing her every chance he got and she loved it.

Once they both noticed the time, they stepped outside and stood under the shimmering moon. Beth Ann could feel the cool fall breeze tickle her nose.

Other kids were running and trying to scare each other. She and Kaylob laughed when someone hit Kathy with a water balloon, which ended up being her sister. Holy water fight, they were drenching each other and laughing about it.

Kaylob moved her off to the side of the street and stood by the pole, then leaned in for another kiss.

"Kaylob …" She pulled away, breathless, and felt her stomach hurting again. Was she coming down with the flu or something? He was such a good kisser and she loved how his tongue glided over hers.

"Yes," Kaylob whispered into her lips.

"How many girls have you kissed like this?" She touched her stomach, wondering if she was allergic to him.

"Beth Ann, I've never spent this much time kissing anyone. I can promise you, I never liked it as much." He pulled her closer and inhaled deeply.

Laughter echoed all around, distracting them from each other. Frankie was laughing and Denny was smacking his arm. In the next instance, Denny was chasing him down the road. It appeared he had her slip on his head and was giving her a bad time.

That Frankie Russo was a prankster.

Kaylob looked at her and laughed. "I guess he's in danger, maybe we should go rescue him."

"No, we need to rescue Denny's slip," Beth Ann said.

They both watched as Denny pretended to beat on him until he finally handed it back to her.

They were pulled away from the entertainment, when a horn honked. "I have to go Kaylob, my mom is here. Talk to you soon."

He nodded and winked. "You sure will."

She waved goodbye to Frankie then noticed Lisa point to Terry as she climbed on the back of his bike.

When Denny and Beth Ann slid into the car, her mom asked, "Did you ladies have fun tonight?"

Denny nodded while Beth Ann touched her lips. "Yes, Mama, I had a great night, but I think I have a flu bug."

"A flu bug?" Her mom questioned then reached over and felt her head. "You don't have a fever. Did you remember to eat?"

Denny leaned up to the front seat and examined Beth Ann. "You look good, but you could've eaten a bit more tonight."

"I ate plenty tonight. It's not that. Every time I get close to Kaylob, my stomach hurts. I think I'm allergic to him or something. This is just awful, because I think he's going to ask me to go steady."

"Well, I don't think it's a bug of the viral kind, my sweet daughter." Her mom chuckled.

Denny giggled and whispered in Beth Ann's ear. "The only bug you have is the love bug."

"The love bug?" Beth Ann repeated. "How long does that last?"

Both Denny and her mom slowly started laughing. Beth Ann sat there, wondering what the heck was so funny. Any kind of bug couldn't be good.

After they dropped Denny off and she got home, she climbed into bed and touched her heart. Yes, her heart was filled with emotions, and maybe having the love bug was not such a bad thing after all. She reached out and turned off the light, then laid her head down, trying to drift off to sleep, but her dad jumped into her head and worry came crawling inside her thoughts.

Maybe her dad was sick and that's why nobody had brought up anything about him. Not even Gram mentioned him on the phone and lately their phone calls had been quick. Could Gram be hiding something from her? That really made her stomach flip just from thinking that.

* * * *

That morning when she woke up, she decided that it was time to ask about her dad. When she made it into the kitchen, she noticed her mom sweeping off the back patio. It was now or never, so with a long, deep breath, she opened the back door and stepped outside in her robe.

Her mom stopped and grinned. "Good morning, sunshine. I thought you'd never get up." She started sweeping again. "Good thing Halloween was on a Friday this year." She tried to move a chair.

Beth Ann walked over and pushed it out of the way. "Mom."

"Yes, sweetie." She paused, looking up at Beth Ann.

"Why hasn't daddy contacted me or anything?" Tears welled up. "Doesn't he want to be my daddy anymore?" Her voice cracked.

"Oh baby, he loves you with all his heart." She moved closer and placed

149

her hand on Beth Ann's arm. "He's just trying to find his way right now." Her mom's eyes looked sad. "He's lost his family, at least in the terms he once had us. I'm sure he'll call you soon."

"He didn't even remember my birthday." Beth Ann lowered herself to the lounge chair.

"He remembered, I know he did." She sat down next to Beth Ann. "He just didn't know how to deal with being away from you." She reached out and patted Beth Ann's hand. "Honey, your daddy loves you."

Beth Ann nodded, but still deep inside she didn't get it. If he was so sad about his family, why stay away from his kids? After a few moments of silence Beth Ann stood. "I'm going to finish my homework, so I have the rest of the weekend free."

Her mom held her hand over her eyes to shade them from the sun. "Baby, are you okay now?"

Beth Ann pasted a smile on her face. "Sure, Mama, I'm fine." She turned and left.

Beth Ann was anything but okay. She was hurt and felt her mom was just trying to protect her from her dad being irresponsible. Of course, he had never been the most attentive father, but at least he'd always made sure to be around on her birthday, until now.

Maybe she should call her Gram and see what she had to say.

Chapter Twenty Three

A few weeks went by and Beth Ann decided against talking to her grandmother on the phone. A face to face chat would be better. It wasn't that much longer until Thanksgiving, so she could wait.

Anyway, why the heck was she awake so early when she could have been sleeping in? As much as Beth Ann loved singing and acting, it was nice to have a full week off from rehearsing. She thought about the A she made on the English test and felt proud. All that studying had paid off.

She could hear the muffled sounds of a few neighborhood dogs and cars starting their engines. Ah, the sounds of home, those things were the very things she had grown to love.

While she lay in bed, she glanced around at all her decorations and no matter how much she tried to push her dad out of her heart, she couldn't. This would be her first Thanksgiving without him. Well, sort of her first. In truth, she couldn't remember the last time they sat down and had a real dinner.

There were times her dad got gigs and they had hotels with a kitchen. Her mom had done the best she could to make a special dinner. One time she remembered her mom lighting candles and buying a pretty tablecloth. Beth Ann had gone outside, gathered some colorful leaves, and found a glass to make a nice centerpiece. Her brothers had found a piece of driftwood and done a carving that said, Happy Thanksgiving. Her mom had gotten weepy when they all chipped in and decorated the table.

They didn't even have five matching plates, so her mom had to use a paper one. A memory floated back of the way her mom had seemed to enjoy the day. Her dad had shown up for dinner and stayed for a short time, but as usual, he had left that evening to go play music. Beth Ann was beginning to understand more and more why her mama had to leave.

Beth Ann wouldn't want a husband who was never home. Was she being like that about her life and her desire to be a Broadway star? Would she put that before her family?

Well, number one, Beth Ann would never have children, and number two, she would make time for her husband, even more so if that husband were Kaylob. And threely, well, never mind. She felt her stomach growl and knew she needed food.

Speaking of Kaylob, he was taking her to Novato Theater this evening. It was the first time she would go to the movies with him and she wondered if they would hold hands. This was like a real date, at least in her mind it was, so she needed to find something nice to wear.

There was a tap on her door.

"Come in," she said as she slipped on her robe.

The door opened and there he stood. "Hey, sis." It was James and he looked so handsome in his Navy uniform.

"James, you're home!" She flew into his arms. Excitement with instant tears bestowed her.

He gave her a hug back. "I'm only home for Thanksgiving. I have to go back."

"Aren't you coming home for Christmas?" Beth Ann wanted the whole family together.

"No, I can't have both holidays." He released her and looked around. "How do you like your bedroom?"

She spun around. "I love it. I just wish you were here."

James nodded. "I'm here, silly." He touched the tip of her nose. "I'll let you get dressed and meet you in the kitchen. Mom's making pancakes."

Beth Ann watched him shut the door. The whole family was going to be together for Thanksgiving. She felt her heart skip. Well, not really the whole family, because her dad was away. But Gram was coming and both her brothers were home. She flung open her closet, slipped on her pink top, and pants that matched. Today was most definitely a happy pink day and she was not going to let her daddy take it away.

The morning was filled with laughter and blueberry pancakes. Stanley seemed to get along with James after all. Beth Ann had built up things in her mind that they didn't like each other. However, the more she observed the two of them, the more she knew they were good friends.

After breakfast, the guys were talking about sports and Beth Ann sat out back, listening to the chatter while letting the sun warm her face.

Her mom was humming while she did the dishes. Seems these days she was always happy and humming, which pleased Beth Ann.

"Mama." Beth Ann called out through the open back door.

"Yes."

"Are you sure you don't want me to help with the dishes?"

"I'm positive. What time do you go to the movies tonight?" her mom asked.

Beth Ann wondered if it would be rude to leave home with James visiting. So she got up from the lounge chair and headed inside to where her mom stood doing the dishes.

"I'm wondering if I should cancel tonight, since James is home."

"I think he's got a date so don't change your plans." She winked, then turned back and started cleaning a big bowl.

Beth Ann walked next to her mom and picked up the kitchen towel. "I guess I sort of have a date, too."

Her mom nodded. "Just don't tell Cole." Their eyes met and instantly they started to laugh.

Cole was just so darn protective and would have gone with her to the movies if he thought it was a date. Beth Ann ended up helping her mom clean the kitchen and together they harmonized to the old tune of Doris Days, 'Que Sera, Sera' 'Whatever will be will be.'

After spending the day with the family, it was time for her to get ready. Kaylob had called and said he'd be there at five thirty and she decided to wear her cute yellow dress with the spaghetti straps that had a tiny sweater to match. She had the perfect shoes to go with it and even a yellow headband.

That evening when the doorbell rang, she heard her mom open it.

"Hello, Kaylob," her mom said in her southern drawl. "Why don't you come on in and have a seat, I'll go get Beth Ann. Would you like a pop or something to drink?"

"No, thank you. I'm good."

Beth Ann headed down the hall and turned the corner to the formal living room. "Hi, Kaylob." She felt herself flush.

Her mom nodded and left, heading towards the family room.

Kaylob stood. "You look great." His eyes skimmed over her, and then his hands went inside his pants pockets.

"Thanks. So do you." She loved his blue jeans and light blue shirt. She couldn't help but notice how it enhanced the color of his eyes and made his hair look even blonder.

After a few seconds of silence, Beth Ann yelled to her mom. "We're leaving Mama, we're walking." She realized how young she sounded calling her mom that.

Her mom walked into the living room. "Do you want a ride?" She looked between Kaylob and Beth Ann.

Kaylob nodded. "Sure, if it's not any trouble."

Beth Ann was okay with getting a ride, so they could hang out before the movie started.

"You can call me when the movie's over and I'll pick you up if you want," her mama offered.

Beth Ann shrugged. "Okay, but sometimes we like to walk."

Her mom nodded in agreement and grabbed her keys.

They arrived at the theater ten minutes later and stepped out of the car. The night was brisk and a slight breeze chilled her. Beth Ann didn't mind because Kaylob wrapped his arm around her until they stepped inside. The movie was one they had both wanted to see, From Russia with Love, starring Sean Connery, who was almost as dreamy as Kaylob and had a voice that was deep and sexy. Beth Ann was glancing up at his name in lights, when out of the blue she saw her name only it read, Elizabeth Ann Rose. She shook her head and brought herself back to reality. What the heck? She was seeing things.

During the movie, Kaylob put his arm around Beth Ann and somehow even though she loved James Bond, she drifted to sleep. When she woke up Kaylob was watching her with a look that did something special to her heart.

"Hey, sleeping beauty." He moved the hair away from her face and leaned towards her ear. "I thought you were going to miss the entire movie, but I'm glad you woke up during the break, at least you can catch the second half." The sound of his deep voice tickled her ear, but in a good way.

As much as Beth Ann hated to leave the warmth of Kaylob's arms, she sat up and looked around. Wow, she hadn't even noticed that Lisa and Terry had come in and were sitting right next to her.

Lisa held up her popcorn. "Want some now that you're awake?"

"Sure. Thanks." Beth Ann took a small handful and almost melted from the taste of the buttery flavor that dissolved in her mouth. As she crunched on each piece, a little sting would bite her lips from all the salt. Before she knew it, she'd eaten almost half of the popcorn and figured she must be really hungry. It left a little oil on her fingers from the butter, so she used her dress to wipe it off the best she could, then offered some to Kaylob. However, he chuckled and showed her the empty box. He had eaten the entire thing while she dozed.

Fifteen minutes later the movie started up again and Beth Ann liked it a lot. What she enjoyed even more, was how Kaylob kept whispering in her ear, filling her in on what had happened before intermission.

Once the movie ended, they all walked out into the lobby where Kaylob held her hand the entire time. Beth Ann turned to him. "Can we please just walk home or do you think it's too cold?"

"I'm okay, but all you have is that little sweater and I didn't bring a jacket."

"I'm okay if you are."

They both waved goodbye to Terry and Lisa as they climbed on his bike.

He nodded. "I'm good."

Just as they turned to leave, a noise behind them made them both look.

"Hey, beautiful." Blake raised his eyebrows and shot a nasty look to Kaylob.

"Hi, Blake," she said then turned and looked away.

There was no way to miss the look between the two guys. Blake approached and Kaylob's eyes narrowed.

Kaylob dropped her hand. "What do you want, Blake?"

"I just wanted to ask Beth Ann a question in private." He sneered. "I mean you don't own her, isn't that right?"

Beth Ann shook her head. "Sorry Blake, but we were just leaving." She took Kaylob's hand.

"I could give you a ride since Kaylob lives right down the street and he doesn't own a car. Wouldn't want this beautiful girl to freeze just because you don't drive yet. Right, Kaylob?"

Beth Ann spoke up before a fight broke out. "Blake, I want to walk, but thank you," she said with a shaky voice.

Beth Ann latched on to Kaylob's hand and pulled him away. It wasn't easy because it felt like his feet were stuck to the ground, but he finally gave in and followed.

They took about five steps before Blake yelled out, "You're not going steady yet." He glared at Kaylob. "Beth Ann, don't let him control you and remember you deserve the best."

Kaylob let go of her hand. "You better back off, Tanner."

"Or what?" He laughed. "You're such a loser."

Kaylob marched towards him. "Yeah, you think so, huh?"

Before Beth Ann could try to come between them, the owner of the theater came out. "Do we have a problem here, boys? Do I need to call the police?"

Beth Ann let out the air that was clogged in her throat.

"We're just having a few words, sir. I'm leaving anyway." Blake took off around the corner, but not before he stopped and said, "O'Brien this is for you." He held up a middle finger.

Kaylob laughed and said out loud. "Such intelligence."

He took her hand again and while they walked, he was quiet. Beth Ann wondered what the heck Blake had meant by that.

Once they got near the old train station Beth Ann pointed to the steps. "Can we sit for a minute?"

Kaylob nodded, walked to the steps and sat down, then she leaned on his shoulder and said, "Are you mad at me?" She looked up and studied his face.

"No," he said in a soft voice. "I was quiet because, I don't like getting angry." He turned towards her and tucked a fly-away strand of hair behind her ear.

Just that simple action caused her heart to swell. So she moved closer and placed her lips on his.

They deepened the kiss and he pulled her up. "Beth Ann, we can't make out in public." He looked around. Then started pulling her towards the train.

A few minutes later he reached up and yanked the doors open to the one and only stock car. He climbed inside and reached down for her. "Come on. We can kiss without an audience."

Without blinking an eye, she reached for him and he lifted her. Once inside she saw bales of hay all over the place. She had read a book once about trains because she loved the sound of the air horns.

"I hope we don't step in anything." She glanced around.

"We won't." He pulled her close. "This hay was put here last year on Halloween for a haunted house." He scooped her up in his arms and dropped backwards on the hay. She screamed and they both laughed.

Beth Ann turned over and propped her head on her hand. "Why didn't I see this car before?"

"Because they took it somewhere. Sometimes they bring them back and park them here." He wrapped his arms around her and buried his nose in her neck. "Beth Ann you always smell so sweet. Like strawberries and vanilla."

"Because I use strawberry shampoo," she said and giggled.

The look in his eyes made her heart beat faster.

"Kaylob," she whispered.

He leaned in and gave her a deep kiss. She never wanted it to end, but far too soon, he pulled away and stood.

"No, please just a little longer."

"Come on, Beth Ann. I need to keep my promise." He nodded towards the door. "Your mom will be expecting us and I want to get you home on time. I don't want to lose future chances to go out with you.

"Okay." She pouted, which did no good. "But, what promise?"

"Just to myself." He pulled her towards the door. "Just forgot it. I was talking to myself."

"Can I at least ask you one more question before we leave?"

"Yes," he said.

"What did that mean," She flew her finger in the air. "What Blake did?"

Kaylob's eyes opened wide. "You don't know what that means?" He grabbed her hand. "For real?"

"No." She shook her head. "Should I?"

"Okay. It's a way to say something bad to someone. It's called flipping the bird. Don't ever do it again," he said, then wrapped his arm around her. "Let's get you home."

"I like birds," she said and meant it.

He chuckled, then leaned down and kissed her cheek. "You're adorable."

Beth Ann couldn't describe the feeling that night as she and Kaylob strolled hand in hand to her house under the moonlit sky. His hand was warm and gentle, yet had strength that made her feel protected. It was like they had done it a million times. Once they arrived at her house the look he gave her melted her soul, and even more so when he gave her a gentle kiss good night.

The next morning Beth Ann awoke and wanted to savor the memory of last night, but she kept thinking about what he said about a promise. Maybe she'd be able to figure it out later.

It was her first date and small kissing session, at least one where they were completely alone. She inhaled deeply, placing her hand across her heart and thought of the way they had kissed. Then she leaned over, picked up the movie tickets off her nightstand. She would keep those for always, as a token of their first real date.

The next day was so much fun. They spent time hanging around the house and just being together as a family. She tried very hard to push her daddy out of her mind, but it wasn't easy with all of them together. James was especially happy and just by the grin stuck on his face, she figured the date must have gone really well, because he looked like the canary who'd eaten the worm.

Chapter Twenty-Four

Days later, she awoke and realized it was getting closer to Gram coming and staying through Christmas. Beth Ann could hardly wait. Her daddy was still traveling and her mom said he was supposed to call her Thanksgiving Day. She'd have to hear his voice to believe it.

There was noise coming from somewhere in the house, and whatever it was, must be good. She threw back the covers and slipped on her robe. Once she entered the kitchen, she could see that her mom was laughing and crying at the same time.

"What's going on?" Beth Ann asked.

Her Mom nodded towards James. "Tell her."

"I got engaged last night." He picked Beth Ann up and swung her around.

"Engaged to whom?" Beth Ann giggled after James set her down.

"Marsha. From down the street. We've been seeing each other for a while now."

"You have?" Beth Ann glanced between the two of them. "Mama, you're happy about this?"

She nodded, with tears pooling in her eyes. "I love Marsha. We went out to lunch the other day, and she's so special. I know she loves your brother."

Beth Ann was stunned; she had been out of the loop about this.

"When's the date?"

James grinned. "Soon as possible." He sat back down. "She wants to come with me when I get stationed, so we will do a fast little ceremony and have a reception."

"When?" Beth Ann asked again.

"This week before I leave."

"Holy matrimony," Beth Ann exclaimed. "I'll have a sister."

They both laughed, so there was only one thing for Beth Ann to do, she giggled with them.

A few days later Gram arrived just in time for the wedding. It took place in San Rafael at the Justice of the Peace, and afterwards they had gone out and had a great time at Camelia Dining Room. James seemed really happy and so did his new wife. Beth Ann was thrilled for them.

Thanksgiving had been wonderful. All except her dad, who still had not called. It made her cry when James left a day early to get Marsha settled into their new apartment. He had tried to cheer her up, but she knew deep inside that wasn't the only reason she was crying. The main reason was *because* of her dad. Every time the phone rang, she thought it would be him, but it wasn't. Even when Kaylob called, she was gloomy. He had asked her twice if she was okay and she fibbed and said she was just fine.

The next morning the sun was peeking through curtains once again. It made Beth Ann open her eyes. Today she was going to have a long talk with Gram and nothing would stop her. She had waited long enough.

She started to turn on her side and caught sight of the statue that now sat on her bedside table. The one Kaylob had bought her. Why hadn't he asked her to go steady, maybe she should have a heart to heart with him as well? They hung out all the time, but he had avoided being alone with her since the movie date. The only moments they had without the world being around was at Sawyers pond, but with winter approaching, it was too chilly to be down there much.

Did he really like her? He always said he liked her *a lot*, but never told her that he loved her. There was no doubt in Beth Ann's mind how deeply she felt. He had told her once on the tracks, that someday she'd be his wife. So shouldn't they go steady first?

She stared at the phone and made her decision. Without missing a beat, she dialed his number and waited for him to answer.

"Hello."

"Hi, it's me." She swallowed.

"Hello me." He chuckled. "You're up early."

She paused. "I called ... because; I wanted to talk to you." Her stomach fluttered.

"On the phone?" he asked quietly.

"Yes. Is there something wrong with the phone?"

"No. But let me go into my room."

She could hear him shuffling, then a few seconds later a door shut.

"My mom was sitting right by me, so I had to move. I'm ready now." She heard him take a breath.

"Kaylob, why haven't you asked me to go steady?"

All she got back was silence.

"Kaylob?"

"Beth Ann you're only twelve," he informed her. "You need to get older before you worry about that."

"I know how old I am," she snapped. "Blake said he'd ask me to be his girl. He doesn't seem to care that he's almost four years older."

"Beth Ann. Is that what you want?"

"No, of course not, but everyone keeps asking me, *are you* going *steady yet*. I'm tired of saying no."

"I'm sorry, baby. But I promise I'm crazy about you."

Hearing him call her baby made her heart flutter. Okay, so maybe she'd have to wait until she was thirteen. And she could, because she wanted to be his girlfriend.

"Okay, I understand." She tried to sound normal, but her heart was sagging.

"Hey, you know what?" He sounded so happy she wanted to throw the phone.

"What?" She sighed.

"I bought you something special for Christmas and you will never guess what it is."

"Really? Can you give me a hint?" She really wanted to know.

"No way, baby girl. You have to wait." He laughed.

"Now, you're just being mean to me," she said with a giggle.

Beth Ann never did have that talk with Gram. Instead, she daydreamed the morning away, thinking about turning thirteen and wondering what Kaylob had bought her for Christmas. That afternoon her friends came by to meet Gram. Everyone loved her and enjoyed her old sayings. Later that afternoon, all the girls went shopping and it ended up being a fun filled day. Plus her mom helped her pick out Kaylob's Christmas present.

* * * *

The Christmas season was dashing by and more new memories were being made. The amazing flocked tree stood tall in the formal living room. It was the most gorgeous tree they'd ever had. Her mom had decorated it all in red. Now, it was easy to believe in Santa Claus all over again.

Beth Ann knocked lightly on Gram's door.

"Come on in, Beth Ann," Gram called out.

Beth Ann opened the door and glanced around. Every morning she went into the guest bedroom to see Gram. Her mom had decorated it so nice; there were fresh flowers and a new lavender bedspread. On the dresser were pictures of the family during the holidays. It was rare when they got to spend it with Gram, but when they did it had always been fun. One of the Christmas pictures displayed Gram's big wrap around porch, decorated with southern flare. It had always made her feel at home.

Gram was sitting in front of the Antique vanity dresser, finishing her hair.

"Hi, Gram. How did you know it was me?"

She turned to meet Beth Ann's eyes. "I know your knock, sweetness."

Beth Ann walked over, bent down and kissed her cheek. Gram was so pretty with her snow white hair and a rosy complexion. They were close to the same size, but Gram had these beautiful blue eyes that always had a special shine whenever Beth Ann came into a room, something Beth Ann wished she had.

"I didn't know I had a unique knock." Beth Ann tilted her head.

"It's a delicate knock." She stood. "How about we go make some breakfast together. I'm worried about you sweetness, have you been eating enough?"

Beth Ann tried to paste on a happy face. "Yes, I'm eating just fine."

Gram arched a brow. "I'm glad to hear that, and I can see how much you love the idea of cooking."

"Well, if I learned to cook, I might put on weight." She wished everyone would leave her alone about food. "Then I'd eat too much and everyone would start telling me to cut back because I'd be too heavy."

"You eat too much and get heavy? I guess pigs will fly, too," Gram said and stared at her.

They walked into the kitchen and Gram started pulling out pots and pans, then headed over to the refrigerator and took out some food. Since Gram had been there for a while, she already knew her way around.

Beth Ann wanted to help with something, so she went into the refrigerator and pulled out the barbecue sauce.

"Here you go, Gram. Anything else you need?"

Gram looked at the bottle and arched a brow. "Beth Ann, what do you propose I use this for?"

"The eggs," Beth Ann said. "I love barbecue chicken."

Gram looked at her and started to chuckle. "We need to get you in some cooking classes." She shook her head.

"What are you cooking then?" Beth Ann really wanted to know.

"I'm going to make chocolate chip pancakes and scrambled eggs, without barbecue sauce." She chuckled again.

Beth Ann plopped down at the kitchen table and decided now would be a good time, since Gram was in a pretty good mood.

"Gram." Beth Ann swallowed.

"Yes." She went on, getting things set up for breakfast.

Beth Ann felt her stomach flip and fidgeted.

"What is it?" Her gram stopped what she was doing and met her gaze.

"Daddy hasn't called me in months and he didn't even wish me a happy birthday." She tried not to let any tears escape.

"I know, honey." Gram's eyes turned gentle. "When I spoke to him last, he heard all about it. You know he's on the darn road again."

"Did he say why?" Beth Ann felt her lip tremble.

Gram strolled over and lifted Beth Ann's chin. "No. But I know he loves you more than you know." She pulled up another chair and sat down. "He's going through something right now." Her eyes fell. "He'll come back around. I do have a Christmas card for you. He wanted me to wait, but I think you should have it now. What do you think?"

Beth Ann nodded. "I would like that." Her daddy had remembered to send her a card; that was good.

Gram left the room and returned a few minutes later with a card in her hand.

"Why don't you take this into another room and read it. I heard your mama and Stanley getting up."

Beth Ann nodded and headed out back. It was chilly because of a slight breeze in the air, which made her shiver. The dogs in the neighborhood were barking and the sounds of kids fighting over something permeated around her. She glanced up at the blue sky and thought about all the wonderful days she'd had since moving to Novato.

The card was in her hand and she studied his handwriting. Where was he when he wrote this? Was he alone and sad? She swallowed the lump that was stuck in her throat. After a few minutes passed, she opened it up.

To my sweet little girl,

I just wanted you to know that I love you and miss you very much. Here is a check for your birthday and Christmas. I want you to go buy whatever you need.

She held the check in her hand and was shocked at the amount.

You are very special Beth Ann, always know that and always remember that you mean the world to me.

Love Daddy

Beth Ann couldn't stop the tears that sprang from her eyes. "I love you, too, Daddy," she whispered, then added. "The card would have been *enough*."

Chapter Twenty-Five

The next week went by in a flash and Christmas day had finally arrived. The house smelled so good that it was making everyone complain about their hunger pains. Finally, after hours of torture they sat down at the dinner table; everything looked like Christmas. Candles flickered while Bing Crosby serenaded them with 'I'm dreaming of a White Christmas.' The tablecloth was snow white with a silver snowflake pattern and napkins that matched. It was lovely and Beth Ann couldn't remember a time when her mom had decorated and made everything look so perfect.

Beth Ann glanced around at all the faces of people she loved and her heart swelled. Gram was seated next to her, in her cute little red dress and her snow white hair pulled back in a bun that was accented with golden leaves.

Cole was all dressed up in his white shirt and nice slacks. He was so handsome. Stanley had on a green dinner jacket and had a wide grin across his face. Her mom gave him a look of pure joy, and never had she seen her mom look as beautiful as she did in that moment with her white sparkly dress.

"I'm just so thrilled we're all together," her mom said. "I wondered if Gram would lead us in prayer." She gave Gram a tender look.

Gram nodded and held out her hands. "Let's all join together."

"Dear Lord, I thank you for giving us this time to spend the day of your birth together. Thank you for giving me the chance to be here with this family. Please keep my son safe and help him find the right path, and help all those who are alone and hungry today find shelter and a loving hand to feed them.

"Also, help us put an end to this war and bring our soldiers home safe and sound. This I pray in your name. Amen."

"Amen," said everyone in unison.

Stanley stood, picked up a large fork and knife and started carving the bird. "Now. Let's chow down on this wonderful looking meal." He winked at Beth Ann's mom and nodded to Gram. "You two lovely ladies have prepared one of the best looking meals I've ever seen."

When her mom handed him Gram's plate, he sliced the first piece, walked over, and set it in front of her.

"I hope it's okay for me to say this." He glanced around at everyone. "Gram, I am so very happy that you're here." He paused. "I know this must have been a little odd for you, so thank you for spending these holidays with us." He leaned down and kissed her cheek.

She nodded and mist laced her eyelashes. "I'm happy to be a part of this amazing family."

Beth Ann felt tears, but swallowed them back. She was happy, but at the same time, she missed her dad, and was incredibly relieved that Stanley treated her Grandma so wonderful. This was a special moment and she would choke on something before she ruined it by crying over the sentiment, or not eating enough and making everyone worry.

The phone shrilled so she jumped up. "I'll get it."

She ran into the room and picked it up. "Hello."

"Hi, Beth Ann, you little beauty," Frankie said with his oh so charming and wonderful voice. He'd been gone the entire Christmas holiday.

"Frankie! When are you coming home?"

"Next week. I just wanted to call and wish my best girl a Merry Christmas."

Beth Ann's heart tugged. "Merry Christmas, Frankie."

"I can't talk long, we're about to have dinner. I miss you like crazy," he said.

"I miss you, too. It hasn't been the same without you."

"I miss you more," he replied. "I'll call you as soon as we get home."

"Okay." She paused. "You have a wonderful time."

"You too, and give your family, my best wishes."

Beth Ann said goodbye.

Novato *wasn't* the same without him. Besides Lisa, Frankie was her best friend in the world. No matter what he was doing, if she needed him, he was there in minutes. Kaylob and Frankie were good pals, too, which made things nice.

As she reentered the room, everyone was laughing and talking as the food was passed around, and her stomach growled right on cue.

Cole looked up at her, winked, and took a giant bite. "So is Frankie having a good day?" He spoke with his mouth full.

Beth Ann nodded. "He is. They were getting ready to eat."

Gram stared at Cole as he spoke. "Cole, wait for your sister to sit down and do not talk with your mouth full."

Everyone chuckled as Beth Ann sat down and tried to hide her laughter. Then she witnessed the look on Cole's face as he laid down his fork. Holy cornbread stuffing, He was trying to hide his jaw, crammed with so much food, he looked like a chipmunk.

Beth Ann snickered. "Yes, Cole have some manners." She arched an eyebrow. "Were you raised by heathens?"

Cole shot her a look, but laughed in spite of himself.

At that point, Beth Ann burst out in laughter and watched everyone else crack up, too.

The dinner ended on a wonderful note and Beth Ann ate herself into another dress size. She was glad she got to wear her holiday dress at least once. As she plunked down on the living room couch, she felt her stomach then sighed. "I feel like a stuffed turkey."

Gram touched her arm. "I love that white dress with the red sash around your waist, makes my grand baby look all grown up," she said. "You're starting to fill out a tiny bit, and I was happy to see you eat a whole plate of food."

Beth Ann adored her Gram so much, she didn't even care about being called a baby or that she was gaining weight, but she might just have to cut back again.

Later that day, Kaylob came over with his own homemade fudge. There was no doubt that he would be a chef someday, because the taste was rich, dark chocolate and mouth-watering good.

When they were finally alone, sitting on her bed, he pulled out a small box and handed it to her.

She opened it. "Oh, Kaylob." She flung her arms around his neck. "I love it!" It was an ivory butterfly necklace and gorgeous, she thought as she ran her fingers across the smooth shape of the butterfly.

Kaylob helped place it around her neck.

"I love it so much." She lifted the butterfly and held it in her hand.

The way he looked was beyond charming. "I'm glad," he whispered in her ear.

"Now." She ran over to her bedroom closet. "Let me get yours."

She handed him the big box that had been gift wrapped by the store. "Open it."

"Okay, okay." He laughed.

She almost wanted to help him rip it open, but refrained. "Hurry, Kaylob."

"Why, does it have legs?" He met her gaze.

Finally, he unwrapped it and opened the box. His eyes told her everything.

"Wow!" He lifted up the top of the line skillet. "This is unreal."

"I saw the one you used. I also heard you say, someday you'd have a real, honest to goodness, skillet. My mom helped me pick it out."

He continued to stare and hold it. "I can't believe this." He set it down and gazed at her.

Holy midnight, he had tears over a skillet.

He wiped at his eyes and embraced her. "Thank you, baby." He held her tight. "That is the best gift I've ever received."

He stood. "I need to go thank your parents." He took her hand, held it up to his lips and kissed her palm.

After he thanked her family, they spent the rest of the day watching movies and eating pie. Beth Ann had never eaten so much in her entire life.

The next morning they were all off to San Francisco and had a great time seeing the Christmas decorations and having dinner out on the wharf. It was wonderful, even more so because her parents had invited Kaylob. They loved him, but nobody loved him more than she did.

Gram had told her how handsome he was, but more than that, Gram had said he was a special guy and a keeper.

Beth Ann had also spent an evening with Kaylob's parents and couldn't get over how different they were. Kaylob was tall with golden skin and blond hair. Whereas, his parents were short with dark hair and he looked nothing like them. Were they his real parents? Maybe he was adopted. It wasn't nice for her to think that way, but she couldn't help it.

She understood how it felt to be different, her brothers had dark hair, brown skin, and she was the only redhead in the family, with pale skin and freckles. How lucky for her, she tried to find humor in the situation.

This was the holidays that Beth Ann would remember for always. Her Gram, a card from her dad, and the wonderful time with her family. Yes, life had indeed changed for Beth Ann.

There was still one lingering question. Why did Kaylob treat her so much like a little girl? She wanted to go steady with him. It wasn't just about the ring; he could give her one from a bubble gum machine and besides, she loved the necklace and wore it all the time. It was about being a steady couple and nothing more. Well, he'd ask her soon, wouldn't he?

* * * *

Almost two years had passed and October was the month Kaylob had been waiting for. He stood at Beth Ann's door, knocking, waiting for the birthday girl to answer. He had come a little early to spend time with her before her party. He'd bought her a gorgeous ring that cost him more than a few bucks.

Finally, the door opened and Cole stood staring. "Hey Kaylob, you're a little early. Beth Ann is downtown with our mom. Come on in." He waved him inside.

Kaylob walked in and was actually happy they could have a minute alone.

He was going to ask Beth Ann to go steady tonight and wanted to be sure Cole was okay with that now. After all, she was fourteen and they had been together for two years. Kaylob wanted her to officially be his girl.

"I'm glad we get a minute alone," Kaylob said. "I wanted to show you the ring I bought for Beth Ann.

"A ring?" Cole frowned.

"Yeah, I figure she's fourteen now and I could ask her to be my girl."

"Kaylob, I thought I made myself clear about this. She's too young. You know she's innocent and I want her to stay that way. She's just a baby."

Kaylob felt his heart sink. "I just thought maybe it would be okay." He opened the case and showed Cole. "I bought it downtown at Novato Jewelry."

"It's nice, Kaylob, but you need to return it." He sat on the couch. "I want you to promise me that you won't ask her to go steady until she's older."

"But I thought fourteen was old enough. I waited."

"No." Cole shook his head. "I want you to promise me you won't ask her to go steady without talking to me first. One more thing, don't even think about going all the way with my sister until she's at least twenty."

"I'm not talking about going all the way. I just want her to be my girl, Cole, I love her."

"No," he said again. "I will break this whole thing apart, if you push this. I'll make her go live with gram in Salem."

Kaylob felt the air leave his lungs. "Cut her off from me? Send her away from all her friends and her home."

"Yes, where Beth Ann is concerned, I have the say so. She's my little sister and I've watched over her since she was a baby. Give me your word, Kaylob. I trust that you will keep your promise." He stood and met Kaylob's gaze dead on. "I'll cover for you while you take that back and get her something else."

Kaylob turned when he got to the door. "She's going to hate me, you know."

"She'll understand. Just make up something. But do not tell her about this conversation."

"Cole," Kaylob said. "Is it because I'm not good enough for her? I know I live on the wrong side of the tracks."

Kaylob watched Cole's eyes fall. "Hell, no. You are a good guy. If it were anyone else, they wouldn't be standing here having this conversation. I would have cut her off from seeing another guy. I trust you Kaylob, and I know you will respect my sister and wait."

"Okay." Kaylob swallowed his disappointment. "I'll buy her something else and you have my word. But if you trust me, why not trust that it's just

167

going steady."

"Because, she would want more. I see the way she looks at you. And Kaylob, I've noticed how you look at her. I'm a guy you know. I also know you dated older girls and Beth Ann is still a kid. She's had a tough life and I honestly don't want her to get so involved. She needs to be a kid a while longer."

"I know you guys traveled around a lot. I know that would be hard," Kaylob said.

"You might say that." Cole looked down.

"I just hope I don't lose her because of this." Kaylob opened the door and left.

Kaylob was feeling anything but happy. He was also having a hard time believing that it was just because of the things Cole had said. There had to be more. Most likely it was because of where he lived and the fact that he was a nobody. Hell, he had little to offer Beth Ann, other than love.

Not only couldn't he ask Beth Ann to go steady, he couldn't tell her why. He hit the steering wheel and felt a tear trail down his cheek. "She's going to dump me before she turns eighteen," he said to nobody.

Kaylob sat in his truck after exchanging the ring, feeling the weight of sadness on his shoulders. He ended up buying her a beautiful pair of birthstone earrings and made sure they were in a big box, so it wouldn't look like a ring. The last thing he wanted to do was disappoint her. Now he'd have to ask her when she turned eighteen and not a minute sooner. He sat in his truck, fantasizing about the day they could run away together.

* * * *

The passage of time flew by and summertime once again blanketed the town of Novato. Beth Ann was way past fourteen and still no going steady ring. She spent many summer days at the ocean, watching Kaylob surf and he was the best. He cooked new recipes a lot and worked many hours while she poured almost all her spare time into training. The performances they put on were every three months and although she loved everything, she missed her friends and Kaylob. When she did have spare time, she and Kaylob had gone to parties and even learned to sing together. It was always fun being with the whole gang.

As she lay in her bedroom that morning, watching the lacy curtains flutter, the phone's shrill almost jarred her off the bed. Why hadn't she turned that thing down?

"Hello."

"Hey, it's me." Frankie's voice sounded different.

"What are you doing up so early?" Beth Ann questioned.

"I need to talk to you." His voice dipped.

"Frankie, is everything okay?"

"I have something I need to tell you." He sighed.

"What is it?" Her stomach flipped upside down.

"We are being transferred to another place." His voice broke. "I'm not happy about it."

Beth Ann instantly felt tears fill her eyes. "No, you can't go." She was trying not to break down. "I want you to stay, Frankie, please. Maybe you could live with us. We have a spare room."

"I can't leave my parents and they wouldn't go for that anyway. I don't want to leave either. You mean the world to me and Kaylob has become my best bud."

Beth Ann whispered. "Frankie, no."

"My dad got transferred and we have no choice. They own him."

"When are you leaving?"

"In a few days, we're already packing," he said. "Listen, can you meet me at our usual spot."

Beth Ann's throat clogged. She was trying not to bawl, but was finding it hard to maintain balance.

"Beth Ann," said Frankie. "Please don't cry."

She swiped the tears from her face. "I'll try." She inhaled deeply. "What time do you want to meet?"

"At noon," he said. "The rest of the day will be filled with packing and helping my parents."

After they hung up, Beth Ann placed her face in the pillow and sobbed. What would her life look like without Frankie?

A knock at the door had her trying to wipe off all the tears.

"Come in," she said.

When she glanced up, she met Stanley's eyes.

"Sweetheart, I heard you crying. What's the matter?"

Her voice choked. "Frankie's ... dad. Frankie's leaving."

"Can I come in?" He waited.

She nodded and invited him in.

That morning sitting on her bed, her stepdad rocked and soothed her, until all the tears had dried. A little while later, he made her pancakes for breakfast. While they were eating, her mom strolled into the kitchen still in her robe.

She looked into Beth Ann's eyes. "Sorry, I slept in. Is there something wrong?"

Beth Ann was afraid to speak for fear she'd start crying like a big old baby all over again. Thank God for Stanley, he spoke up for her.

"Frankie's dad got a transfer and they're leaving in a few days."

"Oh, sweetie." Her mom gave her a big hug, and brushed the hair out of her eyes. "I'm sorry. I know how close you and Frankie are."

Beth Ann nodded and leaned into her mom while she stroked her hair. "Mama, I don't want him to go."

"I know, I know, sweetie. Why don't you invite him over for dinner tonight?"

"He has to help his parents pack and I'm meeting him at noon to say goodbye." Beth Ann stood. "I'm going to start getting ready."

"Okay." Her mom embraced her.

Beth Ann went into her room and sighed deeply. Besides saying goodbye to Rusty when she was a kid, she couldn't imagine anything being harder. It just seemed that she always had to say goodbye to the people she loved.

She and Frankie had done everything together, before her time got so limited. They went to the movies, skate night, cardboard sliding. He was always with her and Lisa. Now that Denny was involved and going steady with Andre, nobody saw her as much anymore. Nowadays, Frankie hung out a lot with Kaylob and they had become best buddies.

She thought about the day at the pond. It had been a hot one in Novato and her and Frankie decided to go to Sawyers pond. That was the day she admitted to Frankie just how upset she was that Kaylob had not asked her to go steady.

Frankie's words rang in her memory.

"Beth Ann, Kaylob's crazy about you, so be more patient. He's turned into an old-fashioned guy with you. I already told you way back when that he liked you for more than a friend."

"Yes, you told me that." Beth Ann kissed his cheek.

"Well, even a blind man would know that. So stop your whining and let's go swimming." He'd pulled her up, and holding hands, they jumped into the cold water at Sawyers pond. She screamed and he laughed. That afternoon was spent drifting around together on an inner tube under the blue skies, and now it would be sealed away as a special memory.

The memory faded and she felt her heart slump as she finished getting dressed. She had to get out of the house so she could breathe. It was early, but she didn't care. That would give her time to spend with Sally Mae. There was no question that she was the best horse in the world.

Once she followed the path up the hill, she saw Sally and called out her name. In an instant, the horse came trotting over. The smell of hay blew through the air and sadness seemed all around.

Beth Ann reached out and touched the horse's head while tears filled her eyes.

"He's leaving Sally Mae, and I'm going to miss him so bad." She leaned her head against the horse's and cried.

There was no explanation how that moment eased some of the pain, but it did. As Beth Ann stood amongst the swaying trees and the blue sky, feeling as though her heart was being ripped apart, she knew deep down that Sally Mae sensed her sadness. Then when Sally Mae moved her head down, and made a quiet whinny sound, Beth Ann was hundred percent sure she had just been horse hugged.

She approached their special spot and the memories of her and Frankie were all around. The sounds of joy and laughter floated through the air. Those moments were keepsakes that she would bury deep in her heart, like a secret treasure.

"Beth Ann!" She looked up and saw Frankie pacing towards her.

There was no waiting, and Beth Ann ran and jumped into his arms. "Frankie, I love you," she cried. "I hate that you're leaving."

"I know." His voice trembled. "I hate it too." He held her tight and then pointed to the cardboard lying by the big old oak tree. "For old time sakes." He gave her a slight grin.

"Yes." She tried her best to look happy.

After thirty minutes of flying down the hill and running back up like they had done so many times, Frankie pulled her up off the ground. "I have to get back and help my parents." His eyes turned misty. "I hate saying goodbye to you."

"Frankie, don't say it." Beth Ann went into his arms again. "Let's just say later." She stared into his green eyes.

"I have a great idea," Frankie said with a spark in his eyes.

"What?" She inquired.

"When I turn eighteen, I'll meet you right here two days later." He pointed to the old tree stump. "I'll write to you every week and two days after my birthday, I'll come back to this spot," he promised. "We can set up a time."

Beth Ann laid her head across his heart. "I'll be here waiting for you. Let's say noon on June 20th, two days after your eighteenth birthday. Please, don't forget me, Frankie."

"Forget you. I could never ever forget you, Elizabeth Ann Rose." He took a long deep breath. "If you hadn't been Kaylob's girl, I would have asked you to be mine." He held her gaze. "I know you two are perfect for each other, so I never made a move. Just like I didn't with Lisa. In truth, I was going to ask Lisa to be my girl, when she started seeing Terry years ago. I had it bad for her. Well, the truth is, I still do in a way. But she's in love and taken."

Beth Ann was surprised. "Wow, I never knew that. You hid it well."

"I did the same with you." He looked down. "That first day I saw you, I had a crush. But you were already hooked on Kaylob and he was hooked right back on you. So instead, I gained the best friend a guy could ever ask for." He kissed the top of her head. "Besides, I had a secret girlfriend for a long time and she kept me busy."

"You did? Really, and why the secret?"

Frankie stood, gazing down at the ground. "Because she was a lot older than me and she didn't want anyone to know." He glanced towards the house with Sallie Mae. "As a matter of fact." He handed her a note. "Could you put this on the front door on your way back down?" His lips trembled.

"Sure." Beth Ann knew for sure who the older woman was. She felt bad because he looked so hurt, so she made a quick decision.

"Frankie ... would you kiss me goodbye?"

And she didn't have to ask twice. In that sweet moment as the trees rustled at their special spot, Frankie gave her a gentle but long kiss. After he was done, he put his hands in his pockets and stepped back.

"Later, Beth Ann."

Tears burned and she tried her best to force them back, but once again failed.

Frankie reached out and wiped her tears away. "Don't cry. I love you, my little chickadee." He grinned, but it faded fast.

With that, he turned and ran away.

The weight of the world was heavy when she turned to walk down the hill. Once she reached the house, she left the note on the front door and wondered how long they had been involved. She also thought about what Frankie's parents might do if they found out that their son was involved with a girl in her twenties.

Once she arrived at the bottom of the hill all the sounds were the same. A little boy whizzed by on his skateboard, yelling at his friend to keep up. Nothing could take her mind off the fact that her best friend was moving so far away.

A few minutes after, strolling along and feeling like she was dragging her heart behind her, she heard a horn honk and looked up to find a familiar set of twin dimples.

"Howdy there, young lady." His smile vanished when he saw her face. "Hey, what's wrong? Want to go out to the pond and hang out for a bit?"

For a minute she stood there, wondering if she should or shouldn't. Kaylob was off with his parents for another week, she needed someone to talk to, and Blake was a good friend.

"Sure." She nodded and climbed inside his Nomad.

Blake leaned over and kissed her cheek. "You smell good, kinda like a horse." He cracked up. "Did you bring your swimsuit?"

She held up her hands. "Does it look like I brought my swimsuit?"

"No, I guess not." He lifted a brow. "Do you want to go get one?"

"No." She shrugged. "I actually have it under my clothes. I thought maybe Frankie and I would go swimming, but …" She took a long deep breath. "We didn't have time."

"Frankie must have another date with his hot girlfriend." He drove off. "I saw him once when I was jogging over the hill. Yeah, I was surprised to see him kissing some fine looking older chick."

"No, he didn't have a hot date. He's moving away. His dad got a transfer." Her voice quivered. "Don't tell anyone about seeing that, it could get her in trouble."

"I won't. I'm sorry, Beth Ann. I know you two were close." His eyes showed sadness as he reached over and held her hand. "It's hard to say goodbye to people you love." His expression appeared genuine.

"Did you lose someone, Blake?" she questioned.

Before he could answer, they pulled up to Sawyers pond and it was busy. Kids were running from the deck and jumping into the water, while others floated around on inner tubes. The place made her miss Kaylob so much that her heart did a belly flop.

Blake opened his door and walked around to Beth Ann's side. After she slid out, he asked, "Are you okay?"

"I will be in time." She looked into his soft blue eyes.

Blake went to the back and pulled out a blanket and a cute little ice chest, then they found a quiet spot under a weeping willow tree.

They sat down on the blanket as the warm breeze made its way through the trees. Beth Ann looked up at the blue sky that held puffy white clouds, which cast shadows across the pond. Laughter and splashing sounded all around as they both lay back, watching the sky above them.

"Blake, who did you lose?" Beth Ann asked in a soothing whisper.

There was a long stretch of silence. "I lost my grandma and she loved me a whole lot. Not like my parents, who don't seem to like me at all."

Beth Ann turned to face him, propping her head in her hand. "Of course your parents love you. Don't be silly."

"They've never acted like it and never really said it." Dark shadows gathered in his eyes.

She leaned over and brushed a kiss across his cheek. "I'm sorry. Maybe they just don't know how to show it." She moved the hair out of his eyes with her fingers.

"You're a sweet girl. Are you sure you want to be with Kaylob?" He lifted a brow.

"Blake. We're good friends and you know he's my guy."

He lifted her hand. "Yeah, well, if that's the case, where's the ring. Maybe he can't afford it?"

Beth Ann pulled her hand away. "Let's go swimming." She changed the subject, jumping to her feet, pulling her dress over her head. "Come on, lazy bones!" She needed to tuck away her own melancholy to help him.

"Lazy bones? Who you calling lazy bones." He picked her up and jumped into the water.

"Let me down, Blake Tanner." She meant it.

"Okay, fine." He released her and laughed.

The day went by and they had a good time swimming and splashing under the sweltering summer sun. Blake had brought two sandwiches, deviled eggs, chips and drinks. At breakfast, she'd only had one pancake, so she was starving. Still, throughout the day, she'd think of Frankie and despair would rush through her. But thanks to Blake, he would cheer her and chase away her sadness.

By late afternoon, Beth Ann was ready to go home. "I need to get back, Blake. I'm not sure if my parents knew I'd be gone this long."

With that, he nodded and gathered his blanket and basket. "Let's get you home."

When Blake dropped her off, she kissed his cheek and waved goodbye. She walked through the door and nobody was there, but there was a note on her pillow.

'Hi sweetie, we had to go to San Francisco and pick up the payroll books, which my husband forgot. But we'll be back in time for dinner. By the way, Kaylob called twice before we left. I didn't want to tell him about Frankie. Love you sweetie, Mommy.'

* * * *

She crawled onto the bed, laying her head on the pillow. The warm summer breeze came flowing through the window, helping her to relax. There was just no way to stop her heart from feeling heavy. Blake had helped a lot and she was very happy they were friends, but she knew he wanted much more. Many times, she had made it clear that she was Kaylob's girl. Even though, she had no ring, she glanced at her ring-less finger. Maybe he couldn't afford a ring? That was fine by her; he could just ask her to go steady without a stupid ring.

Just as she was drifting off, the phone's loud shrill jarred her back.

"Hello!" She wanted to choke the phone.

"Beth Ann, it's me."

"Hi, Kaylob. Are you having a good time up there with your family?"

"It's okay. I just miss you."

Beth Ann let out a deep sigh. "I miss you too." She felt her voice tremble.

"Baby, is something wrong?"

"Yes … Frankie's dad got orders and they are leaving right away. I said goodbye to him today."

"Crap. I won't even get a chance to say goodbye. Do you mind if I call him right now?"

"No. I'm happy you're going to call him." She sighed. "I miss you."

"Ah, I miss you, too, and I'm sorry about not being there."

After a few more minutes of sharing what they had been doing, she hung up the phone and moved back down on the bed. Within a few minutes, she was out like a light.

Chapter Twenty-Six

Kaylob hung up the phone, feeling sick about Frankie leaving. He considered him one of his best friends. "Damn it," he said into the phone as he dialed.

"Hello?" Frankie's dad answered.

"Hello, Mr. Russo, is Frankie there?"

"Sure thing, Kaylob, hang on."

"Frankie, phone! It's Kaylob!" his dad called out.

After a few seconds of noises, Kaylob heard Frankie pick up the phone. "Kaylob, what's cooking?"

"Man, I heard about you leaving. That sucks."

"I know it does. But I'll be back. You better take good care of our girl," Frankie said with a laugh. "You're one lucky bastard."

"Frankie Russo, don't you curse in this house!" a woman's voice rang out in the background.

"Okay, Ma, sorry." Both guys laughed.

They went on to share stories about the past. Kaylob felt bad, not only was he losing one of his best friends, but Beth Ann was, too. She loved Frankie like a brother. No matter how someone looked at it, the fact that he was moving away sucked. There had been times when he experienced a little jealousy, but now he had complete trust in Frankie.

He walked outside to the barn and sat on a bale of hay. His family was behind the farmhouse and he could hear them laughing and carrying on. The aroma made him raise his nose. God, how he'd always loved the fresh sweetness in the air, even if the barn had seen better days.

"Kaylob, what are you doing out here?" He looked up toward the voice standing by the barn pole, and found Mary Ann observing him.

"Just thinking." He watched as she walked over and sat down on the bale across from him, she slung her dark hair across her very tanned shoulders.

"I was hoping we could go down to the swimming hole today, just the two of us, please."

"No, Mary Ann. I already told you I have a girlfriend, and you're my cousin now." He shook his head as he held her gaze. "We've been over this."

"Not by blood." She moved in front of him and her brown eyes pleaded. "Kaylob, come on. What she doesn't know won't hurt her." She touched his hair.

"Mary Ann, this is why I stopped coming around." He caught her wrist then gently let go. "Now you need to find yourself a boyfriend and stop this."

He stood and left the barn without looking back. Once he was outside, he glanced around, realizing just how much he missed this place. He loved Sonora, but Mary Ann was the reason he stopped coming to his Aunt and Uncle's without his parents. Even the smell from the chicken coop brought back childhood memories. The old barn is where he spent a lot of time, and really, the only time he was allowed to be a kid. When he was home, he had to take care of his mom and do all the work that a dad is supposed to do.

But here, surrounded by the mountains and sycamore trees, he got to be a kid. The days were spent on rope swings and swimming in the water hole. He would ride the old mule that made him crack up every time she did her heehaw. This place was his youth and the only place he could remember feeling light and free.

Now, though, Mary Ann just didn't want to take no for an answer. Sure, there was a time when they fooled around, but that was before his aunt and uncle adopted her. It just wasn't right to do that with a cousin, blood or not. Besides, he was in love with Beth Ann and the one thing Kaylob knew was he wasn't a cheating kind of guy.

Deep down he knew there would be temptations in life, however, the only one he had right now was to get home and be with his girl. He could hear how upset she was on the phone, and he should be there with her.

It was going to be another week before they left. Maybe he could take the bus. After all, one of his best friends was moving away. Plus, he had his own money from working at the store. All he had to do was convince his mom and dad that he needed to get back.

* * * *

Beth Ann fought to wake up as the scent of savory cooking filled her room. It smelled like one of her favorite things. She jumped off the bed and dashed into the kitchen. There, she found her mom frying chicken with a big grin plastered across her face. Something was making her happy.

Her mom dried off her hands and gave her a big hug. "How are you doing, sweetie?"

Beth Ann tried to feel good. "I'm better, but I'm going to miss him so much."

"You want a glass?" Her mom released her and picked up her sun tea. "Maybe we could sit down and talk before dinner's ready."

Beth Ann nodded and watched her mom pull the chicken out of the frying pan, then she placed each piece on paper towels. Afterwards, she took down a glass and filled it with the tea. "Here you go. Now let's sit."

Beth Ann plopped down next to her mom at the kitchen table and smelled the fragrance of the fruity sun tea. There was nothing in the world so refreshing as the lemony taste of her mother's tea and the chill of the ice cubes that grazed her teeth while sipping on it.

"Baby," Her mom paused, and took another long sip. "I know you're sad about Frankie and I understand. You've never had the kind of friends you have here. But sweetheart, people will come and go in your life. It's part of what happens around us, and I just want you to be okay with it."

"Mama, I can't be okay with losing Frankie." She inhaled. "I know all too well how hard it feels to say goodbye. I've been doing that since I was little."

Her mom nodded. "Yes, you have, and it's been hard on you. Frankie will always be your best friend. I just want you to be prepared for other losses in life." Her mom reached across the table and brushed the hair out of her eyes. "I would never want it to destroy you or make you fall apart. That's all."

Beth Ann met her mom's gaze. "I won't ever let it destroy my life, mama. I promise."

"Good." She nodded. "I'm sure you saw that I am making your favorite food tonight. I know it can't bring back Frankie, but it is my way of telling you I'm sorry and I love you."

Beth Ann looked into her mom's soft gaze. "I love you too, Mama."

Later that evening, while they were eating dinner, there was a knock on the door.

Stanley stood up. "I'll go get it. Maybe someone's trying to sell us something."

A few minutes later, he walked in with a big grin on his face. "It's for you, Beth Ann."

"For me?" She was confused, knowing that most her friends didn't stop by during dinnertime. "Who is it?"

Stanley pointed. "Someone who wants to see you."

Beth Ann got up, caught Stanley winking at her mom, and wondered what the heck was going on. She headed to the living room.

"Kaylob!" She ran and threw herself into his arms.

He fell backwards into the door. "Wow. You're strong for being so little."

"I missed you so much." She swept a kiss across his lips.

"Are you okay?" He put his large hands on her shoulders and looked up into her eyes.

"I'm better now." She pointed towards the kitchen. "Want some dinner? My mom made her southern fried chicken."

"Yes and yes, if it's okay." He lifted his nose in the air. "Man, that smells incredible."

Beth Ann got up, then helped him to his feet. She took him by the hand and he willingly let her drag him into the kitchen.

"Hello Jean," he said, then nodded to Stanley.

Beth Ann's mom rose from the table. "My gracious, I'm so glad you're here." She stood and gave his cheek a kiss. "How about we dish you up some food?"

"You don't have to ask me twice." Kaylob grinned. "Everything smells wonderful."

That evening at dinner, Beth Ann found out that Kaylob had taken a bus from Sonora, California to Novato. At that moment, Beth Ann decided to stop worrying about him asking her to go steady, at least for a while.

Chapter Twenty-Seven

A few days later, she was cleaning the hall bathroom when the phone's shrill almost knocked her in the toilet.

She dried her hands. "Hello."

"Hey, baby," said Kaybob. "Want to come and have lunch with me today? I get the rest of the day off."

"Sure, where do you want to go?"

"I thought I'd pick up some of Perry's sandwiches and we could meet at my house. I have some chores I have to take care of."

"What time?" She couldn't believe they were having lunch alone.

"How about noon?"

"That would be great."

They hung up and her heart skipped several beats. In two hours, she'd be meeting him alone for lunch. She couldn't remember the last time they had done that.

Her stomach did the tango, thinking about what might be going on. Maybe, just maybe, something was up.

Now that she was a few months away from fifteen, dare she dream he might be asking her to go steady?

When she arrived, he was cutting the grass. The vision of him shirtless with tight shorts on, made her heart stutter.

Holy muscle alert, he had to have the best arms and chest of any guy in the world. She couldn't swallow because drool got caught in her windpipe. When he glanced up and saw her standing there gawking at him, a slow smile spread across his face. She was sure as heck glad the saliva went backwards and wasn't hanging from her mouth. She subtly wiped her lips. Just in case.

His eyes met hers and heat crawled up her neck like a burning ember.

Dang it, why couldn't she control that?

His stifled laugh, told her she was busted. After he stopped pushing the lawn mower, he pulled his shirt out of his back pocket, and wiped his face before he headed towards her.

Beth Ann bent over and picked up a blade of grass, trying not to stare anymore.

"Hey you," he said with a chuckle. "Your face sure is red."

Beth Ann looked up and lied. "It's hot outside today."

"You're so damn cute." Kaylob threw his head back and laughed. He took her hands and pulled her close. "Have I told you that I'm crazy for you?" He leaned down, buried his face in her neck and inhaled.

She moved her hands up his bare back then shifted even closer. Before she could focus on how good it felt, he backed away and stuck his hands in his pockets.

"Let me go wash up and I'll finish this later." He nodded towards the unfinished lawn. "I have our lunch all set up." He took her hand and led her up the stairs into his house.

Once inside, they stepped into the kitchen and everything was perfect; a pretty orange tablecloth with matching napkins was laid out on the table. She couldn't help but feel giddy when she saw the wild daisies that were placed in a coke bottle, with candles on each side. There were matching glasses, filled with ice, and sandwiches that looked yummy.

"Kaylob, this is so lovely. Thank you."

He pulled up a chair and she eased down, taking in everything he had done.

"I'm going to go clean off this sweat and grime and I'll be right back." He leaned over and gave her a tender kiss.

The masculine aroma of grass and his unique woodsy fragrance filled her with something she didn't understand. Then, when he walked out of the room, the view sent goose bumps dancing across her arms.

Beth Ann picked up her soda and tried to pour it over the ice, but her hands were trembling. For reasons she couldn't explain, she made a choice to do something that she'd never done. She stood and walked down the hall where she observed him pulling off his shorts. The sight almost took her breath away. He was in his underwear that left nothing to the imagination.

She inched closer and that's when he looked up and saw her.

"Beth Ann," he almost whispered in his deep, husky voice, then reached for his pants.

"No." She moved closer and pushed them away. "Please, Kaylob." After a few seconds, she melted her lips on top of his and a deep groan came from his throat.

"Baby, what are you doing to me?" He kissed her deeper and used his tongue to trail the inside of her lips.

After a few minutes of kissing, he lifted the beautiful butterfly necklace she never took off. "This looks so pretty on you."

"Kaylob, please at least touch me," she pleaded and placed his hand on her breast.

His eyes heated as he left his hand where she placed it, so she slid down her bra so he could touch her bare skin. The sound he made did something to her that made her ache with desire.

He withdrew his hand. "Beth Ann, no." He stood and stumbled backwards against the wall. "We have to stop." He slipped on his pants, but there was no way he could hide his excitement.

"But, why?" She rose up looking at him breathlessly. "I liked it, you liked it."

"Because you're too young and I shouldn't have let it get this far. Beth Ann, I could go to jail."

"Jail? I would never tell, and my parents would never send you to jail. They know I love you."

She had just blown it, and used the L word. Leave it to her to scare him away.

Kaylob went to the closet and found a shirt. "Beth Ann, you're too young to know what you want. Let's go eat." He walked over and took her hand.

She felt like punching him, he was making her feel like a child. First, he'd just touched her in a way she'd never experienced. Then she told him she loved him and now he wanted to go eat.

"You go ahead and eat your food! I'm leaving!" She turned and stomped towards the front door. How could he ignore what she just said and not want to touch her more?

This was it. It was over! Kaput! Wait, though; she couldn't even break up, or could she?

"Beth Ann, please, don't leave," he said.

Without giving him a second glance, she opened the door and said four words. "I'm done, it's over!"

"Beth Ann." He called after her and headed towards the door. "You don't understand what I'm up against."

"What you're up against?" She felt her face heating. "You always have some excuse or reason why you don't want me as your girlfriend."

She stepped outside and slammed the door. Surprisingly, he didn't come after her. With tears streaming down her face, she tried to convince herself that it was for the best.

When she finally made it home, her mom was inside dusting. "Hi sweetie, you're back early." She put down her dust rag. "What's wrong?" She moved closer. "Did something happen?"

"Yes, I hate Kaylob Shawn O'Brien and I never want to speak to him again." She had more tears spring from her eyes.

"What happened?" Her mother looked concerned.

"He barely kisses me! I told him I loved him, and he said I was too young to know what I felt. Mama, I'm fourteen now, almost fifteen, I know what I want." She turned to leave. "He can go to hell." She tore off her butterfly necklace and threw it at the wall. "I need to be alone." She ran to her room and slammed the door, then threw herself on the bed and cried herself to sleep.

* * * *

Across town, Kaylob finished mowing the lawn and wondered what the hell he was going to do. When Beth Ann turned fourteen, Cole had made it clear that he couldn't let things go too far, he flat out said, *no sex, no going steady, nothing too serious or I'll send her away.*

He made Kaylob give his word and he'd already done things with her he shouldn't. It was getting harder to resist what she wanted. How was he going to make it until she was twenty. Not only that, but she had just dumped him.

Cole had made Kaylob promise, not to tell her about any of their conversations.

Now, though, he might lose her. No way in hell would he let that happen. He loved Beth Ann with all his heart, but felt he couldn't even tell her that, because she'd want to know why he didn't ask her to go steady. He couldn't chance her being sent away and losing everything she had in her life.

He'd screwed up big time and had touched her in a way he shouldn't have, even after he gave his word. What kind of guy did that make him? Maybe Blake was right, he was a loser.

Man, if Cole found out what he'd just done, shit would hit the fan and smack him in the face. He'd never let that happen again, so he'd find a way to make sure they were never alone.

After he finished raking the grass and doing the edging, he went inside and plunked down on the couch. He needed to go talk to her and try to make things okay again, but he thought he'd better give her some time to cool down.

Maybe, he should go shoot some pool after he ate his sandwich. Beth Ann had left and not touched her lunch. He sure hoped she would remember to eat something; he worried about her small appetite.

He finished eating and put everything back in place, then headed out. When he arrived at the pool hall Blake was there, playing pool with a tall dark haired beauty. He did his best not to look their way. Now that Frankie was gone, he'd have to find someone else to hang out with. Bruce, his other buddy, had a girlfriend now and they were pretty serious.

He racked the balls, picked up a cue stick, and started a game. The minute Blake walked up to the table he knew there would be trouble.

"So you lost her. Your loss, my gain." He grinned slyly.

"Screw you, Blake. Get away from me." He wondered how he found out.

"She told me everything, and she's free and clear, because she ended it with you. You made her cry, you jackass."

"Shut up, Blake. You don't know everything." He bent down and hit another ball.

"I know enough to know that I'm taking her out to the movies tomorrow night. And, I know that I'll ask her to be my girl soon enough. I'll help her forget all about you."

Kaylob felt his insides boil. "You better not touch her." He stood straight up, glaring.

"You have no claim on her. She's done with you. Don't you think you've jerked her around long enough? Besides. I've already said it. She deserves someone who can give her everything and we both know that ain't you."

Kaylob had to clench his fist not to deck Blake.

He snickered. "I'm going to teach her what a real guy does to make his girl happy."

That did it; Kaylob flew into Blake and grabbed him by the shirt. "Shut your fucking mouth, Blake Tanner."

Blake pushed Kaylob backwards and held up his fists. "Come on, asshole."

Before Kaylob could react, Harry pulled them apart.

"Now, you two hoodlums knock this shit off. What's gotten into you guys?" Harry stood looking back and forth between the two of them. "You're acting like a couple Neanderthals."

Blake laughed. "Oh, Kaylob's a sore loser. I won the girl and he can't handle it."

Kaylob reached around Harry and pulled at Blake's shirt. "I'm going to pummel you."

Blake tried to push Harry out the way, but Harry yelled, "If you two don't knock it off, I'm having you both thrown out for good. You know the rules here."

Kaylob turned and stormed out of the pool hall. Once he got to the corner of the street, he saw Blake coming in his fancy car. Kaylob stopped and glared at him, wishing he'd try to fight now, but Blake gave him the bird and squealed his tires.

The only word that came to Kaylob's mind was asshole. He sure as hell hoped Blake was lying about taking Beth Ann out tomorrow night. He was upset with Beth Ann for sharing everything with his archenemy. Of course,

Beth Ann didn't know the full extent of how much they hated each other. But if Blake touched her, she might just find out. He made a choice to call her as soon as he walked in the door.

He picked up the phone and dialed.

Jean answered in her cute southern accent. "Hello."

"Hi Jean, is Beth Ann around?"

"Yes, she is, but she is really upset. Let me go tell her you're on the phone."

Kaylob heard her mom. "Beth Ann, honey, Kaylob's on the phone."

"Tell him to go away," she told her mom.

"Honey, that's not my job. This is between you and Kaylob."

He heard Beth Ann plod to the phone. "Go away, Kaylob!" She hung up.

Damn, she was mad. But he needed to talk to her so he called back.

"Hello!" She hurt his ear.

"I'm sorry. I'm crazy about you and you know it."

"Is that what you call crazy? Always pushing me away." He heard her sigh. "I'm done, Kaylob. Go back to one of your high school girlfriends who are old enough to kiss, go steady, or do whatever!" She hung up again.

Kaylob stood staring at the receiver, feeling like his heart was just ripped from his chest. How could she tell him that? Did she really hate him now?

He decided he'd give her a few days to cool off, but he was going to go see her, and they were going to talk.

He walked over and kicked the couch. "Shit." He grabbed his big toe and almost fell over.

* * * *

The next night, Beth Ann was getting ready to go the movies with Blake and was picking out a dress when she heard a knock on her door.

"Come in," she said.

"Hey, sis. I heard you are going to the movies with Blake tonight." Cole stepped into the room.

"Yep, sure am." She tried to act happier than she felt.

"Can we talk for a minute?" His voice softened and his lips were turned downward.

"Sure." She went and sat on her bed and watched him ease down by her.

"Sis, don't you think you're being a little hard on Kaylob?" he questioned.

"No, why would you say that?" She tilted her head and thought she saw guilt flash in his eyes.

Mom told me that you're upset that Kaylob won't …well, hardly kiss you, or ask you to go steady." He paused and pushed some imaginary lint off his

185

pants. "Don't you see that you're being a little harsh on him?"

"No way. He never wants to be alone with me. I told him I love him and he wanted to go eat lunch."

"Maybe, he's just waiting because of your age, Beth Ann. You know, I can tell he cares deeply for you." He cleared his throat.

"He has a funny way of showing it," Beth Ann said.

"He's respecting you, and in my book that makes him an exceptionally good man. He's protecting you, Beth Ann, and I would bet he loves you."

She stared down at her hands and felt some of her own guilt.

Cole turned her to look at him. "He's a good guy, and I think you're making a giant mistake, giving up on him and going out with Blake, who's a known playboy and I don't want you going out alone with him anywhere, but to the movies."

With that, he got up and moved to the door. "It's your call about Kaylob, but don't throw away someone you love, and you know you do, just because you can't have what you want this minute. Don't be a spoiled brat." He stared at her with a pointed look, then opened the door and left.

Beth Ann sat there with tears in her eyes. What had she done? Cole was right. She was acting like a spoiled brat because Kaylob wouldn't do what she wanted. He had fixed a beautiful day for her, the pretty flowers and tablecloth and she'd gotten mad because he wouldn't touch her sexually. That was it; she made up her mind she couldn't go out with Blake.

If she were being completely honest, she'd tell herself the truth. She had loved Kaylob from the first minute she laid eyes on him, and nobody else would do.

She remembered Charlie's words again. *"You will meet your prince charming."*

Kaylob was always so good to her. She moved over to the nightstand and lifted her shattered necklace. It was made from ivory and broken into pieces. "Oh Kaylob." She was feeling a bit shattered herself.

As she sat there crying, she lost track of time. There was a knock at the door, and she tried her best to wipe away her tears.

"Beth Ann, it's me, Blake. Your mom sent me back here to see if you're ready."

Oh, my God, she wasn't. She hadn't even thought about Blake since she picked up the necklace. She stood, opened the door, and waved for him to come in.

"Blake, I'm so sorry." She couldn't look at him. "I just can't go out with you tonight."

He stepped closer. "What's wrong? Did he hurt you again?"

"No. As a matter of fact, I haven't heard from him since I hung up last."
She felt her heart tug.

"Come on, Beth Ann, let's get you out of this room and to the movies."

"Blake, I love Kaylob. I can't go out with you."

He paused, but a slow smiled spread. "We're friends, right?"

"Yes. Good friends," she agreed.

"Well then. As a friend, I want to take you to the movies."

Beth Ann thought about that. They were friends. She was just honest with
him, and told him she loved Kaylob. So of course, she'd go with him.

"Okay, you're right. Two friends going to the movies might be fun and
maybe take my mind off things."

His dimples flashed. "There ya go. Now you get dressed and I'll wait in
the living room." He kissed her cheek and left the bedroom.

Thirty minutes later, they left the house and walked into the Novato
Theater. The aroma from the popcorn smelled heavenly, so they stopped at the
concession stand. As they left, holding their snacks, they saw a couple of kids
from school and said hello. Beth Ann was excited about seeing A Patch of Blue
with Sidney Poitier. The movie was about a girl who was blind and had an
abusive family. She hoped that it had a good ending; she took a bite of the
buttery popcorn and almost couldn't swallow it.

Chapter Twenty-Eight

Kaylob sat in the back where nobody noticed him, thinking they might show up after dinner. He had to see if Beth Ann really had a date. Before he could give it too much thought, they walked in. A thousand horses stampeded across his heart, and he could almost feel the blood loss. The minute Blake's arm went across the back of the seat he almost stood. There was no doubt in his mind that if they kissed he'd cause a scene and not a small one either.

Thank God, Beth Ann moved Blake's arm down and shook her head. Then she took her fingers and brushed the hair out of his eyes. Kaylob's hands were shaking bad, so bad, in fact, he couldn't hold onto to his pop. He had to get out of there so he left and walked into the restroom.

He headed over to the sink and splashed water on his face. What the hell was he going to do? He took a paper towel from the dispenser and wiped his forehead.

"What are you doing? Spying on her?" Blake asked and stepped closer. "I saw you when we walked in, but thankfully Beth Ann has no clue you're here."

"Spying." Kaylob stood straight and started to leave, but Blake stepped in his path.

"Get out of my way," Kaylob demanded. "Don't make me do something we'll both regret."

"Look, you might as well get over it. She's going to be mine soon enough." He grinned at Kaylob.

Kaylob opened the door to leave when Blake pushed him. "You're such a jerk."

Kaylob felt his fists clench and his jaw tightened. "Keep your hands to yourself, asshole." He pushed him back.

Blake got in his face. "Why don't you go back to the side of the tracks where you belong. She deserves better than you and you damn well know it."

That did it. Kaylob grabbed him by the shirt and shoved his ass against the wall. "You better get away from me and get away now!"

"I can't, you dick weed, you're holding me." He pulled away from Kaylob and got in his face once again. "She's going to be mine because I'm not afraid to give her what she wants." He wiggled his brows.

That did it. Kaylob picked him up with one hand, and had his fist drawn back, ready to nail him. He hoped all of Blake's teeth would fall out. Before he could punch him, Kaylob was jerked back.

"Get out, both of you." The owner stared at Kaylob and then at Blake. "You're both yelling loud and using language that's not permitted. You're both banned for thirty days." He grabbed them by the shirts and led them to the front door. "Don't try to come back, or I'll call the police."

Blake held up his hands. "Wait, I left someone in there."

"You should have thought about that before you caused a scene and tried to tear down my bathroom. She'll figure it out soon enough." He turned and left.

Kaylob couldn't believe how he'd just acted. He'd always been a calm guy. Why the hell was he letting Blake push his buttons? He needed to get a grip.

Blake turned, his face twisted with anger. "You are a complete ass and now Beth Ann is sitting in there all alone." He rubbed his hand through his hair. "Do you know how bad she was torn up when I picked her up tonight?" He glared at him. "Her eyes were red, she'd been crying for God knows how long." Blake punched a pole. "Damn it. You're not the only one who ..." He paused. "Who cares about her ... I'm in love with her." He stared right through Kaylob, then took off down the street.

Kaylob stood in shock at what Blake had admitted. Just hearing those words made his head spin. Could Beth Ann be falling for Blake? Should he just let her go?

He was thinking about leaving when he saw Beth Ann talking to Mr. Dunn, then saw him point outside, she instantly turned and saw Kaylob. Her face expressed an emotion he couldn't read.

But it wasn't *joy*, that much he knew.

He braced himself for her wrath when she opened the door and stormed over to him.

"Kaylob what the heck happened?" She held his gaze. "Mr. Dunn said you and Blake had a fight and he had to pull you off him." She shook her head. "Why would you attack Blake?"

Kaylob looked around and rubbed the back of his neck. "I guess, I got jealous," was all he said. "I'm sorry."

Beth Ann's look, shot him right through the heart. "You guess you got jealous. So you attack Blake?"

He didn't say anything.

"Where is he?" She looked around.

Kaylob felt his heart sink. "He took off that way." He pointed.

With that, she turned and headed down the street, without even looking back. For the first time since Kaylob could remember, he had tears running down his cheeks. He had lost her to Blake. There was nothing more for him to do so he turned and headed home. On his way, he fought like hell to keep the tears away, so he started to jog. He needed to get inside where nobody could see him.

When he reached his yard, he opened the gate and stumbled up the stairs into the house. Once inside, he didn't know if he was pissed off or just broken hearted. How could he handle seeing Blake and Beth Ann together? That wasn't even a question, he'd go away. Maybe move up with his aunt and uncle and stop being the boy from the wrong side of the tracks. He slumped down onto the couch and laid his head back, staring at the ceiling. After a few minutes he made the only decision he could, he'd call them tonight and make plans to leave.

Blake was right. He had won Beth Ann and Kaylob was a loser. He looked around and realized Blake was also right about the way he lived. They were poor, and Kaylob had nothing to offer Beth Ann, only love. What good was that since he couldn't even tell her?

"Damn that promise to Cole!" He yelled to nobody. "Why didn't I just tell her the truth about what happened in the bathroom? Better yet, why didn't I tell her about his promise to Cole?" He knew the answer to both, he wasn't going to break his word and he wasn't a rat. She should have more faith in him than to jump to the conclusion that he attacked Blake.

The more he remembered what she'd done, the angrier he got. The last time he spoke to her before she hung up, she'd yelled at him and said he should go back to his high school girlfriends. Maybe, she used that as an excuse so she could be with Blake.

Fine, she could have him; he'd find a way to get over her. How, he hadn't a clue, but he'd figure it out.

Chapter Twenty-Nine

Beth Ann continued to run down the street searching for Blake. She finally spotted him. "Where are you going?"

He turned and shrugged. "I needed to get some fresh air."

"So you just left?" Although, she understood why, because Kaylob had jumped on him.

"I heard about what happened. I'm sorry Blake."

"You're sorry." He stepped closer. "Why are you sorry?"

"Because, my boyfriend, ah, Kaylob attacked you." She walked up and touched his arm.

"Who told you that?" His eyes widened.

"The manager and Kaylob said he got jealous."

"Kaylob told you that?"

Beth Ann saw confusion on Blake's face. "Yes. Why wouldn't he?" She looked around at cars passing by, and felt the chill in the air.

"Well, we were." He paused. "Never mind, it doesn't matter." He took her hand. "Let's get to my car and maybe we can go to the pool hall."

"Blake, I have to go talk to Kaylob," she murmured.

"You want to go see him?" he asked, releasing her hand.

"Yes. I need to see him."

"I'm sure as hell not taking you to his dumpy house." Blake frowned.

"Fine, I'll just walk." She turned to leave. "For your information his house is not a dump!" She felt angry.

"Okay, fine. Hell, I don't want you walking in the dark. I'll take you." He sighed and took her hand, heading towards his car.

Once they were in the car, he turned towards her. "Beth Ann, why the hell do you care about him so much? I mean, he won't ask you to go steady and I would." His eyes softened.

Beth Ann needed to be honest. "Blake, you can have a lot of girls and I'm in love with Kaylob." She tried to act happy, but felt sad for Blake. Sure, he was popular, had girls, but there was pain inside him, and she saw through it.

"I would give them up for you." He leaned over and kissed her cheek. "But I'll take you to Kaylob." He started the car.

He pulled up in front of Kaylob's house and she opened the door. "Thank you, Blake," she said.

"You're welcome," he mumbled under his breath, clearly not happy.

Beth Ann stood by the fence and watched Blake's car drive away. The lights were still on, so she opened up the gate and moved up the steps. Thank goodness, Kaylob's parents were still gone for another week.

With a deep sigh, she knocked lightly on his door and heard footsteps.

When he opened the door, his face sobered.

"Do you want to come in?" His voice was deep and he seemed angry.

She nodded and stepped inside. The place was clean and looked nice with the dimmer lights on. It wasn't a dump. When she met his gaze, her stomach knotted.

"What do you want, Beth Ann?" he asked in a voice she'd never heard. "I think you've made it clear who it is you want. If you've come by to rub it in, it's not necessary."

"What are you talking about Kaylob?" Beth Ann felt confused.

"Just what I said." He pointed to the chair. "Sit if you want."

She sank down and watched him as he took a seat on the couch. Then he just stared at her.

"Kaylob are you going to talk to me?" Her gaze locked with his.

"Sure. Which part you want to talk about?" Kaylob's eyes narrowed.

Beth Ann placed her hands in her lap. "Just talk about whatever you want." She sat back. "I'll wait for you to say whatever's on your mind."

The only sound in the room was the ticking of the wall clock. Beth Ann watched as Kaylob sat staring out the open window. The minutes ticked by, so she adjusted herself, waiting for him to speak. To keep from going crazy, she started twirling her thumbs like Gram had always done. After about five minutes, which seemed like the longest five minutes of her life, she got really bored. So inch by inch, she started slumping and sliding down the chair. It didn't take long for her legs to be sprawled out across the floor, and she was almost on the ground.

When she glanced over at him, he arched a brow and cleared his throat. "You want to sit back up in the chair or fall on the floor?"

"Okay," she said softly. "I'll sit back up, but I've been waiting for you to speak for a hundred hours now."

"Oh, really, a hundred hours?" His gaze was glued to her face. "So let me see if I have this right. You want me to go back to my high school girlfriend, and you want me to ask someone else to go steady, oh wait, you also wanted me to kiss another girl. Do I have all those things correct?" He rubbed his hand through his hair.

She looked at him, but turned away, not wanting to see his scolding look. Her words tumbled right out of her mouth. "I was mad. I didn't mean any of it. I was extra upset because I broke the necklace you gave me. I only meant to throw it, but it broke. I went to the movies with Blake to take my mind off you. I wasn't trying to play games or make you mad. I just felt bad when I found out you attacked him. And I went after him but …"

"Beth Ann, stop rambling."

"I don't ramble," she disagreed. "I was just talking and explaining that it was all an accident."

"Oh, so you didn't mean to run after Blake and leave me standing there?" His voice was deep and laced with bitterness.

"I didn't know what to do, Kaylob. I guess I was confused after I found out you attacked him."

Kaylob stood and moved over to the window. "Confused at who you wanted, me or Blake?" He turned and met her gaze. "You know you weren't in that bathroom … Beth Ann, who was the one waiting for you?"

"You," she whispered. "I don't want Blake. I only want you." She stood and moved closer to him. "I just say mean things when I'm mad. I'm sorry." She looked down and felt tears start to flow.

He took his fingers tilting up her face. "Beth Ann, please don't ever say those things to me again. And, don't ever chase after Blake and leave me standing there. I was ready to move up to my Aunt and Uncle's house."

"I don't want you to leave. Please don't go." She fell into his arms and wept.

"Baby," he locked his tear filled gaze with hers. "I don't want to lose you, but, I can't go through that again, it hurt way too much and I know I don't have a lot to offer you."

"Please tell me you won't go," she pleaded. "I've always lost everything in my life. People are always leaving me and I can't take saying goodbye to you, too, and you have plenty to offer me."

"I won't go." His voice cracked.

"You promise," she said in a faint whisper.

"Yes, and you have to promise me something." Kaylob looked at her and she nodded.

"Promise me you won't say those things to me again. It hurt."

Beth Ann knew he was right. She had flown off the handle and she'd make sure not to do that again. Or at least that's what she told herself. "I promise to try not to do that again."

"I don't want us to fight like that, ever," he continued. "Did you ever eat anything?"

"Some popcorn."

"Okay." He embraced her once again and she melted into his arms. "You're sandwich is still here and Beth Ann, I do wish you would eat more."

"Why? Don't you like the way I look?" Beth Ann asked.

"I love the way you look. I just worry about your health." He pulled her close and lifted her chin with a gentleness that made her knees weak. Then, he gave her a kiss that whispered of hope for an everlasting love.

Chapter Thirty

Time breezed by without much incident. Kaylob and Blake disliked each other, but the fighting had stopped. At least as far as Beth Ann knew. Blake was her friend, and everyone at school and the people of the town knew she was Kaylob's girl. There was still no going steady ring, but Beth Ann had a feeling that he was waiting until she was sixteen, which was right around the corner.

As she sat on the edge of her bed that August morning, she thought about how well they were starting to know each other. When they spent time out at Sawyers pond, it was filled with smooching and a lot of fun, although, it wasn't nearly enough because of their schedules, and Kaylob didn't stay long if there weren't a lot of kids around.

She loved those days when he would pick her up from rehearsal, because they'd get to drive home alone and those rare moments where it was just the two of them, meant everything.

She held up her bare finger. "I don't really care what kind of ring it is, I just want to be his girl and I want it to be official."

Today she was going to hang out with Blake. Kaylob had been working two jobs to help out his parents. Now, that he had graduated, he was taking a couple college classes. It seemed these days they were apart more than together. He called her twice a day on his breaks. She just wished he would say he loved her. It might make all this time apart easier. He did say he was crazy about her and she was his girl. But formally, nothing had been declared.

At least he didn't seem to get upset over her friendship with Blake. Maybe he trusted her, or maybe he respected her choice in friends, even if he didn't like them.

Her mom's laughter interrupted her thoughts. It was Saturday just past eight a.m. She put on her robe and slippers, then shuffled down the hall. The sound was coming from the kitchen.

Her mom was sitting on Stanley's lap, hugging his neck. I have the best husband in the world." She held something in her hand. Her voice trembled and she looked a little misty eyed as she rested her head on his chest. "I can't believe you."

Beth Ann cleared her throat. "Child entering the room," she said. "I woke up and heard something fun going on out here."

Her mom was still staring at what appeared to be tickets.

She glanced up at Beth Ann. "My wonderful husband is taking me to Italy for a long overdue honeymoon." She had a sparkle in her eyes as she handed the tickets to Beth Ann.

"Wow! That's so cool. You two never had a honeymoon?" Beth Ann didn't know because she was at her Gram's when they got married. After she saw the tickets, she handed them back to her mom.

Stanley rose and sat his wife on the chair. "No. I never took Mrs. Cooper on a honeymoon. I think after four years of marriage it's time." He leaned down and kissed her cheek. "Now, I'm going outside and get that yard cleaned up."

He winked at Beth Ann and strolled out of the kitchen.

Beth Ann plopped down in the chair. "Wow." her mom's life had changed so much in four years, but it was still strange to hear her mom being called Mrs. Cooper instead of Rose.

Jean took in a deep breath and held the tickets to her heart. "How did I ever get so lucky?" She glanced at her daughter with a couple of tears trailing down her cheek.

"You're both lucky and what a honeymoon." She stood and hugged her mom. "I'm so happy for you."

"I'm glad, sweetie. I know it was hard on you when I left your daddy." She studied Beth Ann's face.

"True. But now I love Stanley. He's my other dad. It's changed our lives for the better." She sat back down. "Mama, I love Daddy, but he hardly ever calls me. When he does, he's always in a hurry." She sighed. "I sometimes wonder if he even cares about us anymore."

Her mom's eyes drooped. "Of course he loves you. I think he misses you more than he knows how to say." She took a sip of her coffee. "Honey, your daddy cried the day you were born. He will always love his children."

Beth Ann nodded. "Right now, let's just think about your honeymoon and how much fun that's going to be."

Her mom stood. "And, let's not forget someone is turning sixteen very soon." She cupped her daughter's face. "My girl is growing into a beautiful woman." She leaned down and kissed her cheek. "I am so blessed, and you, my sweet girl, are such a good daughter."

Beth Ann felt her own eyes mist up so she stood. "I better get dressed. Blake and I are going out to the pond today."

Her mom tilted her head. "Is Kaylob okay with that?"

"Yes mama, Blake is my friend."

Her mom arched a brow. "And a handsome one at that." She winked. "I wanted to invite him to your birthday party this year, if it wouldn't be a problem."

"He would love that and there's no problem anymore." She kissed her mom and left the room, but turned back around. "Congratulations, Mama."

"Thank you, sweetie."

An hour later, Blake showed up at the door, dressed in his surfer trunks

"Ready to head out?" He grinned.

"Yes, I'm looking forward to it."

The day was hot and sticky, which made it hard to breathe. They lay in the sun, listening to the birds and the laughter of neighborhood kids when Beth Ann sat up and hugged her knees. When she glanced over at Blake. The look on his face about tore her heart out. He really looked sad.

"Blake." She made him jump. "Are you okay today? You're awfully quiet."

He tried to smile, but his dimples didn't show.

"Just some issues at home, nothing major." He sat up and gazed out at the water. "You know, Beth Ann, I wonder why my parents don't like me. I try to be a good son but nothing is good enough for them."

Beth Ann placed her hand on his arm. "I'm sure they love you, Blake. They just don't know how to show it, that's all." She stood and held out her hand. "Let me show you something."

He gave her a once over and stood, taking her fingers in his. "Sure thing, anything you want to show me I'll take."

She shook her head and scolded, "Blake, it's nothing like that."

"Alright, but … never mind."

She pulled him across the marsh and down by another small area of water. There she plopped down and patted the ground for him to sit.

"See that duck right there with the four babies?" She pointed and waited for him to nod. "Those aren't her real babies."

"How do you know?" He seemed perplexed.

"Because," she said. "I found some eggs abandoned and I was so sad. I came back every day and covered them with a warm towel, waiting for their mom to come back, but she never did. So that duck," she pointed again, "only had one egg, so one day when I saw her leave, I placed the others in her nest, not sure what she would do."

Blake studied the ducks and glanced at Beth Ann. "I don't get it? Does that have something to do with me?"

"Yes. You were adopted and your parents didn't give birth to you, but they love you just the same. Maybe you weren't born in your mom's stomach, but you grew up in her heart." She nodded towards the duck. "Just like her. Those babies are a part of her heart. She doesn't hug them and the only way she shows them love is by taking care of them. Blake, she keeps them safe and look at the way they follow her."

The silence stretched between them, and she noticed Blake taking in the way the mother duck sailed around in the water watching over the babies. At one point she was sure she saw tears fill his eyes.

"Maybe they love me a little," he said a few minutes later, his voice hoarse. "They've always wanted me to have nice things. And, they've always made sure I was healthy and safe."

Beth Ann nodded. "Just like the mother duck." She reached out and took his hand. "Just because they don't tell you, doesn't mean it's not so." She inhaled deeply. "Besides, Blake Tanner, you are a good person." She placed her hand on his heart. "I know that your heart is full of goodness and love," she said then leaned on his arm.

"Beth Ann, how did you get so smart?"

"I don't know, I just am and I'm usually always right." She giggled.

* * * *

The next day Kaylob took off his work jacket and was going to take it home and wash it. He had gotten it messy from stacking meat trays. As he lifted a bag to place it inside, something was in the pocket. What the heck? He pulled it out.

How did that get in there? He unfolded the note.

Kaylob, I'd really like to get to know you more. I know you noticed my lacy bra. Want to see what's under it? Robin

Why was she writing him notes like that? Something didn't feel right. He'd seen her with Blake a few times. That would be so Blake Tanner to put Robin up to this so he could try and steal his girl. A few days ago, Blake had laughed about Kaylob's truck. Hey, it might not be new, but it ran good and it was all paid for. As far as Robin, he wouldn't put anything past Blake.

Sure, she was a foxy chick, but his heart was wrapped up in one tiny redhead. In truth, he didn't care who was wearing the lacy bra or what was underneath. Nobody could hold a candle to Beth Ann because what he had with her wasn't about lacy bras, it was about true love. He stuck the note in his pocket and would have to find a way to tell her he wasn't interested. Too bad Frankie wasn't around, he'd probably like her. After all, she did have some long legs.

On the way home, he made a last minute decision and headed over to see

Beth Ann. When he drove up to her house, he saw Stanley about to get in the car.

"Hey, Kaylob, how are you son? How's that truck running?" he asked.

"All's good." He nodded. "Is Beth Ann inside?"

"Yes." He pointed. "Go on in and when you see my wife could you tell her to get her sweet little self out here? We're running late for lunch with some friends."

Kaylob laughed. "Sure will." He flew up the steps, then opened the door and stepped inside.

"Beth Ann, honey, have you seen my pocketbook?" her mom called out down the hallway. "I can't seem to find that darn thing anywhere."

"No, Mama. Why don't you start putting it in the same place?"

Jean turned and spotted Kaylob and her hand went across her heart. "Goodness gracious. You just about scared the life out of me."

"Hi, Jean." Kaylob chuckled. "Stanley told me to come on in and ask that you get your sweet self out there."

"Heavens to Betsy, I just can't find my pocketbook." She looked around.

"I could help you. But what does it look like?" Kaylob had no clue what to look for.

A serious look washed across her face. "It's brown and holds my entire world." She placed her hand across her head. "I think I left it on the commode." She turned and ran down the other end of the house.

Beth Ann yelled out, "Kaylob, is that you?"

"Yes, it's me." He laughed when Jean ran out with her purse in her hand. "Beth Ann, honey, I found my pocketbook on the back of the commode. We'll be back later." She waved to Kaylob and rushed out the door.

Beth Ann came walking around the corner. "Hey, you." She hurried over, stood on her toes and gave him a heart-melting kiss. "I've missed you so much."

"I've missed you too, baby."

He wrapped his arms around her and pulled her close. Just touching her skin drove him wild. That was nothing compared to the heat he felt from looking at her in those shorts, and bathing suit top. It made him think about doing things that might not be considered nice. He backed up and stuck his hands in his pockets.

"Your mom was really frustrated. She couldn't find her pocketbook."

"She's always losing that thing." Beth Ann laughed. "She leaves it lying around everywhere. I always put mine in my bedroom. That way I don't lose it."

"Can I see what yours looks like?" he asked, not wanting to sound dumb.

199

He had no idea what a pocketbook was.

"Why? You've seen it before. It's the same one I had when we went to the movies last." She tilted her head.

"I didn't notice it. Can you show me?"

"Well, okay, if you really want to see my purse, then I guess I can go get it." She turned to leave.

"Not your purse, your pocketbook," he informed. "And while you're at it, could you show me the commode?" He didn't think these were difficult tasks.

Then he watched the strangest thing, Beth Ann fell backwards on the couch with her hand covering her mouth.

After a few seconds laughter echoed throughout the room.

"Beth Ann, what's so funny?" He crossed his arms over his chest, while he waited for her to stop.

Finally, she stood. "Follow me." She continued to chuckle.

Beth Ann took his hand and led him to the bathroom. "This is the commode." She pointed to the toilet. "And now," she dragged him to her room and picked up her purse. "This is a pocketbook." She laughed harder.

"I see." He arched a brow and wanted to get her for laughing at him.

"Kaylob Shawn O'Brien, I can't believe you didn't know what a commode and pocketbook was."

With that, he gave her the look that he knew she had grown to understand. He was going to get her and get her good.

She pointed her finger at him with a scolding look. "Don't you dare, Kaylob." She took off running. "I'm going to get mad if you do." She giggled.

Once he chased her into the family room, she went behind the couch where he caught her and picked her up in his arms.

"You little redheaded brat, now you're going to get it." He carried her to the center of the floor and sat her down. Then, like always, he climbed on top and started tickling her knees.

"Say, Kaylob is the smartest guy I know."

"No." She laughed hard and squirmed. "You didn't even know what a commode or pocketbook was." She squealed with laughter.

Kaylob tickled her knees and knew just the right spot. "Say it now or I won't stop." He knew she'd say it soon.

"NO!" She wiggled harder.

He tickled her more and got her right in the place that made her scream the loudest.

"Okay, okay," she gave in and her voice rippled with laughter. "Kaylob is the smartest guy I know."

He let her go, but not before he gave her a raspberry on her stomach. Then he held out his hand and helped her up. When he pulled her into his arms, the way she smelled almost took him down to his knees.

"Maybe we should go swimming." He placed his hands on her shoulders and held her back.

"Why? You need some cooling off?" She studied his face and let her eyes swim from top to bottom. "Oh, yes, indeed you do. You need some major cooling off." She turned to leave, but he caught her.

"Anyone ever tell you that you're a little tiger?" he whispered in her ear.

"Yep." She stuck her nose in the air. "Lots of guys."

He knew darn well she was trying to make him jealous.

"Oh, and who are these guys? Do I need to go beat them up?" He winked.

They both laughed and headed out to the pool, but not before he changed into his swimming trunks. Lucky for him, he kept a pair in the bathroom closet, for when he did get a chance to come over and go swimming, which lately had not been often enough.

He stepped outside and watched as Beth Ann slipped off her shorts. Man oh man, the sight of her in that bikini was making his hormones run wild, maybe they should leave and go to the pool hall.

They spent a good hour swimming and basking in the sun, keeping things at bay, when he heard her sweet voice.

"Kaylob, are you awake?"

He opened one eye. "Yes."

"Do you want some sun tea? My mom made some and added blackberries to it. It's really good and we have some homemade oatmeal cookies."

"I'll take both," he said. "You need any help?"

"No. I got it." She turned and sauntered off.

"Hell, I better eat a lot of cookies," he muttered to himself while he watched her cute and sexy bottom wiggle away.

A while later, he heard the door open and by the look on her face he knew something was wrong. Oh crap, she was holding that damn note.

"Who is this?" Her face was blood red. "Why is she writing notes to you and why are you checking out her lacy bra." Beth Ann threw the note at him and stomped off into the house.

He got up and followed behind her. "Beth Ann." He turned her around. "Listen, I just got that note today and I was going to tell her I'm not interested." He snuggled close to her. "You know you're the only girl I care about." He kissed her neck. "I'm crazy about you."

"Did you notice her lacy bra? She said you did."

"Well. I noticed, but I didn't care about it." He held her gaze. "Beth Ann, she came into the store asking me questions, wearing a see through top. As soon as I saw that, I wouldn't even look at her again, not below her neckline anyway."

In a voice slightly above a whisper, she responded, "Okay, I believe you." She leaned on his chest. "I hope she leaves you alone."

"Me too." He laughed. "Don't need my redhead throwing any tantrums."

"Well, I'd like to take her lacy bra and shove it up ..." Kaylob put a finger across her mouth just before he leaned down and kissed her.

She definitely stopped talking and he felt the world spinning out of control. Then when she brushed her tongue over his and let him suckle on it, he knew he had to stop and stop now. Her hand moved down under his swim trunks and the way she touched him, slowly moving back and forth, oh my god, that just about paralyzed him; he didn't want her to stop.

With every normal brain cell he had left, he removed her hand and backed away. Then ran out the back door and dove into the pool, but it was dreadfully close to being too late. That was it; he would never let that happen again. From that moment on, he'd learn how to be the master of control, because if Cole found out, he'd send her away and that was something he couldn't take a chance happening.

Chapter Thirty-One

Beth Ann couldn't believe another summer vacation was over, but she wouldn't know it by the heat in Novato, which had scorched everyone. That sure as heck made her glad they had a swimming pool.

Beth Ann lay on the bed, counting on her fingers. Holy adulthood, she was weeks away from turning sixteen. Wow! A driver's license and maybe her parents would let her use their car. There was no doubt it was exciting. Learning to drive had been fun with Kaylob. He was so patient and explained everything. With her mom, it had been a bit more stressful, she could feel the tension.

This would be the year Kaylob would ask her to go steady. They were already boyfriend and girlfriend and he was crazy for her. But did he love her like she loved him? It was hard to know for sure these days. With her training and shows and his working and surfing, they hardly had any time together.

The phone rang so loud that it echoed in her head. "Why in the world does that thing have to be so dang loud?"

"Hello," she almost grumbled.

"Hello, beautiful, is something wrong?" Kaylob chuckled. "Let me guess, the darn phone is too loud."

"I do need to turn down this dumb phone." She sighed. "It's so loud."

"Elizabeth Ann Rose. You've been saying that for over two years," he told her. "Want to get away from that loud noise maker and go out to the pond today? I took the day off from work."

"You did?" She felt her voice go up a few notches. "It's been months since we went out somewhere together."

"Sounds like that might be a yes."

"Yes, yes and did I say yes." They both laughed. "What time are you picking me up?"

"In about an hour."

"Sounds good, I'll see you then."

She hung up and flopped backwards on the bed, holding the phone to her heart. "I love him so much."

A knock at the door made her jump. "Come in."

Her mom peeked in the door. "I heard the phone ring so I knew you were awake."

Beth Ann sat up and inspected her mom. She was radiant, with her dark curly hair hanging free, which usually she kept up or in a ponytail. She wore a yellow dress that showed off her amazing figure.

"Beth Ann, honey, are you okay? You're staring at me?" She walked over and sat on the bed.

"I'm fine, Mama. I was just noticing how pretty you are."

Jean leaned over and hugged her daughter. "Thank you, honey. Stanley said he likes my hair down, so today I wore it down." She touched her hair. "I feel kind of silly, like I'm trying to be young or something." She kissed Beth Ann's cheek and stood.

"Mama, you do look young, so why not?" Beth Ann grinned.

"All that as it may be. I am thirty eight years old."

"Guess it's time to pull out the walker." Beth Ann giggled along with her mom.

"I wanted to let you know that Stanley and I are heading to San Francisco. I want to get his office cleaned and he has some inventory to do. We are getting everything tidy before we take off to Italy. Afterwards, we are meeting some friends for dinner." She stood and smoothed out her dress. "Now, I left some lasagna unthawing on the kitchen counter. Cole said he'd be home this weekend. He's found a place in San Diego." Her mom's smile faded. "The University of San Diego sent him an acceptance letter. And, he's met a special lady down there. He says she's really something." Her mom's eyes filled with tears. "That's so far away. But he said he would stay here while we're on our honeymoon."

Beth Ann felt her throat clog, but needed to be supportive for her mom. "It's not that far away, Mama, and it will be fun to go there and visit." She tried to sound happier than she felt. "You know that Lisa's parents said I could stay with her while you're gone."

"They did? That might be better for your brother so he doesn't miss school. Are you okay with it?" she asked.

"Yes, we were excited about it," Beth Ann said.

"Okay then. I'll call and make sure to let your brother know." There was no missing the sadness in her eyes.

"Mama, we are going to go see him and we'll enjoy San Diego, you just wait and see. By the way, you meant to say you left the lasagna thawing out on the counter. Right?" She giggled.

"No, it's unthawing," she said. "You have our number in the city if you need us and Beth Ann, Please eat some of the food. You hardly eat anything lately and I worry about you."

"Yes, Mama, I will eat, I promise." She watched her mom walk out the door and felt her heart drop.

Cole was moving to San Diego? Why hadn't she known about this? He had been going to a College in San Rafael and who was this new girl? Beth Ann didn't even know her name. With that thought, she climbed off the bed and would find out everything when she called him.

She got ready for her day and wore her holey cut offs with her bikini underneath. Afterwards, she rushed out to eat some cereal. Just as she finished, the doorbell rang. Kaylob was early; she jumped up and swung the door open.

"Hey, Beth Ann." Blake looked her up and down. "Wanted to stop by and ask you something." His expression got serious.

"Okay." Beth Ann waved him inside. "Is everything okay?"

"Glad to see you care." He met her gaze. "I just wanted to know if you'd like to hang out today, and maybe go to a movie later."

"I can't. Kaylob is on his way over. We are going to hang out at Sawyers Pond."

Blake nodded. "Okay, how about tomorrow?"

"I'm not sure. I can call you later?"

Blake stepped closer. "Beth Ann ..." He swallowed hard and looked her straight in the eye. "I'm not asking you out as a friend. I want to go on a date."

"Blake, you know I'm seeing Kaylob, and can't do that. We've been through this over and over again." She was tired of telling him no. "I have a boyfriend."

"Is that right?" He lifted her hand. "I don't see a ring there yet. Come on, it's been way too long."

"I could go with you as a friend, but nothing more."

He nodded. "Alright, fine." He scuffed the floor with his foot.

"I'll call and let you know if I can go or not," Beth Ann said.

Blake reached for the door. "I have to take off anyway, but don't forget to call me later." The minute he opened the door, Kaylob was standing there with a smile that faded when he saw Blake.

Blake turned back to Beth Ann. "Catch you later." He winked, then nodded to Kaylob as he stepped off the porch, but not before he said, "I see you're still driving the truck."

Kaylob snarled and watched him walk away, then glanced up at Beth Ann. His eyes narrowed.

"What did Mr. Playboy want?"

Summoning her most innocent look, she said, "he wanted to take me to the movies and not just as a friend." She headed towards her room.

Before she could take another step, Kaylob was in front of her. "And what did you say?"

"That I was spending it with you." She held his gaze. "I've been excited about us having the whole day and evening together."

Kaylob leaned in and gave her a gentle kiss. "I like that answer a lot." He winked.

Beth Ann placed her head on his chest and could hear his heart beat. "Are you sure you want to go to the pond? We have a pool and the house to ourselves." She peeked up into his eyes and knew what he wanted, but he whispered, "No."

"I have a picnic in the truck and it will be nice out at the pond today." He backed away from her and pointed towards her room. "Are you ready? Do you need to get anything?" He turned and headed towards the couch.

She knew there was no sense in arguing. He hardly ever wanted to be alone with her at the house and now that she was almost sixteen, she wondered if he would ever cave in because they had less time alone now than when she was younger.

She changed into her pink sundress, pulling it over her bathing suit, grabbed her towel, and put on her flip flops, then headed to the living room. There she saw Kaylob with his head back on the couch staring up at the ceiling. So she strolled over and sat on his lap.

"Kaylob" She played with his shirt.

"Yes." He looked like he wasn't feeling well, so she touched his face.

"Are you okay?" She leaned in and kissed his neck.

"Not really." He lifted her off his lap and grunted. "We should get going."

"Kaylob. I'm almost sixteen. I could make you feel better."

He stared at her for a long moment. "Beth Ann, don't. I don't feel like being teased all day."

"I'm not teasing, Kaylob. I am offering." She meant it. "I want to be with you."

"I know you do, but we aren't going to talk about that." He nodded towards the front door.

"I guess you just don't get that I'm almost sixteen," Beth Ann said again.

"Yes, I do get it. If I didn't, I wouldn't have already got you a gift. But since I know you and how nosey you are," He pointed at her, "I have it hid. Now, let's go."

"Nosey." She crossed her arms over her chest. "How special."

He threw his head back and laughed as he pulled her towards the front door.

Once outside, she couldn't control the urge to instigate. "Wonder if Blake would've run away if I asked him to be alone with me?"

"You don't really want to go there, do you?" Kaylob held up his hand and cut her off. Shadows darkened his blue eyes.

"Well, why won't you be alone with me? Every time we have a chance for the two of us, you almost run away. Why Kaylob?"

"I just want to go to the pond today. Is that okay?" Kaylob said.

"No, the pool is cleaner and we could be alone," Beth Ann snapped. "Maybe I'm tired of never being alone."

"Maybe some other day, not today." Kaylob held her gaze.

When they climbed into his old Ford pickup and headed off to the pond, she felt him glancing at her, but she was angry. She was starting to wonder why he spent time alone with Dusty at her house when her parents were gone, but never wanted them to spend time alone.

When she glanced over at his face, he was not smiling. "Kaylob, are you mad?"

"I don't know? So long as you don't bring up Mr. Butt wipe, I'm fine," he practically growled.

Maybe he wasn't over the whole Blake thing after all.

"Well, I have a question," Beth Ann said.

"Okay." Kaylob glanced at her then turned his eyes back on the road.

"Why did you spend so much time alone with Dusty and you avoid it with me?" she questioned.

"Beth Ann, Dusty was older. She was eighteen."

"I see, so I have to wait until I'm eighteen to be alone with you?" She crossed her arms over her chest and sulked.

He reached over and took her hand and just that simple touch sent electrical charges through her. Today since he took the day off, she reluctantly let it drop, but intended to ask again later.

* * * *

They arrived at the pond surrounded by rolling hills. The water was so blue that she couldn't help but notice how it reflected the color of Kaylob's eyes. A few puffy clouds lingered above, casting wayward shadows across the water. From the view, it was hard to tell how hot it was, except she was sure that the weeping willows dipped their branches into the pond so they could take a long sip to cool down.

Kaylob headed towards the back of the truck. "Go ahead. I'll be there in a few."

Looking out across the horizon, thinking of her life in this small northern California town, she felt an ache in her heart. She had a feeling that life in Novato would change in the next couple of years. Her dream had always been Broadway and she was going to leave the only home she'd ever known. They were already sending out applications and one of the schools had responded. It was all the way down in Riverside, California, The Lakeside school of Performing Arts. It had a great reputation and it was the one she wanted.

She gazed into the sky and watched the seagulls dipping and gliding around. The sound of their cries made her feel at home; she'd never find another place that had so much magic.

Kaylob was heading towards her, shirtless and carrying a picnic basket. His body was like a statue of perfection. Holy heat stroke, just checking him out anymore made her temperature rise. Her mouth got dry and her heart sped up. When she thought about what it was going to be like when they finally made love, her body responded in a way it never had before.

He studied her studying him and the amusement in his eyes gave her away.

Just as he winked, a breeze lifted her dress above her head and she tried to hold it down, but the wind had other ideas.

A few younger boys on an inner tube whistled and yelled out, "Ooh wee baby! Nice!"

Kaylob's hands were full, but he managed to point and stare at the two young kids. It didn't take them long to grab their tubes and high tail it to the other side of the pond. Only after they were gone, did he set down the basket, move over, and try to help her, but the wind just wouldn't behave.

"Just forget it, I'm taking it off." She slipped the dress over her head and saw Kaylob's eyes approve of her new bikini. This one was the sexiest yet.

Kaylob arched an eyebrow. "Uh, that's getting kinda skimpy there, Beth Ann. I hope you don't wear that around anyone else."

"I wore it to school the other day. Maybe that's why everyone was staring." She laughed.

With one giant step, he picked her up and held her over the water, pretending like he was going to drop her, but she knew better. Kaylob never let her go unless he jumped in, holding her. That didn't stop her from playing the role.

"Let me down, Kaylob Shawn O'Brien." She pretended to fight him.

He had always loved teasing her, and she knew what came next. He placed her on the deck climbed on top wiggling his fingers.

"Say, Kaylob Shawn O'Brien is the smartest guy you know." He tickled her knees.

"No, you can't make me." She wiggled, acting like she was trying to get away.

"Say it, Beth Ann, or I'm going to …" He tickled her again, making her scream. She noticed some other kids laughing at them so to stop drawing attention she caved.

"Okay, Kaylob Shawn O'Brien is the smartest guy I know," she called out.

His grin grew wide, then he bent down and gave her a raspberry on her neck. "I knew you thought that." He threw his head back and laughed, pulling her up.

She playfully started to smack him, but he caught her wrist. While gazing into his eyes, she snuggled closer. "You are the smartest and most handsome guy I know." She leaned in and nibbled on his ear, I'll only wear this around you," she whispered and moved even closer.

With no warning, he moved away, but she knew why and gave him a mischievous grin.

"You're a brat, Elizabeth Ann Rose." He arched a brow.

"Like I said, I could make you feel better." She moved close and leaned her head on his shoulder.

"I have no doubt that's true." He swooped her up and jumped in the cool water, while she clung on to his neck. It was refreshing compared to the hot sticky day.

"Trying to cool off?" she asked, just before he dunked her.

"No, but you need to be spanked," he said when she came back up.

"Okay." She crossed her arms across her chest. "I dare you."

He shook his head. "No, I think we better forget that." He dove under the water and grabbed her feet, making her scream. Once they both came bobbing up out of the water, they moved behind the dock. He pulled her close and grazed his lips across hers, she responded by gliding her tongue inside. She moved as close to him as she could, and knew the minute he responded. It seemed to her that Kaylob wanted her as bad as she wanted him.

"Beth Ann we need to stop." He moved her and held her back, taking a deep breath. After a few minutes, he pulled her out of the water onto the deck. "Let's get some sun."

Ever since he'd first brought her to this place, it had been their place to have fun, picnics and lazy summer days. This was where Beth Ann and Kaylob shared their hopes and dreams. His were to be a chef and own his own restaurant and she wanted to be a Broadway star.

As she relaxed her head on his knee, listening to him talk about his future, he sprinkled kisses on her eyelids and tucked the hair behind her ear. She could feel his eyes skimming over her body and the way he studied her gave her goose bumps.

"Beth Ann, someday you can sing in my restaurant, and that will help you to become famous," he murmured, looking down into her eyes.

"So if I do, would we be going steady then?" She looked up at his handsome face.

"No." He shook his head. "You'll be my wife by then." He started singing. "Hey, hey, Beth Ann, I want to marry you. Nobody else will ever do."

"Someday, I'll be Mrs. O'Brien and we will make love every day," she said just above a whisper.

"Oh, you bet we will. We're gonna have a lot of making up to do." He chuckled.

"What would the name of the restaurant be?" she asked.

"I don't know. But I know it'll have the word Rose in it." His eyes softened.

She sat up and met his gaze. "Rose? Like my last name?"

He gave her a slow grin and kissed her nose. "Yes, just like your name." He looked around, ensuring they were still alone before pulling her up into his arms and kissing her deeply. She was awash in his scent and knew that she loved him with every bit of her heart. After all, someday, she would be Mrs. O'Brien.

That day she decided she would tell Blake "no" because it was wrong. He wanted more and she never would. She didn't have to go steady with Kaylob to know that he was going to ask her by the time she was eighteen. Besides, later that afternoon when he thought she was asleep, he leaned close to her ear and told her he loved her. Yes, her heart had soared that summer day, because that was the first time she had heard him say those three words.

Chapter Thirty-Two

Two years later, after spending those special moments at Sawyers pond, she thought about how that had been the only time Kaylob had ever said he loved her. Beth Ann stood, gazing in the mirror, feeling like the world was ending, because the very evening she turned eighteen she had broken things off for good. She almost wished Blake was still living in Novato; she missed his friendship. He had left for Texas last year to go to school. He was becoming a realtor and had told her he needed to get away from the town. She had a feeling it was away from her and Kaylob, but couldn't be sure.

Life had rushed by and nothing had turned out like she thought. They had hardly spoken to each other in months, it was over and her heart was dead. Kaylob had tried to call her a few times and wanted to see her, but she had said no. She was done being jerked around.

The good news was she'd been accepted into the Lakeside School of Performing Arts. Everything else had happened like it was supposed to. Her parents had gone to Italy and had a great time. Cole was living in San Diego and was still with his new lady. James had decided to be a lifer in the Navy and was very happily married.

Now she was dealing with a life without Kaylob, not happily ever after for her. For her eighteenth birthday, he'd given her a beautiful hand carved chest and she knew there would be a promise ring inside. But all it had was pictures and trinkets. That had hurt her so deeply that she'd left the box and ran out the door, if only he had asked her to go steady. She didn't care about the ring. It could have been anything, his high school ring, a crackerjack ring; she just wanted him to ask her.

So it was over between them. It was time for her to move on with her life. She would work hard at picking up the pieces of all those wasted years, waiting for him. Maybe Blake had been right, and he was just jerking her along. Kaylob didn't want a commitment. If he did, he would have come after her.

She'd be heading off alone tomorrow for her new school in Riverside. Maybe she'd forget all about her childhood sweetheart. Her parents had bought her the cutest little car and had rented her a small one-bedroom apartment. It was a secure place, meaning she had to enter a code to even get inside the lobby. Riverside didn't have the best reputation.

One special thing that had happened was the meeting with Frankie. It had touched her heart deeply, and the memory floated back in her mind of that day.

Beth Ann had awakened and glanced at her calendar thinking about Frankie. Would he remember? Would he be there at their special spot? Today at noon, they were supposed to meet, but they hadn't spoken in over a year. His dad was getting transferred around a lot, so they hadn't called each other very much. Frankie seemed as busy as Beth Ann. All they'd done was share a letter from time to time and birthday cards.

The phone was quiet these days with her rehearsing and no more Kaylob. It might be better to be in a new place and meeting new people than living in a town where memories of her and Kaylob lived around every corner. If she could stop thinking about him for more than five seconds, she could move on with her life and make new friends.

She rose from the bed and put on a pair of white shorts and pink top. Her stomach had knots just wondering if Frankie would be there, would he remember their childhood promise. She hadn't reminded him in any of the letters she written. Why hadn't she? Maybe she wanted him to remember on his own.

Armed with that knowledge that he might not be there, she left the house. It didn't take long to start the climb up the small hill that led to their special spot. The smell of eucalyptus fanned its way through the air, and the familiar sounds of the neighborhood made her feel at home. If her heart could stop hurting over Kaylob, she might actually have fun again. It would be nice to enjoy the place she had grown to love. In a few days, she'd be going to live in a new town and start a new life, not knowing one person there. Saying she wasn't nervous would be a lie.

Beth Ann paused when she spotted her old friend. Sally was still the most beautiful horse in the world. Rhonda had moved and sold her house a couple years ago. She had married a man from San Francisco. Beth Ann was happy that she hadn't moved Sally away, and the new people adored her. The kids were always out riding her and she had tons of attention, which made Beth Ann smile. Sally turned her head, saw Beth Ann, and of course started walking towards her.

Once she reached the gate, she gave the horse a hug and stroked her mane. "Hey girl, you look like you just got brushed." Beth Ann kissed her nose. "Frankie is supposed to be here today, but I don't think he's coming." She leaned her head into Sally and felt her heart sink.

One of the kids came out the front door and waved as they ran to the barn. Sally stayed with Beth Ann and walked up to the edge of her fence with her. After a few minutes she heard her galloping off to the barn and running around with the young boy.

Beth Ann sat there, remembering all the secrets this place held. Charlie had always said San Diego knew her name. That might be true, but Novato held all her secrets and memories of her first love. She swallowed the tears that burned her throat just thinking about how everything had changed. Kaylob was no longer her guy. Blake was gone away and Frankie she missed every day since he left.

She looked down at her shoes, hearing Frankie's voice in her head. "Come on, Beth Ann, grab that cardboard, hold on to me." The laughter echoed all around, almost like it was happening. "Beth Ann, call me later."

Her mind drifted back to the long talks, sitting on the grass and rolling down the hill, even catching poison oak. She had to laugh at the memory of him chasing her with grasshoppers; she hadn't even known that she was afraid of them, until he tried to get her to hold one.

For a long while, she sat waiting and reminiscing of all the yesterdays. After a while, she glanced at her watch and knew he wasn't coming. It was one thirty and Frankie was never late.

With tears in her eyes and her heart breaking, she stood and took one last look around at the place she would miss so very much. She inhaled deeply and headed back down the hill. A few times, she would stop and listen to the sounds of the birds singing and try to get her emotions in check. Maybe someday she and Frankie would meet up again, she spotted a butterfly and watched it dipping and landing on a few wild flowers.

"Beth Ann!" a voice called out, winded.

Slowly she turned and saw him, the tears filled her eyes. "Oh, my god, Frankie." She ran towards him.

The minute they met, neither one of them could hold back the tears. Frankie picked her up and swung her around.

"I'm sorry I'm late, traffic." He wiped away his own tear. "Look at you. You're gorgeous," he said. "And just look at how much you've filled out." He laughed and hugged her again.

"Look at you. You're not so bad yourself and so tall." She went back into his arms and started to cry. "I've missed you every day, Frankie."

He held her until her tears dried and took her hand. "I have my car down at the bottom of the hill. Want to go hang out at the pond or your house? We could go see Kaylob."

"No." She shook her head. "We broke up months ago. Well, we're not *together anyway. He never asked me to go steady, and I got tired of waiting around."*

"I'm sorry," Frankie said and lifted her chin. "I just thought you two would end up married." He shook his head. "I haven't talked to Kaylob in about eight months." His eyes looked sad.

She went on to tell Frankie about her school and leaving for Riverside. He was not very happy about her going to Riverside alone and wished she were taking a friend. He was on his way to Harvard and would be studying to become an attorney. There was no doubt in her mind he would be wonderful at it.

At the end of the day, she had cried like a baby when he left again, but he told her she would see him sooner than she could imagine. She didn't know how that would happen, but he seemed sure about it. He was upset with Kaylob and said he was going to call him when he got settled. However, she told him to forget about it; what was done was done. He seemed to know her heart was broken, and didn't like it one little bit.

A few days earlier, she had actually seen Kaylob from a distance, but she turned and had gone the other way. There was nothing left to say to him. He had broken her heart and she needed to let it heal. There was just no good reason why he hadn't asked her to go steady, other than he just didn't love her enough, and that's what she told Frankie. He had held her hand and there was no missing the shock on his face. Kaylob had fooled everyone.

She kicked a box full of her stuff and heard a knock on her bedroom door. "Come in."

Her mom stood there with a sandwich and sun tea. "I thought you'd like a snack." She sat it down on the dresser. "Looks like you are just about ready." Her eyes pooled with tears as she looked around.

"Mama, I'm going to be fine and I promise to eat three meals a day." Beth Ann moved closer and gave her a warm hug. "The building is secure and I'll be careful," she promised.

"I know. You're all grown up now. It's just you're my baby and time went by so fast." She backed up and pointed to the dresser. "At least eat your whole sandwich and make me feel better." She wiped a tear from her eye.

"Okay, I am hungry anyway."

The doorbell rang, pulling them both away from their emotions.

"I'll get it. I bet its Denny or Lisa." They weren't taking her leaving so well, either. Lisa had spent a whole two hours crying the day before, while she packed. That had almost made Beth Ann change her mind.

She swung the door open.

"Hi, Beth Ann." Kaylob stood, looking awful.

"Hi." She met his gaze and was shocked at his unshaven face and how pale he was.

"I heard you were leaving, and I didn't want you to leave without this." He held out the handmade chest.

"Oh, thank you." She took it and tried to act happier than she felt. It was going to be hard to just be friends, but she'd do her best, because Kaylob was a wonderful guy. Even if he had broken her heart.

"Would you like to come in? I'm almost all packed. I'm leaving tomorrow morning."

"Sure." He nodded.

As they turned to head towards her room, Beth Ann saw her mom studying Kaylob. "For heaven's sake, Kaylob, are you feeling okay?" She moved up to him and cupped his face. "You're awful pale." She felt his head.

"I'm okay, just working extra hard." His smile didn't reach his eyes.

"Okay." She kissed his cheek. "I'm going to do the dishes if you need me." She turned and left.

Beth Ann waved for Kaylob to follow. "I've been cleaning out my room for days." She led him down the hall and when she entered the room she set the chest on top of a box. "Thank you for the gift. I really do like it." Her fingers touched the hand carved initials E, A, R, with love. It was truly beautiful and she would treasure it for always.

"Beth Ann," he said, his voice trembling.

"Yes." She saw his bloodshot eyes. "Are you okay?"

"No." He shook his head. "I'm a mess, Beth Ann." He took a deep breath. "I love you with all my heart and I ..." He paused. "Would you be my girl?" He met her eyes. "I know I'm late and I'm really sorry, but baby, I love you." He moved closer.

Beth Ann stood in place, stunned. "Why did you wait so long?" Her lip trembled.

"Because, I'm the biggest idiot in the free world and I just felt I wasn't good enough for you." He looked down then glanced up with pleading eyes.

Should she chance it? He didn't think he was good enough? Was he making that up, so she wouldn't date anyone else?

She nodded. "I love you too, but what do you mean you might not be good enough ..." She stepped back. "How do I know that you really want me and you're not just saying that?" She turned and looked straight into his eyes. "Why did you wait, Kaylob?"

He glanced down at the ground. "I didn't trust myself with you anymore, and I really don't have much to offer you."

"Didn't trust yourself and you don't have much to offer?"

"Beth Ann." He swallowed hard. "You know what I mean, my family is poor. I lived on the wrong side of the tracks. I also think we should wait to make love until we're married or until you're twenty."

"Until I'm twenty? Why? And the wrong side of the tracks?"

He moved closer and gazed into her eyes. "Open up the box, please." He pointed and gave her a look she couldn't refuse, even though he hadn't answered her.

She moved over to the chest and eased it open. "Kaylob," she whispered.

"It's my graduation ring and I want you to wear it, I wish it was something nicer, but I've been saving all my money. Will you go steady with me?"

"Yes, I'll go steady with you and the ring is perfect." She couldn't stop the tears. "I would have settled for a dime store ring."

Kaylob wrapped his arms around her. "Oh, baby. I've missed you so much. I've been a big-ass fool. I should have had more faith that me being poor and living in an old worn house wouldn't matter to you."

Beth Ann nodded. "You're right about that, I wouldn't care what kind of house you lived in, purple, green with naked ladies painted on the outside."

They both laughed as he slipped his oversized ring on her finger. "I think we need to get you a chain." He chuckled.

"I hope you can come to see me from time to time." This was all bitter sweet. "Damn it, I do wish you would have asked me sooner. We could have had more time with each other. I do have my own place, so you could come and visit on your days off."

"Come to see you from time to time and visit?" he repeated. "Beth Ann, I want to live in Riverside. I already quit my job. I want to be with you every day. Even if you would have said no, I was leaving anyway. I can't be here without you."

Beth Ann's voice got stuck in her throat. "Where will you stay?"

"I was hoping with you. I want to make sure you eat well. I can sleep on the couch and I'll get a job and help out." He let out a shaky breath. "Please say yes."

"Yes! Yes!" She squealed with joy and jumped into his arms, with her legs wrapped around him.

The next minute, her mom barged into the room. "What in the world?" Her hand went across her heart. "You scared the dickens out of me." She backed up towards the door. "Sorry, I didn't mean to interrupt."

Beth Ann dropped back to the ground. "Mama, Kaylob is going with me tomorrow. He said he would get a job and help out." There was no stopping the tears. "I'm so happy, he asked me to go steady." She held up the ring.

Kaylob nodded. "I promise to kick in for rent and will take over the payments as soon as I make enough. I have two thousand dollars saved up from selling my truck and work money." He pulled it from his pocket. "I could give you rent money now and I promise I'll make something out of myself."

Jean waved him off. "No, no, you two might need that and Kaylob you are something, already. I'm so happy you both stopped all this nonsense and are finally going to be together," she scolded. "Kaylob, I'm happy that you're going to be there with Beth Ann." She put her hand on her heart. "Lord, I was so worried about her going alone."

Kaylob nodded and took Beth Ann's hand. "I promise to take very good care of your daughter. I love her with all my heart."

"I know you do." Her mom's face softened. "I've always known. I saw the way you looked at my daughter that day." She paused. "I was spying, and saw you carry her inside when she fell asleep by the pool. When you laid her down and brushed the hair from her face, it was clear." She held her heart. "My god the way you looked at her." She swallowed, then walked up and hugged him. "I know you'll take good care of Beth Ann and Kaylob, I'm proud of who you are."

Beth Ann felt her lip tremble and a big tear fell from her eye. All this time he didn't think he was good enough. If he only knew what her life had been like when they traveled, he wouldn't have thought that. Someday she'd tell him everything.

"Now, how about let's go in the kitchen and I make you a sandwich, too," Jean offered.

"I can't," he said. "I need to go home and pack." He squeezed Beth Ann's hand. "Tomorrow will be a long drive."

He sealed the deal with a kiss and left in a rush.

The next morning came with blue skies and the wind whispering promises of a new future. Everyone walked them out to the car. Denny and Lisa were both bawling. The three girls stood in a circle and hugged.

"Our phone bills are going to be awful," Beth Ann said, and they all three nodded in agreement.

"I'll be home for Thanksgiving. It's not that long." They wiped the tears off each other's face and tried to smile. Beth Ann lost track of how long she stood in that circle with her two best friends. It was harder than she thought to say goodbye.

When her mom stepped up, there was a gentle strength that Beth Ann could feel coming from her.

"I love you, my sweet daughter." Beth Ann went into her arms, trying to keep from breaking down all over again.

Just above a whisper, Beth Ann said, "I love you too, Mama."

After they released each other, Stanley gave her a big hug and shook Kaylob's hand.

For a few minutes, the girls stood around in silence, watching while the guys finished placing things in the trunk. The back seat was filled with boxes and clothes. Her car was stuffed and they were ready.

"Wait." Jean ran into the house and came back out carrying a big brown bag. "Here's some food for the trip." Her lip trembled as she handed it to Kaylob.

"Thank you, Mama." Beth Ann's voice broke.

They both climbed in the car and Beth Ann was trying hard not to fall apart. Once Kaylob started the car, they both waved goodbye to the people they loved. Beth Ann felt a deep crushing pain in her heart, wondering if they would ever live here again. They made one last stop and she climbed from the vehicle to say goodbye to another love. As if on cue, Sallie Mae ran to her as though she knew Beth Ann was leaving. When their noses touched, Beth Ann couldn't stop from crying like a baby.

"Goodbye, my dear friend," she whispered as Sallie Mae whinnied. They stood together for a long while, loving on each other. One would think that she'd be used to saying goodbye, but she wasn't.

When she climbed back into the car, memories danced all around. She could hear the days of summer laughter and Halloween parties. The flashbacks came like old movies, with her best friends and the fun filled days with Lisa, the girl that had captured her heart.

She remembered her first kiss with Kaylob as they stood under the stars that fall night, with the wind blowing whispers of forever. Another tear fell as she said goodbye to the little town that had shown her how to believe in magic.

The funny thing was, when Kaylob switched on the radio, the song that blasted out was *Do you believe in magic*.

She scooted next to him as they drove down Grant Ave. "I arrived here on a warm sunny day in August, and I'm leaving on a warm sunny day in August." Her voice trembled.

"I'm going to miss this place, too," he said, his eyes glassy.

"It's bittersweet," Beth Ann said.

After a couple miles outside of town, Beth Ann was finally able to talk again. "Kaylob, nothing can ever come between us now. We're heading towards our dreams."

He grinned. "Smooth sailing, baby girl, smooth sailing."

They both laughed and glanced out at the long road before them.

THE END

To find out what happens next and if those dreams come true.

Follow the Seasons of Love and War Saga.

About the Author

Brenda Ashworth Barry's first book was a memoir titled, Healing the Voices Within, which was never published but sponsored on a local TV station and flew off the shelves at her Healing Center in Redding California.

Her most recent work is a six-part saga of star-crossed lovers separated by the war in Vietnam, entitled Seasons of Love and War. Brenda worked for over five years to bring the six part Saga alive.

Brenda lives in Roseburg, Oregon, by the Umpqua River, and has raised four children three birth children and one adopted born in her heart. Her husband, who was in the military for 21 years, gave her help and encouragement while writing her novel. When she's not writing she can normally be found walking the trails with her husband and their little dachshund, or in their RV enjoying nature.

Twitter: @sunsetsky52
Website: http://www.brendaashworthbarry.com
Facebook: www.facebook.com/pages/Seasons-of-Love-and-War-Author-Page/411210412247684
Blog: brendabarry.blogspot.com
Blog: brendabarryashworth.wordpress.com

Other works by the author from Melange

Seasons of Love and War, Book 1 of the Seasons of Love and War Series
December Road, Book 2 of the Seasons of Love and War Series

www.ingramcontent.com/pod-product-compliance
Lightning Source LLC
Chambersburg PA
CBHW032048240626
47154CB00003B/1127